MIRROR X

KARRI THOMPSON

Entangled Publishing, LLC
2614 South Timberline Road
Suite 109
Fort Collins, CO 80525
Visit our website at www.entangledpublishing.com

Ember is an imprint of Entangled Publishing, LLC.

Edited by Liz Pelletier and KL Grady
Cover design by Amber Shah

ISBN 978-1-50055-299-2

Manufactured in the United States of America

First Edition June 2014

For John and Kyle.

...at hearing of these sad changes in his home and friends, and finding himself thus alone in the world—every answer puzzled him by such elapses of time and of matters which he could not understand...he had not courage...but cried out in despair,

"Does nobody here know Rip Van Winkle?"

Chapter One

"Can you see me?" A hand pressed against my forehead for several seconds, leaving a cool spot above my eyebrows.

Blink. Blink. Blink.

Two people stood at my side, blurred like dark smudges on a gray wall. Another series of blinks brought them into focus: one male and one female.

"How about now?" asked the male, holding a small pen-light above my face.

"Yes," I forced through dry lips. "What happened?" My jaw hurt at its hinge, my lips burned with each labored breath, and I could taste blood. The victim was my tongue, swollen and sticky with a puncture wound from my right bicuspid.

"You gave us quite a scare last week, but your vitals have been stable for the last three days. We don't anticipate any more complications."

The center of my chest hurt, a hard and heavy throb,

matching the pain welling in the middle of my forehead. "Where's my mom? Where am I?" I sputtered as the words rapped against my aching throat and the man pulled away.

I was in a room, in an inclined bed, my body tucked cocoon-like in a blanket, but my arms were lying free atop it, positioned on either side of my torso. The blanket pulsed with warmth and emitted a steady beat, creating an intangible, unrestrictive comfort. It was the only thing that kept me from screaming at them.

"I'm Dr. Michael Bennett, and this is Dr. Susanne Love."

But he was too young to be a doctor. He couldn't have been more than twenty-one years old. Dr. Bennett's shoulders were broad, squared sharply under the maroon uniform he wore. The thick fabric, fabric that made a soft, scratchy sound when he moved, clung to his skin from his chest to his waist, hinting at the hard muscle underneath. With golden, smooth skin and controlled, purposeful movements, he looked like a high school football player in disguise.

"Where's my mother?" We were together. She must be here, too. She had to be, but what was this odd place? Nothing looked familiar—the cylindrical lamp to my right, the panel of equipment at the foot of my bed, the domed ceiling infused with tiny lights that glowed like stars.

Dr. Love brushed a strand of hair away from my eyes and tucked it behind my ear. I strained to flinch but couldn't move. She was Dr. Bennett's opposite. She was short, her facial features large and angular. Her uniform was way too tight, accentuating large hips and a protruding belly, but her smile was fantastic: bright teeth behind naturally thick, red lips. "Cassie, you're in a research and treatment hospital in Los Angeles, California."

Hospital? This was unlike any hospital I had ever seen. I swallowed hard, shifting my eyes away from the doctors. The wall to my left was covered with small, flat screens that pulsed with lights and lines that rose and fell and blinked. Two tubes rode up from the floor, draped over the side of my bed, and disappeared under my sheet. What parts of my body they were connected to, I didn't want to know or even think about.

"What's wrong with me? What's…?" But the words rattled into a croak and died.

My hands were usually tanned and calloused from years in the desert wielding pickaxes and shovels, and brushing the dirt away from tiny bits of bone. But the hand I barely managed to lift from my bed was skeletal, soft, and pale.

The effort made me shake. The muscle in my forearm burned. "Ouch," I said, clenching my teeth and letting my hand drop.

"We can give you something for the pain, but only time can bring back your mobility," said Dr. Bennett.

Dr. Love walked around to the other side of the bed, and after pushing a series of colored squares on one of the panels, the pain ceased and my stiff body relaxed and sank into the softness of the sheets.

"What did you do?"

"This machine feeds a series of electronic impulses into your nervous system, blocking your pain receptors," Dr. Bennett replied, his tone controlled but cautious. "Since the human body adapts rather quickly to the stimuli it receives, the pain will eventually come back. When that happens, Dr. Love will reset the system with a new wavelength in order to keep tricking your body. We're doing everything we can to keep you comfortable."

Dr. Love placed her hand on my cheek. "Your muscles haven't moved by your own accord for a very long time. The pain you're experiencing is normal, but don't worry. Soon you'll make a complete recovery, and within a day or two, it'll be easier to speak. Muscle stimulators affixed to each limb will accelerate the healing process."

"Recovery from what? What's happened to me?" A single, hot tear slid down my face, followed by its twin a moment later, but I was unable to move and wipe it away before it left a warm streak on my cheek.

Dr. Bennett put his hand to his chin. "Tell us the last thing you remember."

"Um, well, I was with my mom, and Daniella, and Ian, and…" I swallowed hard. "Where's my mom?"

"Please, just tell us the last thing you can remember, and then we'll tell you about your mother. I promise." Dr. Bennett raised one eyebrow.

"We were on-site. My mother found a tooth, serrated on one side, smooth on the other, most likely from a Ceratosaurus. We were eager to keep digging, but a storm was coming. We worked for another hour, then we secured the site and waited for the helicopter to take us back to Phoenix for the night…" I paused as my throat tightened. "But we never made it to Phoenix."

"There was an accident." Dr. Bennett spoke softly, compassion in every word. I could see it in his eyes and sense his intensity as he furrowed his brow.

"We stayed too long. We should have left earlier." My nostrils flared. I took a deep breath and blinked hard to delay another set of tears, but the effort was futile. Before I could exhale, my cheeks moistened with a steady stream of tears. "The storm arrived just before the helicopter came. Ian tried to talk us into staying, but we were all sick of camping and just wanted dinner at a restaurant and a soft, warm bed. No one would listen to him." I sniffled and coughed to clear my throat. "Within minutes after takeoff, there was a flash, and we dropped from the sky. That's all I know. Now tell me about my mother. Where is she? What happened to her?" I cried with muffled words and a raw tongue.

"Everyone escaped the crash with minor injuries."

"Oh thank God. Then she's okay."

"Everyone survived—except you," said Dr. Bennett slowly.

Except me?

"You had multiple fractures in both legs," the doctor continued, "and a compound fracture of your right forearm." He pointed to where I expected to see a scar, but there wasn't one. "In addition, you had several broken ribs, a punctured lung, and many cuts and abrasions, of course, but your most debilitating injury was an acute subdural hematoma, caused by blunt head trauma. The doctors did everything they could to save you, including surgical decompression, but they were limited in the twenty-first century."

"Limited…what do you mean, limited? You said I'll make a complete recovery." My voice, my arms, my legs—everything started to shake.

"Cassie, when were you born?"

My answer came instantly. "July 16th, 2005. Why?"

"When was the accident?"

My second answer came just as easily. "March 19th." It was Daniella's birthday. After we made it back to Phoenix that night, the team was going to take her out to a fancy dinner and celebrate, so in the days before she turned twenty-three, that was all she could talk about.

"March 19th, yes, but what year?"

"2022."

"Cassie, today is June 4th, 3025."

"What? That's not possible. Why are you…?" The words clogged in my throat. Stabbing the point of my elbow into the mattress, I pushed down hard, hoping the rest of my body would follow in pole vault-like fashion. But my legs, like sticks of lead, remained tethered to the bed while my upper body twisted into a roll, taking me face-first toward the glassy floor.

Dr. Bennett caught me with one arm, and when I gasped, I caught the scent of his cologne, something crisp and spicy.

"I want to see outside," I screamed hoarsely. "Take me to a…" I needed an open window, a surge of natural light or source of fresh air, but as I scanned the room again, I was met with the continued pulse of lights and zigzagged lines on a paneled wall to my left, and two blackened windows to my right. "Please, I just… I have to get out of here."

"You need to rest, Cassie." In one motion, Dr. Bennett lifted me back to the center of the bed, his face looming close to mine. His breath hit my cheek when he pulled his arm from under my shoulders, and our eyes locked before he blinked and stood, facing Dr. Love.

My throat tightening, I clenched the edge of the sheet, and with a deep inhale, fought the surge of panic rising into my chest. "But this isn't possible," I blurted.

Dr. Love set her hand on my arm and gave it a squeeze. "Please listen to Dr. Bennett. He'll tell you everything. It's important that you remain calm."

Remain calm when I'd just been told that I'd awakened one thousand and three years into the future? This had to be some sick joke.

Dr. Bennett licked his lower lip. "It *is* possible. You need to let me explain, and then you'll understand." The corners of his mouth curved into a soft smile, and his eyes, gentle and reassuring, reminded me of Ian's—bright blue with a glimmer of innate intelligence and passion. His soothing expression alone was enough for me to release the clumps of sheet in my fists and steady my breathing.

After pulling a plastic chair closer to the edge of my bed, Dr. Bennett sat down and put his hands together like he was ready to give a sermon. "Have you ever heard of cryogenics?"

"Yeah, why?"

Dr. Bennett's shoulders crumpled before he inhaled deeply and licked his lips again. His eyes looked like mine felt—tired and laden with dark circles.

My only consolation was that I probably still looked worse.

"Well, in your lifetime, there were three private companies that specialized in preserving the body after death and storing it until it could be revived at a later date. People suffering from chronic illness, or those eccentric enough to partake in this fad, made arrangements to have their bodies frozen when they died and put away for the future when advancements made it possible to regenerate and cure them."

"So? Why are you telling me this?" I interrupted, my heartbeat gaining momentum, the monotonous cadence of his voice eroding my spirit with each word.

"One cryogenics company, S.T.A.S.I.S., specialized in those patients suffering from the irreversible termination of all functions of the brain," he continued, ignoring my question.

"And what does this have to do with me?" I asked cautiously, my voice cracking. "Are you trying to say that…?"

Before he spoke again, Dr. Bennett glanced at the lines dancing next to me on the panels. "Cassie, you were brain dead. No one expected you to live, so out of desperation your grandfather purchased a S.T.A.S.I.S. cryonic chamber for your body."

"Brain dead? But that doesn't make sense. Brain cells can't be regenerated." A jolt of panic resurfaced as my words came out as a whisper.

"But not impossible in 3025," said Dr. Bennett, smiling confidently, his eyes as soft and soothing as the tone of his voice. "With the invention of a neurogenic stimulator, brain regeneration is now possible. This procedure was performed on you."

"You're kidding, right?" I tried to smile. The expression on Dr. Bennett's face didn't change. "I'm sorry, but I can't believe any of this. I need to get out of here right now—I have to find my mom!" I said, pushing up onto my palms and rising from my pillow.

"Cassie, be still, please," urged Dr. Love. She lightly held me down, but I continued to struggle, shifting my legs and arching my back until I felt the hard pull of the tubes tethering me to the bed, which ended my fight for freedom.

My brain pulsed with denial, my heart wracked with grief, but they were both prisoners in a body that refused to help me flee. I frantically scanned the room again for something familiar, something from 2022, but the slick walls and suspended tables were alien to me.

All I wanted was to knock Dr. Love away, jump from the bed ninja-like, burst out the door, and run away—to escape this foreign world and Dr. Bennett's jarring words.

When I hit the mattress, Dr. Love dabbed a soft cloth against my forehead, her lips mashed together.

A small wrinkle returned between Dr. Bennett's brows, and when he leaned closer, I noticed that the crisp blue of his eyes were speckled with gold. "Cassie, I know this is difficult to hear, but we're not lying to you. We're here to help you."

I closed my eyes, and the sound of the helicopter returned, its blades whipping around and around in a grating whine, broken and unbalanced like the impending knowledge of my death and the truth of my resurrection.

Lightning cracked. My mother grabbed my arm. Daniella screamed. Ian shouted something at the pilot, and the copter jerked to one side, plunging to the desert floor. The smell of smoke and dust and then darkness—those were the last images to penetrate my thoughts.

If my mom survived, she'd be here now, wouldn't she? She'd be at my side and wouldn't leave me—not for a single minute. But they were all dead—my mom, my grandfather, Daniella, and Ian. Everyone I'd ever known was gone—dead and buried centuries ago.

A cold prickle began at my spine, radiating upward with the words, "But…why so long?"

"You can blame the economy on that. Within ten years, all three cryogenic agencies went bankrupt and were forgotten." He smiled. "Six months ago, your cryonic chamber was discovered in the ruins of a twenty-first-century warehouse."

"So there must be others like me, S.T.A.S.I.S. participants from my time period."

"Unfortunately, no. Your chamber was the only one our team found that was still intact and fully powered, tethered to solar panels and a wind generator. We revived you almost immediately, but we kept you in stasis for several months until all of your injuries were healed."

"So, I'm all alone," I said in a hollow whisper that echoed inside my new emptiness. I tried to draw myself into a ball and hug my knees against my chest, but my atrophied muscles limited me to a slight twist that did little more than allow me to hide half my face in my pillow. "Everyone from 2022 is dead," I said in a weak, stifled whisper.

"I can tell you about your mom, if you like," said Dr. Love, taking the chair next to Dr. Bennett.

I nodded numbly.

"Well, right after you died, your mother found fame when she unearthed the skeletal remains of a female Ceratosaurus that she nicknamed Cassie. Isn't that sweet?" Dr. Love smiled twice as wide, her teeth like stars, but I didn't smile back. "Then two years later, she married one of her colleagues."

"Who?" I asked, quickly rolling onto my back to face her. My mother and father divorced when I was two, so I didn't grow up with the hope of them ever getting back together, and my mother was basically married to her profession.

"A paleontologist named Ian Jeffries."

"Are you sure?" I blurted.

"Yes, Ian Jeffries. They didn't have any children together, but they remained married through the end of their careers and retired in Arizona. Your mother was ninety-four years old when she died. Isn't that wonderful? She lived a very long and productive life and continued to be recognized for many accomplishments in her field."

Ian? My mom was almost twice his age. Sure, he was hotter than your average paleontology grad student, but still... This was all too weird.

I turned to Dr. Bennett. "What am I going to do? I don't belong here. I don't even exist in 3025."

"You're wrong. You do belong here. Your hospital records, birth certificate, high school transcript, and even your driver's license were put in your cryonic chamber," said Dr. Bennett, his eyes gleaming as he pulled a rectangular, metal object from a pocket. "All of your information has been transferred into our system. You exist, Cassie. You're real, and we're here to help you adjust and understand our world."

I wanted to adjust to and understand their world, but my world was gone, dead. I was brought back to life like one of the dinosaurs my mother and I dug up from the earth. How was I going to fit in without my family and friends? Was I going to be treated like an artifact and put on display like the Ceratosaurus nicknamed Cassie? Could I trust Dr. Bennett and Dr. Love?

Chapter Two

"Come on, legs, move!"

It took both of my hands to pull them free from the sheet, first one leg and then the other, while rubbery disks affixed to my body to accelerate my healing clicked and stimulated my muscles. I started sweating from the effort... and then paused, shocked at the sight of my legs. They were so skinny, so pale, so undefined and fragile, like the legs of a porcelain doll.

No matter how many mountains I had climbed, rocks I had scaled, miles I had walked in the dead heat of a desert afternoon, my quads had withered away like the people who had once been a part of my existence.

The door opened with a *ding*.

"Good morning," said Dr. Love.

It was definitely *not* a good morning. "How can it be when I'll never see any of my friends or family again?" I snapped. "And I've been nauseous all morning."

"That's to be expected, considering what you've been through. Soon you'll have plenty of good mornings. It's just a matter of time. This is a beautiful world, Cassie. But you need to get well first."

"What's behind there?" I asked through a yawn, pointing to the black, almond-shaped windows.

"An observation room."

"People are watching me?" Yanking the sheet up to my chin resulted in a sharp pain down my arm.

"Not right now."

"So basically I'm a trapped lab rat," I said, my words as raspy as my nerves.

Dr. Love's red lips wilted. "They were only watching you as a means of documenting your recovery. You're a medical miracle. They wanted to be present during your awakening."

"Who wanted to be present?"

"All three presidents, of course."

"Three?"

"The world is divided into three regions: Los Angeles is in Region One, so our president is William Gifford. Aleksandr Tupolev is the President of Region Two, and Shen-Lung is the president of Region Three. When I said important people" — she laughed — "I meant it."

"All of this is just so hard to believe. I'm sorry." *But was I sorry?* I kept thinking I was going to close my eyes and when I opened them, I'd be somewhere in Tucson on a dig with my mom, or in Connecticut snuggled up on the couch with my grandfather.

"You know, sometimes I wonder what it was like just after the Plague of 2423. There were so many deaths, so many lives lost. I suppose the survivors felt just like you do right now, and I can tell you what they did. They wiped away their tears, thanked God they were still alive, and started all over again. You can't return to the past, so you need to think ahead to the future—your new future."

I leaned forward. "Are you talking about a worldwide pandemic? It must have been a new strain, a superbug, something resistant to our antibiotics and antiviral medications."

"Don't worry about the plague. You have a bright future. You just haven't discovered it yet." Dr. Love fluffed my pillow and replaced it lovingly behind my head.

"It's hard to discover my future lying here miserable all day."

"We're doing everything we can to make you comfortable and happy. Dr. Bennett has been assigned to your case since the beginning. He cares deeply about you. He's taken full responsibility for your progress and has spent many sleepless nights worrying about your recovery. Your life is very precious to all of us." She gave me a smile and a wave as she left the room.

I laid in bed, thinking about my mom and my grandfather until each image morphed into Dr. Bennett. His stoic but gentle smile and cautious bedside manner filled the movie screen in my head until I replaced the view with skepticism. Scientists didn't publish their paleontological findings based on assumptions or hearsay. They required provable facts and first-hand evidence, and that's what I needed.

The door opened and another female of the future entered my room with the same optimistic smile and passionate manner as Dr. Love. But this woman was beyond beautiful. She was drop-dead gorgeous. Unlike Dr. Bennett's and Dr. Love's two-piece uniforms, this woman's was navy blue and fitted like a jumpsuit, perfectly accentuating her thin waist without exaggerating her rounded hips.

"Hello, Cassie. My name is Ella. I'm a physical therapist." She carried the tray with my breakfast in one hand and two metal poles in the other. After leaning the baton-like poles against the wall, she took a seat next to my bed.

Breakfast was scrambled eggs, hash browns, two slices of buttered toast with some kind of jelly on the side—probably blackberry, but I wasn't 100 percent positive about that—a short glass of orange juice, and a tall glass of water. At least the food hadn't changed, and I surprised myself by actually having an appetite, despite an earlier stint of queasiness.

"Hungry?"

"Not really," I lied. My throat hurt, and I wasn't too keen on the idea of possibly being hand-fed like a baby, especially by someone I'd just met.

"Well, then. How about I set your breakfast right over here and we start conditioning?" She positioned the tray on the floating table. "Who knows? Maybe after today's session you'll even be able to feed yourself."

Or maybe I could do more—like walk out of this room.

Ella demonstrated several simple pole exercises that I was supposed to copy, then pulled the clingy sheet away from my body and unhooked my high-tech catheter. *Gross.* "Okay, Cassie. Now it's your turn."

The bar vibrated in my hands, and as the muscles in my arms flexed, a stimulating pulse pinged through, making my hands tingle.

Ella clapped after my third set of what she called "floating curls." "Great job, Cassie. Yesterday you could barely lift your wrists, and now look at you."

"You saw me yesterday?"

"Of course. Everyone wanted to witness your final awakening, but the lounge isn't big enough for everybody, so every monitor in this wing was set to your room."

"Please tell me you're kidding."

"No, I'm not. There are obscuras everywhere. We just can't see most of them." She pointed to the seamless walls.

"Obscuras? You mean as in camera obscura? So anyone in this building could be watching us, even now?" I frowned, setting the resistance bar across my lap and pushing up on my palms to lean forward.

"No, no, honey, only during your awakening. It was a special moment for everyone. We've all worked so hard to bring you back to life. Until a few weeks ago, we weren't even sure if we could do it. You're still being monitored, of course, but only by a few staff members, two of whom you've already met—Dr. Bennett and Dr. Love."

I pulled my sheet up to my lap. *Had Dr. Bennett been watching me this whole time?* "Turn the obscuras off now, please. Having these two windows staring at me all day is bad enough, but hidden cameras? I don't want people watching me all the time." I kicked hard from under the sheet. The pole rolled from my lap and wobbled with a high-pitched hum before rising and stabilizing itself above my calves.

Not the dramatic move I was aiming for.

"It's—it's an invasion of privacy."

"Honey, you're not being observed all the time. There's a sensor on the floor at the foot of your bed. A tap on it with a toe renders this room free, meaning all lenses close and all observation windows blacken."

"Does free mean that Dr. Bennett can't see?"

"Of course."

Thank God. Even though he was a doctor, that would be way too embarrassing. "But I can't reach the sensor."

Ella raised her eyebrows. Her plump lower lip protruded slightly in a pout, but she didn't say anything.

"Is this the only hospital under surveillance?"

"No, that wouldn't be safe. The entire region is being watched: the streets, the buildings, inside and out, even our homes. But don't worry, all bathrooms and bedrooms are free all the time."

"Even your homes? So who does all of this watching?"

"The local government of this division. Each division has its own security patrol, but we're not monitored around the clock. That would be way too expensive and inefficient. The obscuras are activated only when necessary, and random viewings are taken several times during the day and night."

"Doesn't it bother you?" It sure the heck bothered me.

"I don't have anything to hide, so it doesn't matter. Don't worry, sweetie, pretty soon you'll forget all about the obscuras in the walls." Ella fluffed her brown hair. It smoothed in toward her neck and curled out and under at her shoulders, mimicking her hourglass shape.

How could I trust someone who was so trusting of a government that kept track of its citizens 24/7? Were they really all this naïve? Even Dr. Bennett and Dr. Love?

I mumbled, "I hope so."

"Well, I know so. Now, let's work your lower body."

Three sets of floating quads from a lying position made my forehead hot and my armpits sticky, but while the bar's inner workings pulsed against my legs, my muscles felt alive and strong. "So what's going to happen to me? After

I recover, where am I going to live? I don't own anything. I don't have any money. I don't even—"

"Honestly, I don't know what's going to happen. I'm in charge of your physical therapy, but Dr. Bennett's in charge of your recovery and assimilation. Save those questions for him."

"Then tell me about Dr. Bennett." I blushed, but maybe she'd attribute it to my workout. "He just looks so young. I can't believe he's a doctor."

"Dr. Bennett may be young, but he's highly professional. He's a genius, you know, an absolute genius. And I must admit that he's as handsome as he is smart, don't you think?"

"Yeah, I guess." Dr. Bennett was gorgeous, bordering on perfect. I'd never seen anyone so good looking before in my life.

Thinking about Dr. Bennett made this sterile room somewhat bearable, but my lungs craved fresh air—I yearned for a soft breeze and sunshine. If they wanted me to assimilate and adapt to their world, I needed to see it.

I needed proof. "I wish this room had a window."

"There's a balcony at the end of this floor. When you can walk on your own, I'll take you there."

But I wasn't planning on waiting that long. The minute I could plant both feet on the ground and move, I was going to sneak out of this room, find a window, and make my way outdoors for a dose of real air and sunshine before I went stir-crazy. And no one was going to stop me—not even the hot Dr. Bennett.

"Can't you take me there now? You know, put me in a wheelchair or something? I'm not used to being cooped up like this. I need to see trees and flowers. Mountains, or even the sun." I imagined the four glossy walls of the room closing in on me. "I can't stand it in here anymore. Please?"

Ella shook her head. "You haven't been L-Banded yet. You can't leave this room 'til then." She tapped a tight, black bracelet on her right wrist.

"That's an L-Band?" It looked more like a dog collar. "I don't think I want one. It's ugly."

"Every citizen in the world wears an L-Band. You can't drive, shop, or travel without one. It keeps track of your expenses and, like a key, it allows you to enter and exit rooms and buildings. It connects you to the region's computer."

"So I can't refuse to wear one?"

"Why would you?"

Why? Because it didn't just *look* like a dog collar—it was a dog collar with an invisible leash to a computer. But with Ella smiling proudly like it was an honor to wear one, I knew there was no use questioning her about it.

"Then do me a favor. If there *was* a window in this room, and I looked outside, what would I see?"

"How about this? Before we discuss the thirty-first century, why don't you tell me what you'd see in 2022, looking out your window."

"Well," I said, tapping the pole hovering above my legs, which sent it wobbling before it steadied into a rotating blur of silver. "Most of the time, my mom and I traveled and slept in tents, so I guess you could say that my window was always changing." In my mind's eye, I saw the opening of my tent, parted slightly, a ray of sun burning a spot on my sleeping bag. "Hills of sunset-colored sandstone against a white sky. A checkerboard of string below, marking our site. Two additional tents to my left. Two Jeeps, one red, one forest green, both encrusted in orange mud and dust. My mother standing next to a camp chair drinking a cup of black coffee."

My eyes became misty.

The pole slowed and teetered. I hit it again, harder this time, ignoring my muscle pain. "I look a lot like my mother. At least that's what people have always told me."

"Then your mother must have been beautiful because you're a natural beauty with your dark hair, porcelain skin, and red lips."

A natural beauty—I can't tell you how many times people have called me that. But they were all relatives or my mother's friends, people who felt obligated to say something nice.

David Casper, my first crush, was the only person who ever made me feel pretty, and he was dead like everyone else I'd known. We met on my first day at Central. It had been David's first day, too, having just moved to the States from Australia. Within a week, I was smitten.

So while my mother was on a dig in the Middle East, I lived with my grandfather, attended the local high school, and met the guy of my dreams. If only I could have attended Central for more than one semester.

"Thanks," I said, without making eye contact and shaking my head as the memory disappeared. "But she was wrong to do this to me." I should be dead like my mother. I couldn't believe she agreed to freeze me and store me in a warehouse.

Ella smoothed the hair on my forehead. "Sweetheart, this is a wonderful place. I believe that you came to us for a reason. Everyone has a purpose, and soon you'll find yours. Life is oh so precious, Cassie."

"I guess." I groaned. It's not like it wasn't precious back in 2022. Humans have an innate respect for life—all life. My respect just happened to extend back to the Triassic period.

"Now, chin up, hon. Let me tell you what you'd see if there was a window right there."

"You know, you wouldn't have to tell me if you could just show me. Can't you move me to a room with a window? That would be a lot easier." I took a breath and imagined what lay beyond this boring, alien room, a room that seemed to shrink in size and make me break a sweat every time I was seized with the reality of my confinement and physical limitations.

"You know I can't do that."

"I know." I sighed, trying to hide my frustration.

Ella cleared her throat. "Now, the first thing you'd see is the plaza, which lies between this hospital and another building identical to this one, so you'd see lots of people, benches, and outdoor eateries."

"What about trees, flowers, grass, you know, maybe even a mountain or two?"

The fine arches of Ella's eyebrows became more pronounced as she thought for a moment. "Um, no, you couldn't see anything like that from here."

"You're kidding. There has to be a little bit of landscaping somewhere."

"No, this whole compound is set within concrete paths and slabs."

I frowned.

"But it's not ugly," Ella was quick to add. "Much of the concrete has been laser etched and colored with beautiful designs."

"So there isn't a single blade of grass anywhere around here?" I asked, crushed and disgusted.

"Well, there's the botanical building, but no one ever goes in there. Oh yeah, there is one tree. It's—"

"Really? Where?" I asked, bending my knees and scooting forward.

"Behind the hospital next to the Magnolia Café. It's called the Magnolia Café because there's a big magnolia tree growing next to it."

"Oh, I love magnolias. I wish I could see it from here."

"I know, honey, but it wouldn't look like much from up here anyway."

"Why? What floor are we on?"

"Fourteen."

Adios to my idea of jumping from a window. Never mind. "So, what else would I see from this imaginary window?"

"Well, just past this building there are highways, some at ground level and others elevated."

"Except for the lack of fauna and flora, it doesn't sound much different from one thousand years ago."

"After the plague, we experienced a technological recession. At least that's what Dr. Bennett likes to call it. Advancements in technology and medicine suffered. But mankind is back on track, at least on the medical side, thanks to Dr. Bennett and his genius."

"What about the field of paleontology? How has it changed?" I asked, imagining a self-propelled chisel and pickax.

"That occupation no longer exists. This world's focus is on the future. This is a world full of optimism and hope. There's no need to look back."

"So no one studies dinosaurs anymore?"

"There are a few private collectors, but that's all," she said.

"What about museums? Do they still exist?"

Ella shook her head and blinked. "Nope," she added in the same flippant tone.

From under the sheet, I kicked the exercise pole up and away from my ankles, setting it into another wobbly spin. My mother's craft—my future craft—was long gone. There was no one left to brush away the dirt of the past, to complete a picture of the Triassic, Jurassic, or Cretaceous periods.

Those who cared about the mighty Tyrannosaurus Rex or graceful Pteranodon were dead and buried like the extraordinary creatures they studied. Apparently there were more important tasks for this humanity to fulfill, whatever those might be.

The pole finished a last rotation, faltered, and dropped onto my bed.

"Hon, let's continue this conversation tomorrow, okay?"

I didn't answer. Why should I, Cassie Dannacher, the daughter of a lowly paleontologist? This was a society that wanted to forget its past. I was a part of the past, a new plague in this world. I wanted out of this hospital. I couldn't stand it in here one more minute.

"I just don't get it, Ella. The only way a society can properly advance is by exploring and studying its history. There's more to a society's past than what's written in books. There's still so much to learn, to uncover through excavation." I tried to sit up, and my lack of muscle control and coordination sent the table hovering next to my bed into a rhythmic shake with an accidental elbow poke.

"Wait, please, take me to a window before you go," I begged one last time. "This room is making me claustrophobic."

"Oh, stop that Tasma talk. Why don't you try eating your

breakfast? You're more than ready to feed yourself." She returned to my bedside and picked up my tray.

Tasma talk? What in the world was she talking about? The plate Ella set on my lap was cool, but the eggs, hash browns, and toast were as steamy hot as when they arrived. I didn't bother to ask how or why.

"Aren't you hungry?"

I didn't answer.

"You should try to eat something before Dr. Bennett gets here."

"He's coming here today?"

She nodded. "He wants to spend some time with you, so he can see how you're feeling and how you're coping with the new changes in your life."

Time alone with Dr. Bennett. Although I'd hardly met him, my heartbeat quickened and my cheeks erupted with heat.

Chapter Three

Dr. Bennett entered my room carrying a flat, rectangular box under his arm. "How was your first meal in over one thousand years?" He laughed. He was different than he was the last time I saw him, more confident, rested, and poised.

"Good," I said, beginning our conversation like a proper patient.

"How are you feeling?" he asked in doctor-like fashion as he secured the box under his arm, leaned across my bed, and placed his palm on my forehead. It was the same one I'd felt when I first became conscious. I recognized its weight and the gentle spread of his fingers just above my eyebrows.

Taking a deep breath, I studied the curve of his lips, the rise of his cheekbones, and his perfectly proportioned nose as he lifted his hand away.

"Okay, I guess, Dr. Bennett. It's easier to talk today, but my mouth is still really dry."

"Call me Michael."

"Okay. Michael." My stomach did a somersault as Dr. Bennett—no, Michael—approached my bed with a smile.

As he set the box at my feet, I couldn't help but remember his hands at my waist, easing me up from the floor and back onto the bed.

From his pocket, he pulled out the metal object I'd seen him holding yesterday. As it lay in his palm, what began as the size of a half-deck of playing cards, instantly unfolded into a flat, handheld screen, thinner than any computer tablet from 2022. "I'll request a pitcher of water for your room. It'll be delivered with your next meal," he said, tapping the screen with his fingertip.

"What's that thing?"

"It's called a Liaison. It's a communication and informational device, linked to the Region One master computer, Liaison One."

"You have access to the entire region?"

"Some people do, I'm sure, but not me. Although, as a doctor and scientist, my Liaison has more programs than most."

"You don't look like a doctor or a scientist." I smiled.

Michael lowered his head, grinning and releasing his Liaison as it collapsed upon itself and dropped back into the lower pocket on his shirt.

Geez, why did I say that? I am such an idiot. He's going to think I'm hitting on him or something.

"Why not?" he said, crossing his arms but keeping his smile.

"Because you just look so young, that's all. It has nothing to do with the way you act or anything. I'm sure you're older than you look. Let me guess—the fountain of youth isn't a myth. It's been found, right?" I giggled nervously. Oh gosh. I was such a geek. That wasn't flirting, that was making a complete fool of myself.

He didn't laugh but lifted an eyebrow.

Seeing he was not amused, I searched for a way to save the conversation and my dignity. I came up short, dropped my shoulders, and sighed.

"Are you thirsty now?" he asked.

Whew! So glad he changed the subject. "Yeah."

The glass of water brought to me with breakfast was still half full. As he reached across the bed to retrieve it, his abdomen lightly brushed the tops of my knees. Now I really needed to get my hormones in check before I made a total fool out of myself again.

My hand shook as I took the octagon-shaped glass. "Your muscles are tired," he said. "Let me help you." He set the glass against my chapped lips and tilted it until the cool water hit my tongue. I looked up at him from the rim of my glass. He was looking at my chest. Why? I was wearing an ugly hospital gown.

I should have been looking at the glass, not at him. Water leaked from the corner of my mouth, trickling down to my chin. Ignoring the soreness in my bicep, I brushed the drops away with my fingers and caught another with the back of my hand before it reached my neck.

"Sorry about that," he said as he set down the glass, pulled a chair closer to the edge of my bed, and sat down without looking at me.

Totally embarrassing. I took a small breath through my nose and let it out slowly in order to keep my heart rate in check. "No problem," I half mumbled with a forced smile as my lower lip trembled. Now what? Another subject change. "Um, so what's that?" I asked, pointing to the box at the end of my bed.

"It's a game. Ella told me that you were bored, so I thought I'd keep you company for a while—that is, if you don't mind."

"No, I don't mind," I answered, beaming genuinely this time.

He brought the box to my bed, and after lifting the lid, the game board rose into the air.

"Oh my gosh, that's amazing."

With a tap, Michael knocked it into position, where it remained suspended, inches above my lap. "I need to get closer. Do you mind?" he asked, motioning to the edge of my bed.

"No, not at all. It'll be easier to play if I can sit cross-legged." Holding the sheet against my waist, I attempted to get into game-playing position, my movements clumsy and weak at best.

"Let me help you," he said.

"Thanks." I smiled. Bracing my hands, one on each of his shoulders, he helped stabilize my upper body while I scooted into position, our foreheads almost meeting.

While he touched me, a pleasant chill rippled in my chest and I inhaled, filling my lungs with his spicy cologne. I hoped a second breath would ease my pounding heart.

"Thanks," I said again, blushing.

"No problem." He leaned forward to steady the game, and the muscles in his forearms flexed. My lips parted, but I held my breath until he was seated with his heels resting on the bed frame.

Michael cleared his throat and moved his hand until it

was a few inches from my knee. "You're making an excellent recovery, Cassie. Your brain waves are normal, your heart is strong, and your lungs are clear."

"What were you worried about—cardiac pulmonary edema?" I joked.

"Actually, yes, we were," he said, tilting his head. He smiled and set two shiny game pieces, something like a little car and what appeared to be a tiny ring, on a space labeled "Go." "It sounds like you know as much about the human body as you do dinosaurs."

"No, not quite. One of the graduate students who worked with my mother was also studying forensic anthropology and forensic pathology. I used to read her textbooks when I ran out of novels or magazines. I'm a big nerd, I know." I laughed again.

"Nerd? I don't know that word."

"Really? Wow. Um, a nerd is someone who studies a lot. You know, someone who likes to learn."

"Well then, I'm a nerd, too. I've been studying and learning my whole life."

"Is that how you became a doctor at such a young age?" He was at that in-between point where the word "boy" or "man" could be used to describe him. "How old are you anyway?" Part of me was surprised I actually dared to ask. When I get nervous, I get giddy. And when I get giddy, my filter basically disappears. Not a good thing, especially right at that moment as I accidently knocked my knee against his hand.

Oh God, I touched him.

"I'm nineteen, and yes, that's partly how I became a doctor at this age."

"Wow, you're only two years older than me. It's kinda weird calling you 'doctor.'"

"To be honest, I'm not quite used to being called 'doctor' yet, even by my colleagues." He cleared his throat. "So, um, do you want to be the mover or the L-Band?" He asked, pointing to the game pieces.

So it was a type of car. "The mover." Cars were cool. L-Bands were ugly, and I didn't know enough about them. I took the tiny, metallic mover, inspecting its bullet-shaped body and running the tip of my finger against its four fixed wheels. Hmm, I guess their cars don't fly. "So, you're only two years older than me. That's crazy. I mean, you're not old enough to drink alcohol, but you're allowed to diagnose and treat patients."

"Actually, I'm a geneticist, and real alcohol is banned since it's too hard on the liver. No one is allowed to drink it. Artificial alcohol is available, but its impact on the central nervous system is mild compared to the non-synthetics."

Wait. Geneticist? Why was I being seen by a geneticist?

"Is Dr. Love a geneticist, too?"

"No, she's a transplant surgeon."

"A transplant surgeon? Did I need to have a…?"

"No, but she, like Ella, played an integral role in your awakening and now in your recovery. I predict you'll be walking by the end of the week." He brought one leg onto my bed and left the other where it was, the bottom of his hard-soled shoe teetering on the bed frame.

"And then will you give me a tour of this place? I want to go to the botanical building. I can't stand being in this room all day."

Michael smiled, and his right eyebrow lifted. "Sure,

part of your rehabilitation includes a slow immersion into the GenH1 compound." He moved closer to me, and my heart jumped into my throat. "How did you know about the botanical building?"

"Ella. I asked her about trees and flowers."

"When you're ready, I'll take you there. I promise," he said, leaning near enough for his breath to hit my lips. "You can go there right now if you land on it." He set the tiny mover to a square with the picture of a wooden building, and I watched the rise of his cheeks and the light in his eyes dance when he laughed.

"So this game board represents this hospital?" I asked, diverting my eyes from Michael's to study each square outlining the board.

"Yes, but not just the hospital. It includes this subdivision, this division, this sector, this region, and Regions Two and Three." Michael touched the center of the game while he spoke, and what appeared to be a solitary board sliced horizontally into four additional boards. "But since this is your first game, I think we'll just stick to this subdivison." He touched the uppermost board, and they collapsed back into one. His tone was playful, borderline flirtatious—definitely not as doctor-like.

Score.

"Wow, I've never played a game like this before." I grinned and my whole body tingled.

"Now, we both begin with ten thousand credits." He pulled what looked like two mini Liaisons from the box and handed one to me. "The object of the game is to become the wealthiest player by buying and renting property, which is actually kind of ironic considering that the government owns all property."

"Then it's just like Monopoly," I said, scanning the board until I found the words "Community Chest" and "Chance," but instead of the four Railroad spaces and two Utilities, I found the squares "Hoverbus Depot," "Liaison One," and "Obscura Preservation" in a subdivision adjacent to the hospital.

"It's based on an ancient game. I was hoping you'd recognize it." Michael's eyes gleamed. "It's called Ascendancy."

The innocent-sounding word gave me chills, especially when I saw that the "Jail" space was replaced with the not-so-innocent title of "Prison." I wasn't sure what to make of that.

Michael showed me how to navigate through the screens of the mini Liaison, and every time he reached across the game, stretching his muscular arm and letting his shoulders settle back into place, my heart danced, and I caught his gaze looking over my body.

Our eyes met, and he beamed, his knee bobbing up and down a few times during the silence—maybe from nerves. Like being on a first date.

On his next turn, Michael landed on a square labeled "A.G.-lift," an anti-gravity elevator, which allowed him to move his marker to Community Chest. He tapped the game's Liaison to read the card.

Community Chest. In this world, I was no longer a part of *any* community. "So, um, what will happen to me when I'm ready to leave the hospital?" I asked. "I have no money, no home. I don't even have a high school diploma. Wait. You still have high school, right? Can I go to high school?" I asked excitedly. "I still need to finish my senior year."

"That won't be necessary. High school does still exist, but we've seen your digital transcript. It's quite impressive. You could've graduated at the end of your junior year with all of the credits you had. If you want a diploma, we can issue you one, but it really isn't necessary," he said, brushing back a strand of unruly hair that broke away from above his forehead.

"So, that means no prom." I frowned, frustrated, and rolled the dice. Ironically, my marker landed on a government-run high school called "Educator 7."

But who was I kidding? I wouldn't have gone to my prom back home, either. I wasn't affiliated with any particular high school, just a school district, and I would have been stuck in the middle of the desert anyway. A semester at Central only gave me one possibility and that faded the minute my mother landed back in the States and dragged me to her next dig. I knew David Casper would have asked me.

"Prom?" He looked up with a confused expression.

"Oh, um, it's a dance. It's kind of like a rite of passage. You get all dressed up. The guy wears a tux and the girl wears a fancy dress. You rent a limo. You go out to dinner at a fancy restaurant beforehand," I said, beaming, but his expression hadn't changed. "Don't tell me proms don't exist anymore."

"I've never heard of one. The regions' educational systems promote learning, not socializing."

"Never mind then. I don't need a prom. If I was back home…" I dropped my hands in my lap. "What's going to happen to me?"

"Don't worry about your future here. We're going to take care of everything." He held his mini Liaison like it was the real thing.

By what, some kind of welfare system? I didn't want a handout of any kind.

"So if the government owns all property, what happened to the house my mother owned? And my father's? He owned a house, too." My dad, well, we never spoke. He left my mom and me when I was two. Supposedly he was rich and owned several properties, not that I ever saw any of his money. But I must have some relatives or maybe even an inheritance somewhere. "And what about relatives? I must be someone's great, great, great, great, great aunt, or something, right?" My shoulders ached with panic.

"I'm sorry, Cassie, but all property was absorbed and redistributed by the government after the plague, and"— he sighed and set his hand on my knee—"your bloodline ended."

"Ended? Are you sure?" My hands trembled in my lap.

"Yes, we traced your genealogy thoroughly."

"So, now what am I going to do? I just want to go home— to my home in my time."

Michael leaned over the game board and settled his palm on the top of my hand. "People's priorities are different. Our goals are not the same. A new culture has emerged from the old. You and this world do have something in common, though. Life stopped and then started again. And just like this planet, you've been given a second chance. You're going to make this world a better place." He spoke earnestly, his gaze fixed on me, but his words and warm touch weren't enough to smother my fears and confusion.

"A better place? How? Tell me." I struggled to keep the panic from my voice.

Michael bit his bottom lip and drew his hand away,

making the game board teeter. "I can't. I've already said too much, Cassie. I hadn't planned to—"

"What do you mean by too much?" I tossed my mini Liaison onto the bed and folded my arms. "Please, Michael. I want to know everything about this place—the people, the culture—everything."

He rubbed his chin, as if considering my request, took a deep breath, and tugged at his uniform collar, forcing the zipper to give an inch.

I gave him my best imploring look.

"Okay, but please, promise not to freak out or be weird or anything."

I nodded.

The game board dropped into his hands. He folded it, placed it back in the box, and powered down the miniature Liaisons. Though they begged a good stretch, I kept my legs crossed, silently urging him to stay where he was instead of returning to the chair.

"Well, six hundred years ago," he said, taking my cue and remaining on the bed, "the planet was struck with a pneumonic epidemic, a plague, its airborne bacteria resistant to the strongest antibiotics known to man. Due to its four-week incubation period, the infection was worldwide before it was detected." Through several fallen strands of hair on his forehead, I could see a vein pulse, and his voice shook as if the disease still lingered. "It killed over 50 percent of the earth's population."

"I already know about the plague. It's been eradicated, right? Then why is it still such a big deal?"

"Of course it's been eliminated, and now there's a vaccine to prevent it. The entire population is inoculated, including you, just in case. It's considered a dead disease, but we want to make sure it stays that way." Michael licked his lips. The vein on his forehead was no longer visible, but he was pale, and when he swallowed, I could hear it.

"So then what happened?" I asked softly, keeping my uneasiness in check.

"Then we recovered. The best we could. We adapted. We had to. The earth is the only planet capable of sustaining life. Life doesn't exist anywhere else except here. That's why life is so precious."

"How do you know that we're the only planet capable of sustaining life?" I countered as gently as I could.

"Nothing was found to support those claims. Which is one of the reasons why we dropped our space program after the plague."

"No space program? You've got to be kidding." Now that pissed me off.

The idea of humans connecting with an alien race and sharing technology always fascinated me. Spending most of my life uncovering the past and hypothesizing about the world of the dinosaurs definitely kindled my curiosity about space travel and what it held for mankind. The thought of these prospects being abandoned made my stomach turn.

"I know ancient fiction includes humans colonizing other planets, but it simply can't be done. Humans visited every planet in this galaxy and found that we're the only ones in this universe."

"Curiosity doesn't exist in the thirty-first century? I know you don't care about the past, but what about the future? Everybody keeps telling me to look forward and just forget about the past." I didn't bother to hide the anger in my voice.

"Our curiosity didn't die, it just shifted. Now we focus on what we still don't know about the human race. Homo sapiens are the only intelligent life form that exists, so it's our job to make sure that mankind continues to thrive. My life's work is dedicated to this." Michael squared his shoulders, forcing his tunic zipper to drop another inch, revealing the collar of a white undershirt.

I'd obviously touched on a sore spot, but I couldn't help myself. This world didn't make any sense. "Dedicated to preventing another plague or bringing a girl back from the dead?" I asked, tightening my jaw. "What kind of hospital is this anyway?"

"It's a genetics hospital. The answer to your first question is both. If we were struck by another deadly disease, it could cut our population in half again—the recovery process was almost worse than the disease itself." His eyes were serious and unblinking. "And it was very important for me to bring you back to life once you were discovered." He released a breath, and his stiff body wilted.

Calm down, Cassie. None of this is his fault. Don't take it out on him. "What about spacecraft capable of traveling to other planets? Do they still exist?" I asked, my anger replaced with curiosity.

"No, not anymore. There are high flyers, but they're limited to the earth's orbit."

"And apparently, exploring the past is limited, too," I said, deflated, dropping my chin to my chest.

"Like I said before, our focus is on this point in time and in the future. We only examine the past if it's relevant to what we're doing now." His licked his dry lips and the softness in his expression returned. "I know this must be hard for you to hear, especially since you grew up surrounded by people whose livelihood depended upon the past. And I respect that. I do."

His gaze met mine with a fervor that made my heart sail, sending another pleasant shiver through me despite my frustration with his world.

I sat forward against my propped-up pillow, my anger softening, yet I still felt hollow.

"Our ideologies have changed, Cassie," he continued, "but this is also a safe, clean, and nurturing world. Think about it. For someone like you, living in the year 3025 will be like finding and exploring a lost world. There's so much for you to see, and so many people here who care about you and appreciate you, and—"

"And I appreciate you, too," I said, narrowing the distance between us by lifting my back from my pillow. "But—"

Michael straightened. "You asked me to explain why the plague's still a big deal." Sweat formed on his brow. "The human race survived the plague but it left us...scarred. Right now we're continuing to cope with these losses with the work that's being performed right here at this hospital," he said with a hint of pride.

Scarred? Did he mean physically, mentally, or maybe both? I sucked in a deep breath, ready to push him for more, but he glanced at his L-Band and rose from the bed.

"I-I'm sorry, but I need to go. There's somewhere I need to be right now."

"What? You've got to be kidding," I said, slapping my palms against the mattress. "You can't go. Not yet. What do you mean by scarred?"

He put away the game and picked up the box. "I shouldn't be the one to tell you anyway. It's not part of the plan."

"What plan?" I screamed through my teeth. "Wait. I'm sorry."

"There's nothing for you to be sorry about," he said, lifting his head. "I'm the one who should be sorry."

"For what?"

But he was out the door before I'd finished shouting my question.

Why was it a geneticist's responsibility to wake me from the dead?

The whole thing just didn't make any sense, which made me more determined than ever to figure it out.

Chapter Four

"Good morning, Cassie," Dr. Love said when she entered my room the next day.

It wasn't a good morning. I'd spent most of the night thinking about my mom, my grandfather, and of course, Michael—replaying our conversation in my head, back and forth, his turn, my turn, like a game of Ascendancy, and wondering exactly how the plague left these people scarred.

So far, nobody I met looked scarred in any physical way, so what exactly was he talking about? There was no point asking Dr. Love about it. If Michael couldn't or wouldn't tell me, she wouldn't or couldn't tell me, either, and there was no sense getting mad about it all over again or getting him in trouble for mentioning it in the first place.

Dr. Love gave me a considering look, like she could sense my bad mood. "You're getting a massage this afternoon."

I immediately thought of Michael and drew in a quick breath. "By who?"

"A public-service bot."

"Oh, you mean a robot?" Robots? Cool. Besides a hot doctor, at least there were some good things about this world.

"Yes, we've shielded you from them until now. But Dr. Bennett thinks you're ready to experience your first bot." She set a tray of food, a meat dish with noodles, on my lap.

As she handed me my fork, I noticed a peculiar ring on her finger. The metal was soft and silvery, shining like a muted crystal. At the top of the band where one would expect a gem, there was a perfectly shaped bird's egg in miniature. Its surface was lightly frosted, giving it a matte appearance that glistened as she moved. "Your ring is so beautiful. And so unusual."

"Thank you. Eggs are so lovely, so perfect. It's almost a shame to crack one open."

"Oh, I don't have a problem with that. They taste way too good."

Dr. Love's bottom lip stiffened.

"So, um, what other kinds of patients are here?"

"Mainly organ transplant patients, no one whose circumstances are as unique as yours." She never stopped smiling, which was kind of creepy. "We've been cloning organs now for hundreds of years, but when it comes to genetics, there's still a lot we don't know."

"Cloning organs? That's amazing."

She glanced at the table floating next to my bed. "Those flowers sure brighten the room," she said. An arrangement of white, red, purple, pink, and yellow flowers burst from a triangular container, and in the center of blossomy goodness lay one perfect, creamy magnolia bud carefully positioned like a badge on a uniform.

"Yeah, they do. They were here when I woke up. Do you know who brought them?" *Please say Michael.* My chest inflated.

"I think Ella did."

"Oh, that's nice," I said, trying not to sound disappointed.

"I saw her speaking to a GROW, a gardener bot, before she went home yesterday." Her red lips parted into a smile. "Would you like to see a robot now, or do you want to wait until your massage?"

"Oh, I'd love to see one now. When my grandfather retired, he became a self-taught roboteer. He made robots with spikes, daggers, rockets, and other surprise weapons and entered them in local robot-war competitions."

"Robots with exposed weapons and rockets?" She clapped her hand against her chest. "That sounds dangerous and expensive."

"Not really. When I say 'robot,' I'm talking about a remote-controlled metal box with wheels, weighing less than twenty-five pounds. I'm sure our robots were nothing like yours."

"I'll go find a JAN for you now. I can't signal the janitor bot from here. Facility keepers are the only ones with active remotes on their bands."

Dr. Love returned minutes later with a robot in tow. Its arms and legs were made from metal, but when it moved its jointed limbs and fingers, it was graceful instead of clunky. Its face, neck, and torso were covered with thick, peach skin. Overall, it bore a basic human shape without a lot of detail—definitely made for efficiency.

"This is JAN. It's actually one of our more primitive

bots. Like GROW, it's a limited-service bot programmed to complete a variety of specific tasks, and that's it. There're also public-service bots like RELAX, the massage and therapy bot you'll see today. Because RELAX interacts with people, it looks more like a human. But robots will never be able to reason. We're the only beings capable of advanced thought processes. That's why life is so precious."

Dr. Love patted the bot on top of the head like it was a dog, and I dared to poke its rubbery cheek with my finger.

So artificial intelligence was another thing the human race had abandoned.

"Life is precious. I've been hearing that a lot," I said after giving the bot's face another poke and watching the spongy material bounce back into place.

"That's because it's true." There was an almost defensive tone in Dr. Love's voice.

It was true. So why did these people feel the need to repeat it like they were afraid they'd forget? Weird.

Dr. Love's smile reappeared when I nodded in agreement. "RELAX will be here soon. Enjoy your massage."

Just after Dr. Love left with JAN, a heavy knock and a *ding* echoed through my room. I straightened my back and brushed my fingers through my hair, hoping for Michael, but when the door slid open, a young guy carrying a small box entered instead.

"Good morning."

"Good morning," I said, trying not to look disappointed as I pulled my blanket up to my chest.

"I'm Magnum, technician, tier two. I'm here to activate your L-Band. No bots until you're L-Banded." Magnum had a big, schoolboy grin, so he looked close to my age. It was impossible not to smile back at him.

His facial features were small—small nose, small eyes, thin lips, but his smile was wide. He was five-foot-nine or ten, and very masculine in a boyish way.

He pulled back the cuff of his navy uniform sleeve to expose the thick black band encircling his wrist. It was about an inch-and-a-half thick and looked almost spongy to the touch. "This is an L-Band, or Liaison Band. You've probably seen one before. Everybody wears one."

"Yeah. What exactly does it do?" I asked with a hesitant smile.

"Oh, many, many things." Magnum lifted the lid to the lacquered box he was holding and pulled out my L-Band. "First of all, and most importantly, it's a communication device. You can talk to anyone in the world using this. You can view written text, diagrams, photographs, movies, the list goes on, and link to any database. Oh, and it's also a locator." He lifted his eyebrows and smiled. "You can find anyone in this building, and they can find you."

Yeah, but was that a good thing, or a bad thing?

"You need to wear this in order to interact with bots. If RELAX came in right now, it would see you as another object in the room, something it couldn't interact with. With this on, you can speak to any robot, and it will even recognize you by name. I just need your right wrist." Magnum held the L-Band like a prize, delicately and with pride.

I hesitated and then lifted my arm. "But what if…?"

With one quick movement, Magnum fastened the L-Band to my wrist. The material shrank, drawing itself in until it was snug against my skin, and I gasped, pulling my hand from his loose grip.

"Each L-Band is specific to its wearer," continued Magnum, oblivious to my half-question and rising panic. "This L-Band has been programmed with all of your personal information, including medical records, and it's automatically updated when new information is added to the main database."

I turned my hand back and forth, trying to find the place where the two ends joined but couldn't find it. "How do you take it off?"

"You don't." He smiled, but his tone was serious.

"Why not?" The flat, square surface embedded in the fabric stayed perfectly still when I moved, but the material around it flexed and stretched.

"There's no reason to take it off. You can't function in our society without one."

"But—"

"I know you're not used to maintaining a constant inter-personal connection with a regional network, but believe me, there are more advantages than disadvantages, and there's no getting around it. Once you're banded, you're banded, and there are no exemptions—not even for our presidents. Everyone wears an L-Band."

I had to wear it, but I didn't have to like it. "How do I make it work?"

"It's not activated, yet. Here." Magnum tapped his L-Band. "I'm the only one who can do this." He beamed with pride, his stubble-free cheeks dimpled, and he squeezed his eyes almost shut. He was not in charge of waking the dead or fighting a plague, but he obviously enjoyed the power he had when it came to Liaison Bands.

The sound of a soft beep and a short vibration, and then

a flash of color stimulated the muscles in my wrist as the L-Band sparked to life.

"Do you want the sound on or off?"

"Ah…on is fine, I guess."

"Well, there you go. Your L-Band has limited functions at the moment, but it'll eventually be expanded. In the meantime, go ahead and explore. You can't break it, and you can't accidentally call me at three in the morning or hack into confidential records." Magnum grinned.

"Um, actually, I probably won't be calling anybody." I sighed. Who the heck would I call? "Besides, I'd rather explore this hospital. Now that I'm banded, I can leave my room. Show me how to request a wheelchair." A light tap to my L-Band's screen made it glow a soft, rippling blue.

"Now hold on." Magnum laughed. "I know you must be anxious to leave this room, but to do so, you'll need more than an active L-Band. You'll also need permission from someone a lot higher up than me."

"Who? Michael—Dr. Bennett? I'll call him right now." Did I dare? Yeah, why not? He promised to take me to the botanical garden when I was ready.

Magnum searched the walls like he was looking for obscuras and took a short breath before he spoke. "Actually, it goes beyond Dr. Bennett."

"To who?" Michael was my doctor. He should've been able to make that call.

"You'll find out soon enough. In the meantime, if you have any questions about how to use your L-Band, just touch the screen and say my name." He glanced at his own band and smiled. "Hey, your bot's here, right on time."

There was a double *ding* as the door slid open to reveal

RELAX. It walked forward and froze at the side of the bed, its rubbery body clothed in a tight-fitting, gray jumpsuit.

"Good morning, Cassie. I am RELAX, a massage and therapy robot. I have been programmed to aid in your rehabilitation," it said in a voice that could almost be mistaken for a human.

Great. I hoped I'd enjoy this. I needed something to make me forget I was now tethered to a supposedly scarred world with robots, spying obscuras, and a master computer that recorded my every move. This was way too *1984* for me. I had to find out what was up with this world. And that's what I planned to do once I regained my strength.

Chapter Five

While my tight muscles relaxed beneath a set of mechanical hands, my thoughts raced, leaving my body soft and submissive and my mind in the opposite condition.

What was going to happen to me? What kind of job or occupation was I qualified for? Where would I live? According to Michael, I was going to make this world better, but how was that possible when I didn't belong here in the first place?

One thing I did know: I did *not* want to lead a life of dependency upon anyone or anything except myself. I had to make sure that wasn't going to happen.

The session finished, RELAX strolled from my room with a fixed, contented smile, and for a moment I envied the piece of machinery with its simple, inane life.

My body churned hot with anger, starting with my cheeks and melting to my torso, forcing me to untie and open the robe RELAX wrapped me in after the massage. Frustration at my predicament turned to rage, and within minutes the front of my hospital gown was damp, not only with rubbing oil, but perspiration.

With a *ding*, the bedroom door slipped opened, and Michael entered. "Good afternoon. I wanted to find out what you thought of your massage." His smile faded when we made eye contact.

The minute the door slid closed behind him, I shouted, "I don't care about the massage. I care about what's going to happen to me, but you never told me. What will I do when I leave this place, and more importantly, when do I get to leave this room?"

"Calm down." He approached my bed with his arms up and palms facing me "Now that you're banded, you'll be able to leave this room as soon as its determined you're physically ready. And when it comes to your future, we've already made arrangements for you to—"

"To what? Become a productive member of society on someone else's dime?" I sneered.

"That's not quite how I was going to say it, but yes. You'll be given free housing, amenities, and many training and career options to choose from."

"Like what? Apparently paleontologist or museum curator aren't options, right?"

Michael shook his head as if he knew the word "no" would be too blunt. "But there are other jobs that might interest you."

"And who's going to pay for all that?"

"GenH1 is taking care of all of your expenses. We brought you here. It's our duty to make you comfortable and safe. Besides, you're a ward of the region until you turn eighteen. We don't expect you to take care of yourself."

"What if I don't want to be a ward of the region?" I

asked, straightening my back. "I *can* take care of myself. I'll just get a job, and I want to go to college, if it even exists in this world."

"It exists, but it's more complicated than that. You don't under—"

"You're right. I don't understand. Explain whatever that may be."

Michael's shoulders drooped as he took a seat on the edge of my bed instead of the chair. Something about him was different today. He spoke and moved carefully like he was afraid I would break, and his cadence and his words sounded rehearsed.

It was enough to disrupt my outburst. My crossed arms fell to my sides, and I dropped my head. "I have no family, no friends—no one," I said in a half whisper.

"Even though I'm your doctor, I'm also your friend." Michael lifted my right hand from the sheet, taking it in both of his. His hands were warm, soft, and almost twice as large as mine.

I took a deep breath as my heart lurched into a faster beat. "I can handle whatever it is you aren't telling me."

He sighed and loosened his grip.

"What's wrong, Michael?" I leaned toward him and placed my free hand on his shoulder, letting my fingers settle upon the hard muscle that led to his neck.

"There's nothing wrong. Everything about you is right. It's the way it's supposed to be." What was he talking about? He moved close enough for me to see the yellow specks in his eyes. His lips parted, and I let my palm slide down to his elbow.

"Damn, you're about to have some visitors." He glanced

at his L-Band, and I pulled away. "I wanted to prepare you for this. They weren't supposed to come until — " He abruptly put my hand in my lap, gave it a squeeze before he let go, and rose as the hospital door slid open.

Dr. Love entered first, followed by two men wearing tight black uniforms. Michael cleared his throat. "Good afternoon. Um, let's begin with introductions," he said as the two men walked toward me. Dr. Love took a seat at my right. "This is Dr. Simon Little. He's the manager of protocol."

Dr. Little nodded and raised a coffee cup he held in a small salute. He was a short, large-middled man with enough wrinkles around his eyes and on his neck to place him in his early seventies. "And how are you feeling today, Miss Dannacher?"

"Better. Thank you," I said, noting the doctor's L-Band, thick against his wrist.

"And this is Dr. Colin Pickford," he added. "He's the head of the genetics department. They're here to help me tell you a little bit more about our world and about your progress here at GenH1."

Finally. They were probably the men who went beyond Michael's authority. They took seats in a row along the left side of my bed.

Michael continued. "You already know that six hundred years ago, our world was devastated by an inexorable plague, and over 50 percent of the population perished as a result."

I nodded and bent my knees, forming a peak of cotton sheets.

"Well, in time, it was discovered that the plague did more than what the experts initially believed. Every woman on the planet became sterile, and women who were pregnant before the plague either died or miscarried."

I looked at Dr. Love, but she turned her head away from me. "So you're saying that every woman on the planet at the same point in time was infertile?"

"Yes." Michael didn't blink. Now I understood what he'd meant by being scarred.

"But that's not possible because then none of you would be here." My voice trembled, followed by my hands and lower lip.

"Cassie"—he leaned forward—"we've found other ways to replicate life."

"Artificial insemination?" I dropped my jaw. "No, wait, that wouldn't work, right?"

"No, for intrauterine insemination to work, a viable egg is needed." His eyes shifted to the floor. "There were no viable eggs."

"Then how…" I scanned the row of faces, all staid and straightforward. They were telling the truth. "Well, you're definitely not robots."

"No, no."

"Then…?"

He straightened his back, inhaled, and ran his palms against the tops of his thighs, the scrape of stiff fabric audible in the dead-silent room.

"Please. Tell me." The words were thick in my throat as I tilted my head to catch Michael's gaze. My stomach churned with bile, and I became nauseous.

"We've accomplished what was once considered impossible. We've succeeded where your world failed. To put it simply, we're clones."

A chill bit my lower spine, and I wrapped my arms across

my chest as my heartbeat pounded in my ears. As I searched back and forth among them for something that made them different, I consciously controlled my breathing, taking long, slow breaths while the reality of these beings settled in my brain.

But there was nothing unusual. These people were as human as I. An unethical process in my century was now one of success, each person in this world representing a bigger miracle than a biological birth.

Michael, the guy who'd brought me back from death, was the replica of another, something concocted in a lab. He looked away and tapped his foot nervously. It seemed obvious he was embarrassed, if not mortified, by the thought that I knew his secret—their secret. I was one-of-a-kind, of a biological birth, but that did not make me any more human than them.

It only made me a rarity.

I smiled at Michael and his foot tapping ceased.

"Clones? All of you are clones?" Although stunned at this revelation, I was even more impressed with their technology.

Dr. Pickford folded his hands. He was handsome for a man who was probably in his fifties. He looked how I always imagined my dad—lean but athletic with gray hair that made him appear scholarly instead of old. But there was something about him I didn't like. Maybe it was the way his lip curled up on one side when he talked. "Yes, Miss Dannacher. We are genetic replicas derived from—"

"I know what a clone is," I interrupted. "But in my lifetime, it was wrong to clone a human."

"Our decision was not a matter of ethics, Miss Dannacher,

we had no choice." Dr. Pickford shifted in his seat.

"No choice?" I said, directing my question at Michael.

"Cassie, clones cannot reproduce, and—"

"Why can't they?" If the clone is an exact replica of its donor and the donor was fertile, the clone should be, too.

"Underdeveloped ovaries." He shook his head. "We don't know why this disorder occurs. It's a congenital defect present in every clone female. They're all born without eggs."

There was a soft popping sound as Dr. Love cracked the knuckles of her left hand and proceeded to pick at the cuticle of her pinkie, keeping her eyes from mine.

"That doesn't make any sense. During my lifetime, cloned animals could reproduce."

"That's still true today, but for some reason, it's different with humans."

"And what about male clones?" I asked slowly, directing my question toward Dr. Pickford instead of Michael, although Dr. Little answered instead.

"Oh, don't worry about us, Miss Dannacher," he chuckled with pride. "Male clones are not defective. Our fertility is intact."

Infertility does not make a woman defective, I wanted to shout and expected to see Dr. Love doing the same. But she was still focused on her nails.

Michael drew in a long breath and inched away from Dr. Little by shifting to one side of his chair. "And, unfortunately, there's another issue. We can't clone an existing clone. The DNA is too unstable and fragmented. Even first generations have problems, such as organ failure. GenH1 performs over one hundred organ replacements a month due to this problem."

"If all of you are clones, then you're genetic replicas derived from what?" I asked, bringing my knees closer to my chest as my dizziness increased.

"From our ancestors," said Dr. Little after a long gulp from his mug. "I can show you if you like?" He nodded and a cowlick on his head flopped downward. "Monitor down." A thin, gray screen lowered from the ceiling at my left. He tapped on his L-Band until the monitor glowed. "This is a map of our city. The green areas are cemeteries established before 2425."

Michael added, "Before the plague."

The doctor selected one of the green areas and enlarged it. The boundary of the cemetery was rectangular, outlined in black, and inside were tiny rows of colored dots. "Each dot represents a grave." He explained how different colored dots represented tombs with or without workable DNA and those that had already been excavated. "For each yellow dot, the cadaver has not only been recovered and the DNA processed, but the cloned fetus has already been 'born' and released to parents."

My guts clenched. "Born?"

"We use the term loosely. The babies are actually grown in an artificial uterus, so we can monitor them throughout their entire gestation process."

"Without cloning, humans would have been extinct in less than one hundred years," Michael said. "There would have been complete chaos and anarchy until the last surviving human died alone, a miserable death. Our forefathers couldn't let that happen."

Dr. Little coughed into his fist. "The blue dots represent graves with usable DNA. Some of these graves are being excavated as we speak." Out of all of the tiny, uniform rows on the screen, only two of them contained blue dots.

"There aren't very many blue dots left."

"No, there aren't." Dr. Little frowned. "Every cemetery in every city, in every region, has been surveyed and recorded. Now we are systematically going through each graveyard and replicating the number of people needed to replace those who have died each week."

"Whoa. Talk about population control."

"Yes, but because of that, our unemployment rate is zero, which means our poverty rate is zero."

"And this is happening around the world?"

"In all three regions, but our division manages the cloning program for this region." His gray eyes flashed with pride. I focused my attention on the way he kept his hand in a fist while he gestured, and the sudden rise in his voice at the end of each sentence. Like everyone else I'd met so far, everything about Dr. Pickford was human and unique. It was easy to forget I was having a conversation with clones.

Michael rocked forward in his seat. "Not every country had the technology or the resources to facilitate a program on their own. The world was forced to work together. There's something very humbling about the inability to procreate." He continued. "We're not saying that it was easy. Even though it was the only means of saving the human race, some thought the plague was an act of God, and they didn't want to do anything to interfere with His plan. Others thought the disease was sent by aliens, so an alien race could take over the planet."

I wrinkled my nose. "Well, yeah. I wouldn't want to walk down the street and run into a clone of someone I knew.

That would be insane."

I imagined the clone of my mother on the street, politely stopping as I approached but shaking her head and drawing her eyebrows together, perplexed when I called her "Mom." My arms prickled, and a chill exploded at the base of my neck.

"Actually, the oldest DNA was used first to avoid just that."

"And there's still plenty of DNA left, right?" I asked, looking at the two rows of blue dots on the screen. My stomach tightened even more, and I swallowed hard to clear the lump in my throat. "And if you had to, you could replicate the DNA of just one person to make hundreds of clones, right?"

Dr. Little tapped his thick fingers against the top of his thigh. "Even though we are clones, we still harbor the desire to be an original. One clone from one DNA source, and then break the mold, so to speak. But if we had to, we could make an infinite number of clones from one DNA sample."

"Then your population problem would be solved, right? I mean, why wouldn't it be? Just sprinkle them around the world, so they'd be less likely to run into each other."

"It's not that easy. It's becoming more difficult by the day." Michael interlocked his fingers and set his hands in his lap. "Only one in ten clone embryos survives the first ten days in its synthetic uterus, and only one in five makes it to the second trimester. And when it comes to using the same DNA to produce more than one individual, so far, that hasn't been possible due to a phenomenon known as Ancestral Memory. When — "

Dr. Little banged his fist against my end table, sending

it into a lopsided wobble that didn't stop until he grabbed it and pulled it upright. I flinched. He glared at Michael, who hung his head.

Ancestral Memory was obviously a hot button, but Michael's cowed expression kept me from pressing the issue.

"As Dr. Bennett explained," said Dr. Little after clearing his throat, "embryo stability and survival is one of our biggest setbacks. In fact," he added as he tapped his L-Band, "this is something you need to see for yourself."

See for myself? My eyes immediately darted to the ceiling, expecting the monitor to lower, but a *ding* echoed through my room, and seconds later, a security guard entered with a chair, hovering inches from the floor.

"I-I get to leave my room?" I stuttered as my heart jumped.

"Of course, Miss Dannacher, you're a patient, not a prisoner," he chuckled. "You're not physically ready, but I'll make this one exception until the time comes when you are."

Dr. Little stepped back and stood still, holding his coffee mug, while Dr. Love and Michael lifted me from the bed and lowered me into what they called a hoverchair. The chair bobbed with my weight and steadied itself with a hum that grew louder as it rocked. A suck of air from the green cushion held me securely in place.

When I pulled my arm from around Michael's neck, I tried to catch his eyes, but they were focused on first the floor, and then Dr. Little. Dr. Love didn't look at me either—only Dr. Pickford did and his upper lip lifted into a smile.

"So, where are we going?" I asked as Dr. Little guided my chair into the hall with a push from one index finger.

"The prenatal ward."

Honestly, I didn't care where I went. I was finally out of

my room. The milky ceiling burned with light, but I needed more—a window—but every twist and turn resulted in a stark wall with gray doors.

Before I could beg the team to take me to a window first, Dr. Little said, "And here we are, Miss Dannacher."

My hoverchair steadied itself in front of a door labeled "PNW One." The door slid open, and as my escorts took a few steps forward, Dr. Little put up his arm and announced, "I'll do the honors. Wait for us here," with a sternness that made Michael's lips tighten.

The rectangular room we entered held long tables that ran parallel to one another, each holding a row of clear, fluid-filled vessels containing an embryo or fetus in various stages of development. A foggy red tube extended from each small being, beginning at the belly button and ending at the machinery mounted below each table, equipment that spun, sucked, and turned.

Some babies were right-side up, some upside down, but all of them were curled with their knees toward their chests, and their tiny hands at their mouths. One was even sucking its thumb. Even the smaller fetuses with translucent skin and Martian-shaped heads, I found adorable.

"Oh, they're so cute," I said.

"And each one a miracle." I heard Dr. Little's teeth click against his coffee mug, followed by a gulp.

In contrast to the sterile environment, the room smelled like baby powder and roses, and the far wall was decorated in a floral design of red tulips and yellow daffodils. Two female workers dressed in pink-and-blue-patterned smocks took turns inspecting each artificial uterus, tapping buttons and turning knobs on the machinery below, and after exchanging frowns, one of the women pulled a rubber glove from her pocket and stretched it over her hand.

"What's she going to do?" I whispered to Dr. Little.

"Remember, Miss Dannacher, only one in five fetuses lives past the second trimester," he said, and took another sip of coffee.

The woman dipped her gloved hand into the vessel and cupped the baby's head with her palm. She lifted the dripping baby from the container and delicately set it into a pink blanket that lay like a hammock between the other lady's opened arms.

"So it's dead?" My throat tightened, making it hard to take my next breath.

Dr. Little nodded, lowered his head, and closed his eyes like he was saying a silent prayer. When his eyes popped open, my chair jerked, and he pushed it forward until we met the women at a long table by the flowered wall where tiny wooden boxes lay neatly arranged in a single row.

As we passed the tables of artificial uteruses, I couldn't help but wonder which would and wouldn't survive. My stomach soured, and while I watched the synthetic placentas suck like leeches against the inside of each tank, I swallowed hard to keep myself from gagging.

Each box was a tiny coffin. The worker holding the swaddled baby wiped a tear from the corner of her eye and lovingly placed the fetus into its final resting place. The other employee covered her mouth with one hand, and with the other, dabbed her tear-damp cheeks before stroking the preemie's delicate chin.

"There're so many of them," I said slowly.

"Yes, there are. One in five, Miss Dannacher."

My hoverchair vibrated, rose farther from the ground, and didn't stop until I was just high enough to see the contents of every shoebox-size casket. Each baby was wrapped in either blue or pink, the soft blanket exposing the angelic face. Some fetuses were small, their eyelids paper thin, their heads larger than their wrapped bodies, while others looked close to an expected birth weight, being the size of a baby doll.

"I've seen enough, please lower my chair," I said, turning to Dr. Little, whose eyes were now level with mine. My bottom lip quivered, and a warm tear hit my upper lip. "I want to go now."

"As you wish, Miss Dannacher." He blinked his own watery eyes, and with a tap to the back of the hoverchair, it dropped to its original hoverment.

He guided my chair from the room, nudging it slowly, and just before the door closed behind us, I heard the snap of another rubber glove. One in five—one in five thousand was way too many.

When we entered the hall, I kept my head down. A set of last tears dropped to my lap, and I quickly rubbed them into my pants. Dr. Love and Dr. Pickford didn't speak while they walked, but I heard Michael whisper behind me, "That wasn't necessary, Simon. You shouldn't have done that to her."

"I only do what's necessary. Don't question my good judgment, Michael," answered Dr. Little, increasing the volume of his voice as he spoke.

Once we were in my room, Michael and Dr. Love lifted me back onto my bed. Michael flashed me an apologetic smile, and Dr. Love brushed the hair from my face with her fingertips before pulling the sheet up to my waist.

Dr. Little was the first to speak. "One in five, and that's only one of many issues. As Dr. Bennett explained before, another one of our obstacles is DNA instability. We're running out of workable samples. Dr. Bennett, why don't you explain this additional problem to our patient?"

Michael took a deep breath and rubbed his palms on his pant legs. "The older the DNA, the less likely we'll be able to replicate it. In addition, we're often stuck working with tombs so ancient that the cadavers have turned to dust. Many of our ancestors also chose cremation, and now that decision is hurting us, too."

"Continue, Dr. Bennett." Dr. Little's eyes gleamed as he set his coffee mug on the table next to my bed.

"We don't have a lot of time. The last effective DNA will run out within ten to fifteen years. If we can't figure out how to successfully clone a clone then…"

A chill crept along the back of my neck. I couldn't look at any of them, not even Michael.

"We're sorry to have to tell you this, Cassie…" said Dr. Little. He paused and set his jaw. "You've entered an advanced world, but it's also a world on the verge of extinction. However, I'm sure we'll crack the code to produce reclones, or improve the artificial uteruses. Or we'll simply come up with another plan."

My life had been cut short before, and now it was possibly going to be cut short again? The fate of the world depended on a team of geneticists? And what about those poor babies dying in their artificial uteruses? One bombshell after another—I couldn't take another hit.

Yes, they needed another plan. But what kind of plan? My breath burned in my lungs and the tiny blood vessels in my cheeks fired with heat.

Oh my God! I was the only fertile female on the planet. Why didn't I think of this before? But no…it wouldn't be possible…one female couldn't do it alone. The idea was barbaric and beyond immoral. They had to come up with something else. I couldn't be their alternative plan. Would they dare do something so vile?

My eyes darted from one doctor to the other, and with a quick shake of my head, I attempted to bury my speculations deep into the back of my mind as a cold prickle worked its way up my spine.

No, they wouldn't. The idea was preposterous. Life was too precious to them.

Dr. Little and Dr. Pickford left my room with nods, smiles in my direction, and another, "Don't let this knowledge be of your concern," but it did little to put me at ease.

Don't let it be of concern. Then why tell me in the first place and show me the prenatal ward? The world was on the brink of falling apart, and I wasn't supposed to think about it? I scrubbed my face to hide my tears. This was way too much information to take in all at once, especially when the images of those babies were so fresh in my mind.

Dr. Love blinked at me with a softness in her eyes. As she passed Michael, she placed her hand on his shoulder, and I could have sworn she whispered something like, "We need a place like Tasma right now."

Tasma. I heard that before when Ella had mentioned it casually, like it was some kind of a joke. Strange.

Michael stayed behind, making the room free from the spying obscuras with the swipe of his foot, then took the chair closest to my bed.

Free. The opposite of restricted, limited, bound. When clones weren't in a free zone, they were controlled by the mere fact that someone could be watching and judging their every move. These people weren't stupid. They were naïve, content with the only way of life they knew.

But even without Big Brother, wouldn't those who knew about the failing DNA feel panicked by the impending doom? These clones were enthusiastic and hopeful, too optimistic to make sense to me.

"I hope you're not angry with me," Michael said, staring at the space on the floor between his feet.

"For what? Not telling me that you're a clone, or not telling me that the world will probably end in anarchy, chaos, and civil wars before I hit the ripe old age of thirty?"

"Both." He inched his chair closer to my bed and took my hand. "I'm sorry, but we were more concerned with your recovery than burdening you with the truth of our existence. And about taking you to PNW One, I was against it from the start. But it was Dr. Little's call to make—not mine."

"I'm not mad." I smiled. "And I know you wouldn't have taken me there if you had a choice. I'm actually happy to finally know the truth, but I still can't help feeling a little deceived." Michael stiffened and slid his hand from mine. "Life is precious—yeah I get that—but I don't have a great future ahead of me like Dr. Love and Ella keep telling me. You told me I could make the world a better place, but in less than two decades, we could all be dead."

"Dr. Love and Ella are thinking positively. You can't blame them for that. Besides, the average citizen isn't privy to the data we shared with you today, and they've been led to believe there's an endless supply of DNA at our disposal."

"So why would Dr. Little trust me? He's not afraid I'll tell the average citizen?"

"No," he half laughed. "First of all, no one would believe you, and secondly, we'll find a solution to our problem before our population noticeably begins to shrink."

"So you think there's a geneticist out there—maybe even you—who will crack the code or design a new and improved artificial uterus?" I asked, trying to disguise my horror at his casual tone as I remembered the rows of Plexiglas containers with fetuses floating in them.

"Maybe," he smiled coyly. "Apparently my donor was a genius in the field of genetics. I was cloned and schooled here at GenH1 without parents and without friends so I could do what I'm doing now—advance our genetics program. My whole life has been dedicated to this. I guess I'm just a… what did you call it…a nerd?"

We had a lot more in common than I realized, his youth also stifled by homeschooling and alienation from his peers. "No, you're definitely not a nerd." I laughed.

"Why not?"

"Well, because you don't look like one. You look like a *GQ* model." *Did I really just say that?* Maybe he had no idea what I was talking about and wouldn't equate it with me basically saying he was so hot he took my breath away.

"You don't look like a nerd, either, Cassie," said Michael, smiling as he moved to the edge of my bed.

"Oh yes, I do." My chest burst with a pleasant fire.

"When you called yourself a nerd the other day, I looked up the term in our databanks. A nerd is also defined as being shy and unattractive. You're not a nerd. You're definitely not shy, and you're definitely not unattractive. You're gorgeous."

Michael pushed my hair away from my forehead and took my hand in both of his. I tightened my fingers around the back of his hand and leaned toward him.

"No, I'm not." Welcomed warmth radiated through the rest of my body.

"When the team opened your S.T.A.S.I.S. chamber, there was a collective sigh, not just because your body was intact, but because you were so incredibly beautiful. As we lifted you from the cryonic chamber and placed you on an examination table, your medical records fell to the floor. I picked them up, and that's when I saw your date of birth and your date of death. You are only seventeen years old. I couldn't help but think you were a gift sent here just for..." He licked his lips.

"For who?" Mesmerized by his words, I wrapped one arm around my bent knees and pulled myself closer.

"But then again," he continued, "you were brain dead, unresponsive to the touch, and even after you were revived and placed in stasis, your eyes, your beautiful blue eyes, were vacant, still frozen in time. You weren't a person then. You were a thing, a pretty piece of history, an artifact, making it easy for me to work with the team and come up with a plan, but now..."

Michael's hand melted against mine. His grip tightened and I felt his skin, damp and warm. I squeezed back. "Now?"

"Look," he said intently, his eyes unblinking. "You asked me if I had hope for the future, and the answer is that I do. I do because I believe in miracles, Cassie. You're proof of that."

This world had ten to fifteen years to come up with a plan. It took centuries for scientists to find a cure for cancer, and these clones thought they could solve their DNA issue in a decade? Was there another plan I didn't know about?

Why use artificial uteruses instead of clone women for surrogates? How was cloning even possible without donated eggs? And what about me? Would they dare to do the unthinkable?

The questions teetering on my tongue vanished when Michael's thumb rubbed circles on my palm. Instead of saying good-bye, he gently kissed my hand before he stood and walked to the door. My heart pitter-pattered, and I tingled all over from the feel of his lips and tickle of his breath.

Like Dr. Love had said, Michael cared deeply for me, although I didn't know how much until now. Just hearing his name made my insides swirl and my heart swell all over again.

With a *ding* he left, and with a second *ding* the door slid open minutes later. I lifted my back from the inclined bed, hoping it was Michael, returning to continue where we left off. But it was Ella, balancing an exercise pole on her finger, ready for my afternoon physical therapy session.

Damn. It would be hard to concentrate when all I could think about was Michael and the soft kiss he left on my hand.

Chapter Six

"Are you ready for your dinner?" The voice came from my L-Band. It was the first time it did anything other than light up when I looked at it.

An orange dot glowed on the tiny screen. "Um, yeah, can you hear me?"

"Yes. Are you ready for dinner?"

"Um, sure," I answered, even though I didn't recognize the voice. It was female and human.

The door slid open to reveal an elderly Asian lady with gray hair at her temples and a plump, round face. Her roundness continued from her face down the rest of her five-foot-two frame, and from her big round bosom to her big round bottom.

"Hello. I'm Kale. You were asleep during Dr. Love's shift, so she asked me to bring you your dinner." Kale's uniform was blue, marked with a darker blue stripe.

"Thank you."

"Do you need help?" she asked, positioning the tray on my lap.

"No, my arms are sore, but I can do it," I answered, piercing a chunk of potato with a fork.

"Would you like me to stay and visit for a while?"

"Are you a psychologist?"

"No. I am a medical assistant, tier two." She walked to the side of my bed and took a big whiff of my flower bouquet. While she bumbled about, shifting her weight from one foot to the other, the questions I had before continued to burn in my brain.

"Can I ask you something?" But did she even know what I'd been told? Did she know I was from 2022? "Do you know how I ended up in this hospital?"

"I certainly do. Everyone who has contact with you has been briefed on your unique circumstances."

Okay, so maybe she knows more. "So, um, do you think there's enough useable DNA left to keep up with the current population? I mean, what if there isn't? Then what would happen?"

Her eyes flashed. "That's something I never think about. Do you know why?"

"No."

"Because I have faith in the program. We all need to have faith in something, but we have to remember this: we are not the definitive creators of life. The human being is the ultimate invention."

The hair on my arms became erect, and I shivered.

"Faith and hope are all we need." She lightly patted my arm. The lines on her round forehead became more pronounced, and she lowered her voice until it was almost inaudible. "Hope for the future, hope for all of mankind. And I have it. Do you have hope, Cassie?"

"I guess." She was right. Hope was all I had. Hope and memories of what could have been if I had survived the helicopter crash.

"Then that is all you need. You need to feel this deep down in your soul. Everything happens for a reason. That is what I believe. You died when you did, and we found you when we did for some very important reason. You need to believe that, too, and do what you've been destined to do." Her eyes squinted and her cheeks dimpled with a smile.

But I couldn't think of any important reason why I was here. What was she talking about? "Like what? I'm so sick of not knowing what's going to happen to me. I want out of this bed and out of this hospital." A pathetic kick at my sheets was solid reminder that I was still too weak to ditch this place on my own. Too bad Dr. Little didn't leave that hoverchair behind.

Kale's expression didn't change despite the flare of anger in my voice. "Has anyone shown you how to access our system?" She asked, avoiding my question with an eager grin like she was waiting for me to open a present.

"No," I answered, crossing my arms.

"Well, you can, now that you're banded and connected to the region's main Liaison computer." Kale held up her wrist. "And now that you know our little secret"—she laughed—"you can watch our entertainment channels, but most importantly, you can retrieve information from it at any time no matter where you are. Unless, of course, the information is restricted. You can speak as loudly or as softly as you want, even whisper so no one else can hear, and Liaison One will hear it because it reads the sound vibrations that travel through your body."

"That's awesome, I guess, but doesn't this thing come in any other colors? Black is so drab."

Kale laughed, a big guffaw that matched her size. "No, only if you become a resident in another region. Black is Region One, blue is Region Two, and red is Region Three. And who knows what they wear in Tasma," she laughed.

"Tasma? So it's a place?"

"An imaginary place. Who told you about it?"

"No one. I just heard it mentioned a few times."

"Tasma is supposed to be a top-secret, clone-run facility hidden from the government, but it doesn't really exist, something made up to give the plague survivors hope while they healed from the tragedy. Now it's just an expression— kind of like 'the grass is greener on the other side.' It's also the subject of an old schoolyard song I used to sing when I was a kid. We'd sing it while playing flutter rope on the pavement."

"That's cool. Can you sing it to me now?"

"Oh, I don't know. If I can remember all of the words. Let me see."

In a sing-song voice, her tone child-like, she began a clone's version of something similar to the nineteenth century "Ring Around the Rosie:"

"Dirty socks, purple pox—take me away to Tasma,

Slimy skin, no more kin—take me away to Tasma,

Puss-filled dots, broken bots—take me away to Tasma,

Bloodshot eyes, a world of spies—take me away to Tasma,

Forefathers, forefathers, hear my cries—please take me

away to Tasma.

"That's a pretty depressing song, Kale."

"Well, that's what's to be expected. Young survivors of the plague made that one up, the idea that there was a place called Tasma, a secret paradise free of the plague and its aftermath. Like I said, the song is based on an old myth, a myth born from hope."

That made sense in terms of how Ella and Dr. Love both referred to it.

"Um, I guess black is not so bad. If I have to wear this forever then I guess black is the best color to have. It goes with everything, right?"

"Right," said Kale

"And now that I have access to Liaison One, I can order a hoverchair," I said in a half-serious tone. "I've used one before. I'm sure Dr. Little won't mind if you take me on a tour of the hospital."

She gave me a sympathetic frown. "And I'm sure he will."

"Yeah, I know." I sighed.

After Kale left, I tapped the L-Band's magical screen and figured out how to listen to a song called "New World" by a band called Plague Party. At first, the volume was way too loud and the chorus "New world corruption; What's you're assumption" rocked my room for two minutes, making the suspended table gyrate until I figured out how to turn it down.

Then I watched ten minutes worth of a soap opera on a monitor that lowered from the ceiling. And I thought twenty-first century soap operas were cheesy, although it did give me the opportunity to find out that their vehicles did, in fact, fly after all. A character named Phoebe ran out of credits, so when she tried to board a hoverbus, she was turned away. Boyfriend George tried to come to her rescue by holding up his wrist and saying, "If only my band would work for you." In the end, George offered Phoebe the use of his personal mover, and Phoebe showed her gratitude by complaining about the mover's low hoverment.

Talk about boring. On a positive note, it did give me a bigger glimpse into the world of clones, and by the end of thirty minutes, I wished I had an L-Bud, a small, optional earpiece that everyone appeared to own and wear.

With my L-Band, I could practically locate and talk to anyone in the world, but that also meant I could be located and talked to at any time. Was there any comfort in knowing I was part of their Liaison One system, attached to their society in a way that made me one of them despite not being a clone? No, there wasn't. This was their world—not mine.

What else could an L-Band do?

"Liaison One, where's Dr. Michael Bennett?"

"Miss Dannacher, Dr. Michael Bennett has left GenH1, but I can give you his current location." Liaison One's voice was distinctive but genderless.

"Um, okay."

"Michael Bennett is on Hoverbus 23, heading south above 21st and B Street. Would you like me to connect you?"

"No, no, please don't do that." My face flushed, and a funny, delightful feeling ran through my chest.

Um, how about, "Liaison One, where is Cassie Dannacher?" Having my exact location could help me navigate my way to a window.

"I am sorry, Miss Dannacher, but that information is

restricted."

"Restricted? But I am Cassie Dannacher." Why all the secrecy?

"A VWP clearance is required in order to access any information regarding Cassie Dannacher." That's weird. So not everyone is supposed to know about me?

"Who has VWP clearance?"

"I'm sorry, Miss Dannacher, but that information is also restricted."

VWP clearance. The "P" could stand for "project" or "plan," but what about the "VW?" I couldn't think of any words from my past or any from my present situation that related to me and started with a "V" or a "W."

What in the world could VWP mean and what did those three letters have to do with me?

Chapter Seven

"How are you doing? I haven't been in to see you in a few days," said Dr. Love.

Just a few days? It seemed like forever. Michael hadn't paid me a visit, either. I missed him and couldn't help wondering if he was purposely avoiding me. Did he think I was still harboring disappointment toward him for not telling me earlier this was a world of clones living in mock hope, or was he having second thoughts about his unrestricted gush of emotions toward me?

"Well, let's see. Boredom, breakfast, physical therapy with Ella, boredom, lunch, boredom, dinner, boredom, bed, and two bouts of claustrophobia. Times that by however many days I've been here. Overall, I feel dismified," I said, a bit proud of myself for using a coined word from this century, something I learned from the government-run soap operas.

"It's been ten days since your awakening."

"Then I'm way overdue for some fresh air. I'm banded

now. Can't you at least take me to an opened window in a hoverchair? I was told that once I was banded…"

"I'm sorry, Cassie, but Dr. Little thinks it's best you stay put until you're further along in your recovery. Your trip to PNW One was an exception." Dr. Love smiled sympathetically. Dr. Little apparently held my freedom in his hands. Damn.

"Yeah, I know. That's what Ella keeps telling me."

But how long could I stay put without going mad? Doubt was starting to take root in my soul, growing into a thorny weed of suspicion. Tearing that notion aside by reflecting on the clones' kindness and vulnerability was no longer enough, my skepticism springing back again, fresh, ripe, and ready to play upon my emotions every time I convinced myself everything would be okay.

"But he does think you're ready for another meeting with the team."

"Today?"

"Today."

"Meeting about what?" Could it have something to do with VWP? Maybe it was about the alternative plans? My apprehension doubled.

She drew in a deep breath, checked her L-Band, and sighed. "You'll find out soon enough. They're just down the hall."

She adjusted my bunched-up pillow, but my muscles were so tight with the thought of another visit it made it difficult for her to prop me up. She added two stim patches to my shoulder blades, but their systematic array of shocks did little to give me any relief.

The last meeting bore many unwelcomed surprises, but

I'd get to see Michael again, and in his eyes, I'd be able to read either apology or repentance over the last time we saw each other.

"Miss Dannacher, Dr. Love." Dr. Little nodded, lifting his coffee cup, and Dr. Pickford mirrored his greeting. Michael restricted his eye contact with me, giving one brief smile before looking away. Dr. Love nodded at the three men and made her exit without saying good-bye to me or to them.

The two men took chairs opposite Michael, and Dr. Little set his mug on my table. "Dr. Pickford and I wanted to delay this meeting, giving you a little more recovery time, but Dr. Bennett insisted we make this visit today."

When Michael refused to look at me, the hair on my arms rose.

"During our last meeting, we told you we might need to come up with an alternate plan, and I'm here to inform you that we've done just that. It's a plan that needs to begin as soon as possible, in case our other research fails to produce results."

"And what's that?" Everyone scrutinized me except Michael.

"Miss Dannacher," said Dr. Little. "During your lifetime, females were born with all of their eggs intact. They—"

"I know how the reproductive system works." My stomach turned.

"Then you know that right now you are carrying hundreds of eggs."

My stomach flipped again as fire ignited in my gut. No! He couldn't be suggesting…? I didn't think they'd stoop this low.

"Female clones are infertile, but not our males," he said with a brazen smile. "Miss Dannacher, *you* are the answer to our prayers. You can save the human race." The eagerness in his face contorted the smile stretching between his creased cheeks.

Dr. Pickford's lip curled with pleasure, but Michael's posture hadn't changed.

The muscles in my neck twinged, and a headache the size of a tennis ball developed in the center of my forehead. They couldn't be serious. I tried to speak, but the words clogged my throat and never came.

"But it won't work. I can't do it alone. It's impossible," I said, wiping the sweat from the back of my neck and looking back and forth among the doctors.

Dr. Little rubbed his hands together and rotated his shoulders. "That is where you're wrong. The genetics team has already made the calculations. Using your eggs, a team of surrogates, and a gender selection process assuring the birth of only females, within one hundred years, there would be enough fertile women on this planet to sustain our population naturally."

"A team of surrogates?" I asked after a swallow.

"Our women menstruate despite the lack of an ovum."

My stomach did another cartwheel. Every month the clone women were given a red reminder of their sad fate, making me one to envy and secretly despise. Maybe that was why I was being kept a secret? But they didn't need to wait for me. They could be using them as surrogates now, couldn't they?

"So, you're going to force me to give you my eggs?" My heartbeat quickened as the thought filled my being.

"Force is a strong word," said Dr. Pickford, twiddling his thumbs. Dr. Little's smile turned into a sneer. "'Donate' is a better word. And in the meantime we want you to…" Dr. Pickford's lips curled, twitching into a half smile.

"You want me to have a baby, too?" I shouted. Everything tightened—my shoulders, my neck, my jaw.

"Yes, babies," he said. "We want you to have babies, but only until we can successfully implement a surrogate program using your eggs. Then your reproduction rate can slow to a stop."

Babies. Surrogate program. Reproduction rate. The words rattled in my head. This couldn't be happening. "I won't do it." The room started to spin. "You can't make me!"

"Miss Dannacher, you and your offspring will be treated with the utmost respect and consideration during this process," Dr. Pickford interjected. His tone was fatherly, marked with sincerity, creating deep wrinkles at the corners of his eyes, but his upper lip continued to curve, making him appear sinister. "All of your needs, wants, and desires will be met. Our budget is unlimited when it comes to your well-being. Our goal is to keep you happy and reproductive."

Happy and reproductive. That was what he said, but in his tone and eyes lay a threatening flash of evil, warning me not to trust him.

Two deep breaths made the room stop spinning. "You think forcing me to get pregnant is going to keep me happy? I'm sorry but that's not possible," I snapped.

"Miss Dannacher," said Dr. Little. "You need to think of this as your contribution to the world. We were desperate and out of ideas until we found your cryonic chamber. This is your destiny. You're the woman who's going to save the earth. You'll inspire our clone women to join the surrogate program in an act of patriotism and honor. Your daughters will follow your lead and accept their duty with gusto."

"I can't. I won't." I trembled. "I'd never lead anyone into that fate."

"You'll make it an honor and a privilege for our women to play an active role in the project, thus ending our future struggle for survival. We've created a wonderful place here. It's a world of peace, not war, abundance, not deficiency. There's no poverty, prejudice, or suffering." Dr. Little's eyes widened to their limit. "And they'll be no more one-in-five babies meeting such sad, pathetic fates. Using your eggs will prevent this."

"I don't care. I don't want to provide this—honor." I swallowed and pushed back against my pillow, inching as far away from them as I could as the face of an innocent baby burned in my brain. "No. No." Did he really think he'd be able to guilt me into being cooperative by showing me the prenatal ward?

"We've been able to cure every disease and heal the most debilitating injuries," he said a bit arrogantly. "But there's only one thing we can't do, Miss Dannacher—guarantee the future of the human race without your help."

"Recloning. Recloning is the answer, not this. And,... and improving the artificial uterus."

"No, Miss Dannacher. *You* are our only solution at this point in time. Recloning may prove to be an impossibility and—"

"But, I-I…"

"Without your cooperation, our children will grow up in a world of unbridled desperation and fear, a world with a survival-of-the-fittest mentality. We can't let that happen now can we, Miss Dannacher. You can't let that happen to this wonderful society we've created." Dr. Little shook his head from side to side.

I shrunk away in horror. I didn't want to be the woman who was going to save the earth. Babies? They wanted me to have babies? That's the last thing I wanted to do. What about the training and career opportunities Michael said I would be given to become a so-called productive member of society? And what about going to college? He lied to me! He'd known their plan for me all along.

Michael caught my stare as my gaze begged for his support, and I glared when he remained unmoved.

"We expect your cooperation, and in doing so, I can guarantee your happiness and the satisfaction in knowing that you rescued mankind from a horrific fate. You'll be treated with fairness and the utmost respect."

But there was something about Dr. Pickford's twitching lip and Dr. Little's condescending, yet sympathetic, attitude. Treated with fairness and respect? Could I believe that? In my gut, I suspected quite the opposite.

"And what if I don't want to cooperate? I'm not going to have a baby, and I'm not giving you my eggs!" I yelled, hitting my fist against the side table like a mallet. Dr. Little's mug teetered and toppled onto its side, leaving a puddle of coffee to half absorb into the cuff of Dr. Little's shirtsleeve.

Sure, I was angry. They'd smiled, seemed concerned, yet all along they plotted without my knowledge, only caring about me as their baby-maker. If they'd told me up front, instead of hiding behind their deceptions, maybe I wouldn't have been so furious. Yet, I wondered whether they would have awakened me otherwise.

Ignoring his soiled uniform, Dr. Little picked up the mug and set it upright. His eyes never left mine. "You have to cooperate. It's your destiny. If you refuse to take part in the program, you'll be required to participate. There's no other solution. The conversation ends here."

My destiny. This was what Kale, a technician, had referred to, proving they'd all known what was intended for me.

The older doctors stood simultaneously as if their shoulders were attached, and as Dr. Little strode stiffly to the door, Dr. Pickford matched his pace. Before I could blink, the door closed behind them, leaving Michael with his hands in his lap, studying the floor.

I was bedridden. An invalid. I couldn't run. I couldn't hide. I was exactly where they wanted me—homeless, vulnerable, L-Banded, and fertile. But they were vulnerable, too, a species doomed to extinction.

Did I feel any sympathy for them? Of course, especially for Ella, Dr. Love, Magnum, and even Michael, though he hadn't been completely honest with me. Was I willing to save their future at my expense? I wasn't sure, though according to them, I didn't have a choice.

They'd strap me down, steal my eggs, and keep me pregnant for the next twenty years.

The clones were like earthworms in the rain, curling and arching, stretching and wiggling to save themselves from drowning in a shallow pool in the sidewalk, a mistake left by a careless concrete finisher. The worms wanted to live, but unfortunately in the end, after all the clouds cleared, the worms were dead, lying like rubber bands hardened in the sun.

A clone could not give birth, but a clone could perpetuate the human race. Like greedy pirates looking for treasure, they had plundered and pillaged every cemetery known to man, leaving their ancestors' caskets defiled and degraded.

I was their Eve. My stomach churned. Who would be my Adam?

I was the first to speak, and at this point, I was filled with too much turmoil and betrayal to even raise my voice. "You should have told me, Michael, from the very beginning that being a productive member of society meant being a *reproductive* member of society. All that talk about training and career opportunities was a big lie."

He bent forward, his eyes continually aimed at the gray floor as I watched his back rise with each breath.

"I'm sorry, Cassie. You have no idea how hard that was for me. I wanted to tell you the truth, but I had no choice. Until you were told about the project, we had to keep you from asking questions we weren't ready to answer. There was nothing I could do. They were going to wait another week, but I couldn't lie to you one more minute, let alone a week or even a day. Thankfully, I was able to talk them into telling you today."

I folded my arms against my chest and sighed. "Even so, how can I not be pissed? I'm being forced into doing something I don't want to do, and I've been manipulated and deceived by people I thought I could trust."

"I don't know what to say other than that I am sorry. We were never trying to deceive you. We needed to wait until you were stronger. It didn't seem right to tell you so soon after your awakening. You were too vulnerable."

"And I'm not vulnerable now? Look at me." I said, raising my frail arms and letting them drop limply to the bed.

"We're all vulnerable. We're desperate. We're running out of time, and recloning and the artificial uterus probably won't be perfected before then. We're not trying to take advantage of you. You just happen to be the best and possibly our only solution. Can't you understand that at all? Try to see if from our point of view," said Michael desperately.

"Is this coming from you or the team?" I huffed.

"Both. I don't want our society to end."

"I don't want it to end, either, but I shouldn't be *forced* to participate." I sighed. "They should have given me a choice." Not that I would have agreed.

"That's what I wanted them to do."

"Then why didn't you do it?"

"Because it wasn't up to me. As much as I wanted to tell you about it, I couldn't. I signed a contract with GenH1. If I reneged, I would have lost everything I'd worked so hard for, and then I wouldn't be here to protect you. I wanted them to explain our situation first and then ask for your help, but the other members of the team predicted you'd say no."

Would I have said no? Now that they'd done the opposite, it was too hard to go back in my mind and predict an answer.

"Would you have said yes or no?" asked Michael earnestly, inching closer and taking my hand in his.

"I'm not sure," I admitted, and yanked my hand away.

"Then you might have been forced to anyway. So either way, we'd be where we are right now."

He was right. Without a good comeback, I shifted the subject. "I still don't understand why you need my eggs. The ovaries of cloned females don't produce eggs, but you've obviously found a way to clone without using an ovum, right?"

"Yes, we found a way," he said with conviction, "but it's still not enough."

"Was my cryo chamber discovered by accident, or was I knowingly brought here for this purpose?"

He didn't answer.

"Please!"

He took a deep breath through his nose. "Your cryonic capsule was found by a crew of workers who were in charge of demolishing the warehouse which used to house S.T.A.S.I.S. Your chamber was delivered here, and we found your capsule harbored a human being with all reproductive organs intact and operational. We opened bottles of artificial champagne and celebrated."

"And what if my reproductive organs had been missing, let's say from a hysterectomy or something, or if I was infertile. Then what would you have done with me?"

"You'd still be here. Don't think for one minute that we would have abandoned our mission and let you die." Michael moved closer. "I wouldn't have let you die. You were too important to me, even then."

I was the girl he awakened, his Sleeping Beauty. Like Doctor Frankenstein, he felt an innate responsibility toward the life he helped restore. And, of course, there was a reciprocal effect. Could I be mad at him for going along with this charade?

"Then think about what they're asking me to do—what *you're* asking me to do."

"I was just following the plan—"

"The plan to turn me into a baby-maker."

"I signed the contract before you were 'awakened.' I didn't know you. My feelings for you weren't the same as they are now. It was easy for me to agree with the team, sign the contract, and focus on the future of the project. I never thought about how you'd feel, how'd you'd react to our plan, or what would happen if you refused to participate. But now..." He lowered his head. "Now I care about all of those things."

Michael cared—yes—I didn't doubt his feelings were genuine, but there was no way he could fully understand my reluctance and disgust toward what they were asking me to do. I couldn't expect him to, but I needed him to be on my side now and convince the team to release me from the program.

"My mother became pregnant with me when she was twenty-three," I said, nestling my shoulders into my pillow. "She wasn't married to my dad. In fact, she hardly knew him. He was a paleontologist, too. They were working together on a site in Iran, and one night under the stars, I was conceived. My mom blamed their one-night stand on boredom and the fact that he was extremely handsome. There's not much to do in a tent in the desert without electricity. But that's a lame excuse. Whenever I got bored and tired of hanging out around the campfire, I resorted to reading by flashlight—not having sex."

"No one's asking you to have sex. You'll be artificially inseminated."

A sick feeling rose in my gut, and for a moment, I thought my breakfast would end up in my lap.

"Yeah, well, that doesn't fall into *my* plan either. I always told myself that I wouldn't do what she did. I planned to marry the man of my dreams and wait a few years before having children. And they wouldn't grow up like I did. No homeschooling—they'd go to a public school, so they could be surrounded by kids their own age and have plenty of friends."

"This is a different world. Your plan doesn't fit here," he said softly.

"Then make it fit," I said earnestly. "Tell me that as soon as I'm completely recovered, I can freely walk out of this hospital and restart my life the way I want it to be." My voice cracked and a set of hot tears teetered on my lower lashes.

"I can't. You know I can't. It goes beyond me, beyond this hospital."

"Beyond this hospital to where?" I urged.

"The presidents. All three. I have no authority over any one of them."

"Then I have no choice? This is so wrong on so many levels." I fell back against my propped-up pillow as the cold reality of my new existence in this world settled once again into my bones. I didn't want to have a baby. I didn't want to be a single parent, and I didn't want other women to give birth to my babies either.

"You're right. It's wrong. It's unethical. I'm so sorry." He shook his head and looked up at the ceiling. The twinkle of lights above reflected in his eyes like tiny stars. "There's nothing I can do to change the team's mind. But I can do everything in my power to give you as much freedom as I can. Then maybe you'll be comfortable and happy."

"Comfortable and happy? What a joke," I snapped.

"The program still allows you to get married and have your own children."

"How?"

"The surrogates and their babies will eventually enter the general population under our watchful eye, with the children's fertility remaining a secret. When the surrogate program is firmly established and you've given birth to enough children, you'll also be allowed to enter the population. At that time, you can get married as long as you raise your biological children with an understanding of their future obligations."

"How many children are they going to make me have?" My voice trembled.

"I don't know," Michael said, shaking his head and averting his eyes. "The plan's not specific. There're too many variables when it comes to your future health and fertility. Basically, you'll be expected to give birth to as many children as physically possible before you reach menopause, but through the entire process, the team will do everything they can to give you and your daughters as much autonomy as possible."

Maybe Michael believed that, but I still suspected otherwise.

"Then it'll be *thirty* years before I'm allowed to meet someone, get married, and have my own family." A tear dropped from my lashes, and the sick feeling at the pit of my stomach rose into my throat. "So, is that what you want from me, too? You want me to be pregnant at seventeen and continue to have babies until I'm in my forties and fifties?" I pushed away from my pillow, bringing my face inches from his.

"It's not a matter of want. It's what you have to do. Even if I quit the hospital, it wouldn't matter. It would be more difficult for them, but they already have what they need to start and finish the project without me." His words were gentle, his voice sincere.

Yes, he was part of the team, part of the plan to violate and use me, but so far Michael was different from the others. I truly believed he cared about me more deeply than anyone else here at GenH1, and like me, he was brought to life for the so-called "good" of the world. We had more in common than anyone else on the planet.

"The last thing I want you to do is quit the program, Michael." His face blurred, he was so close. "I need you. I need someone who understands how I feel about this. You understand me better than anyone else."

The sick emptiness returned to my stomach with the reality of what they wanted me to do. "I have to get out of this hospital. I can't stay here another day," I announced.

"You have to participate, Cassie. The team hoped and anticipated that you'd see this as your calling, your duty. That you would willingly sacrifice a bit of yourself for the future of the human race, become an inspiration to your children as they continue the program at your side, and with the same conviction. But I knew it wouldn't be that easy."

He gazed at me so intently it was hard to look away. "I can only hope that in time you'll think of yourself the way I think of you—as a savior instead of a brood mare. And you'll be willing to make great sacrifices for the good of mankind, and find satisfaction in knowing that you've helped save our world. If you do that, we can work together side by side, and maybe then you'll be happy."

"So it's not just Dr. Little and Dr. Pickford? You also want me to eventually find happiness and fulfillment just from knowing that I'm saving the world?" I asked as I broke eye contact and fell back against my pillow.

"It's the only way you'll find peace in the project."

"I want my old life back. I don't want to be here, especially now," I said, ripping my hand away from his. "I'd rather be dead then give birth to a truckload of babies, all girls, who'd then suffer the same fate as me."

"They won't let anything happen to you. *I* won't let anything happen to you." In his eyes, I saw someone who was haunted by not only his own existence but also how it would damage his career if he went against the team. Yet, he also understood how miserable I would be if I didn't accept my fate with an open heart.

"Then I'm stuck." They had me right where they wanted me—without friends or family to fight for my rights. "So, tell me the plan?" My voice cracked as I swallowed hard to suppress my tears.

"Dr. Little wants you to become pregnant as soon as possible through artificial insemination and carry the baby to term."

"And what happens to each baby after I give birth?" The words tugged at my gut, making my whole body shudder.

"You may choose to raise it yourself, or it can be adopted. Either way, the child will be raised in the least restrictive environment as possible, and when the child enters the program at puberty, she'll already have a complete understanding of her role in the process."

A pain developed behind my eyes again, pulsing like a small balloon that inflated and deflated over and over again in my brain.

"I can't do this."

"You can. You're stronger than that," he urged. "You

need to be strong not only for you, but also for me."

Could I?

He stood and took a seat on the edge of my bed, his weight upon the mattress, rocking me toward him. When the side of my thigh met his knee, my heart rate doubled, and I drew in a deep breath.

"Before you were awakened," he continued, "I spent hours at your bedside imaging what you were like, how your voice would sound, how you looked when you smiled. When your red lips pulsed, when your chest heaved, and you took your first breath, I kept my emotions in check. But now, now that you've 'awakened,' everything is different. I'm jealous and angry. I can't sleep. I can't stop thinking about you."

I ignored the pain and tilted closer until the space between our faces was less than a foot. My heart, my mind, my soul— everything yearned for his affection at that moment.

"I feel the same way, too," I said as Michael's sincerity drew me to him and all my anger toward him fled.

I closed my eyes, wanting this handsome, earnest guy to take me into my arms and tell me he'd make them let me go. My lungs expanded with his warm breath and spicy scent. When his lips met mine, every atom in my body danced, urging me to pull him closer and tighten my grip upon his back.

His kissing became more fiery, and I reacted by kissing him harder. It wasn't until his mouth moved to my neck that I came to my senses, bit my bottom lip, and drew away.

"Not yet," I said, scooting away.

"I know," he said between breaths, rising from the bed. His wiped his forehead with the sleeve of his uniform and returned to the chair. "I can't...we can't. We can never..." he said abruptly. "It's against protocol. I-I should go."

He rose stiffly from the bed, brushed the wrinkles from his uniform, and hurried to the door. His lips were tight and his eyes glossy from passion, disappointment, and a loss of self-control. With the sweep of his foot, he enabled the obscuras, and the door closed behind him before I could think of something to say.

Michael, the guy who, like a god, brought me into a new reality, expected me, a seventeen-year-old virgin, to produce children not from love but from necessity in order to quench the selfish desire of man to procreate and rule the planet as the ultimate life form.

Through me, a man could quench his most primordial want, a biological heir. The weight of the world was on my shoulders, but due to GenH1 protocol, Michael couldn't help me through the process as a boyfriend.

The first thing I had to do was get out of this hospital. Where I was going to end up and how I'd do it didn't matter at this point.

Dr. Little's thick-walled coffee mug was still on the hovering table next to my bed. I grabbed it, hurled it across the room, and gave a silent cheer as it shattered into a million pieces. Minutes later, a JAN entered with a vacuum for a hand.

Chapter Eight

Two hours later, Ella was at my bedside, holding an exercise pole. "Good afternoon, Cassie," she said tentatively, like she was trying to gauge my mood.

I rolled onto my side.

"How are you feeling, sweetie?" she asked, sitting next to me on my bed and setting her hand on my shoulder.

"Like my whole world fell apart all over again," I said as calmly as I could. None of this was her fault. She was just following *the plan*.

"A good workout will make you feel better. It'll help take your mind off things," she said with puckered lips and her kitty-cat voice.

"Great! Then maybe after today's session, I'll be strong enough to break out of this place and become a fugitive," I said against my pillow.

"Oh honey, don't even think that way. This isn't a terrible place. Besides, you're L-Banded now, so you wouldn't get that far." She gave the pole a twirl. "Clones who are overly aggressive are considered naturally violent and genetically defective even when the only thing left wounded is someone's pride. If you behaved that way, Dr. Little might think you're a danger to society." She giggled.

Good! I'll let them think that, and let them think I wouldn't get that far.

"The team knows you're opposed to the plan, so they're taking extra steps to ensure everyone's safety, including yours."

I rolled onto my back. "How do they know I'm still 'opposed?' Have they been listening to me? Are they watching me right now?"

"I don't know if anyone from the team is watching or listening to you or not right now, but if someone is, it's because the team is worried about you. You were awakened less than two weeks ago. You're still very fragile."

Yes—let them still think I'm fragile.

"They don't care about me; they only care about my eggs."

"Now that is not true. Life is precious, Cassie, every life, especially yours. How about you do three sets of ten? You'll feel better. I always feel better after I exercise. Then I'll send in a SUDS," she said as she stood.

"Great," I said sarcastically. A sponge bath by a SUDS bot was uncomfortable to say the least. Having my dull hospital gown exchanged with a white, fitted tunic and pants was the only good thing that came out of it.

"Wow. I didn't expect to see so much improvement," said Ella after I completed one set.

Whoops. Time to hide my real strength.

As she jumped and gave me a round of applause, her large breasts jumped, too, shaking a necklace from the folds of her collar.

From a gold chain hung a small, golden egg the size of a jellybean. The egg was shiny and smooth, instead of matte and frosted like the egg on Dr. Love's ring. When Ella moved, it twinkled, swinging like a pendulum.

"What's the egg for?" I asked, pretending to be out of breath and letting my arms drop like my muscles were completely spent.

Ella grasped the charm between two fingers, rubbing it lovingly as if it was the belly of a jade Buddha. "Eggs represent fertility, the source of life. Most women wear egg jewelry. Unlike you, it's the only egg we have," she whimpered.

"That's not *my* fault, Ella." I wasn't the one who caused the plague. I was supposed to give everyone hope. I was their genie in a bottle, but with hope came disappointment, and maybe even jealousy.

"I'm sorry, Cassie." She lowered her head and sobbed, still holding the egg charm delicately. "Dr. Love and I are so sorry we couldn't tell you about the plan. We wanted to, but we had to do what was best for you and the project. In the end, you'll understand why your participation is so important to us."

"I'm not sure I can." I placed my hand over my stomach and was struck by another wave of nausea with the thought of being artificially inseminated.

"I'm curious about something though, and I want you to be completely honest with me."

"Okay, I will."

"If you had a choice of not participating in the program,

and could start a new life without any interference from the government, would you? Or would you choose to help us?" There was pain in her eyes, a yearning for a long, fruitful life for her and a future family.

What if our situations were reversed? Would I want the only living fertile female to prostitute herself for the good of mankind? Yeah, I guessed I would, and if the fertile female did not abide, I probably would label her selfish, egotistical, the destroyer of the human race, the catalyst of Armageddon, and sign a petition for her immediate arrest and forceful participation.

"In the end, I guess I would choose to help," I answered, giving her what she wanted to hear.

She gasped with delight, jumped up from the chair, and threw her arms around my stiff and unsuspecting torso. The hug was clumsy. Her guilt evaporated like a fog hit by the morning sunshine. "I knew you would."

But would I?

"I have a surprise for you in the hall. I wanted to wait until you've warmed up those muscles of yours with the exercise pole before I showed it to you. Close your eyes."

I could definitely use a surprise. The door slid open and closed, but I didn't hear anything else except her footsteps. "Okay, open them," she called.

An apparatus of some kind that looked like a small, green chair standing at attention, minus the salute, was positioned at her side.

"Is it some kind of hoverchair?" I asked.

"No, I think you're beyond the hoverchair. This uses antigravity. It's called a Standup. Standup on." At her command, a hum like a muted whisper filled the room. "It'll hold your body in position, and by reading the electric impulses in your brain, help you use your muscles correctly, so you can walk. That's why we couldn't have you use it until now. There's a minimum amount of muscle control needed for it to work, and you didn't qualify until this week."

A light tap from Ella's hand brought the device to the edge of the bed. "We just need to get you within twelve inches, and then Standup will pull you upright. It'll work best if we angle your back into position." She lifted the corner of the sheet and tossed it away from my body.

As I rotated on the bed and aligned myself with the machine, my back caught the vacuum of the antigravity compulsion, lifted me up and off the bed, and firmly drew my limp body against the molded padding. "This Standup has been synched to your L-Band. It'll only follow your commands and adapt to your body. It has multiple settings, from maximum to minimum support."

"I definitely need the maximum setting," I was quick to add.

"Yes, you do, at least for the first week or two, and then maybe in another month you won't need it at all. Now let me show you how this works."

Fabulous! After a ten-minute tutorial, I could walk, bend over, and lower into a sitting position using Standup, a slab of limber rubber, to obey my movements. Walking was incredibly liberating, but I was embarrassed by how I must look being adhered to an animatronic chair, wearing hospital clothes, and barefooted. I definitely didn't want Michael to see me like this.

"Once you're able to use it on the lowest setting, you can switch to using just the stimulation pack." As I stopped in front of Ella, my muscles burning and twitching, she pushed on the back of the apparatus. "In three to four weeks, this is all you'll need."

Yeah, right. How about in three or four days?

"This is absolutely amazing," I said after a lap of the room with my new mechanical friend. "I can't wait to leave this place. It's so boring in here. I want to go to the botanical garden. That's the first thing I want to do. Can I get dressed and go now?"

"No, I'm sorry. Due to your condition, your activities are still limited to this room, but you won't need a NURSE bot anymore. Now you can go to the bathroom and even take a shower by yourself, so no more SUDS." Thank God for that. "Aren't you anxious to take a proper shower?"

"Yeah, I'd love to take a shower, but I'd rather see the garden."

"When you're physically ready, I'll take you to the garden. And in the meantime, I'll keep bringing you flowers."

"Then what about a window, so I can at least see outside now? You said once I'm L-Banded I—"

"No, honey, not even a window."

"What about the balcony at the end of the hall? Dr. Little allowed me into the hall once before. Can't I just—"

"No, you can't leave this room," she said sternly after I let my fist drop hard against Standup's arm. "You'll see our world soon enough. What you need is a hot shower. Let me show you how to use it."

"Yeah, right," I mumbled.

As she approached the bathroom door, it slid to reveal an all-white room with glossy walls and a smooth, milky floor. It looked spotless and smelled minty clean. A round vessel stood on the floor, its lines fluid and abstract like a statue. In the corner loomed a glass compartment with double doors. When she pushed on one side, both doors sprung outward accompanied by a welcoming *ding-ding*.

After Ella left, I was a naked, semi-invalid with Standup, a giant Gumby, on my back. I drew my arm across my breasts and rounded my shoulders as the shower's lights, set on "tranquility mode," exploded and sparkled against the glass walls like the inside of a geode. A melody echoed from the floor like a distant tribal song, its vibrations invigorating the soles of my feet.

As the blood-warm water pulsed down my back, all I could think about was Michael. There was just something especially alluring about a guy who had the power to wake up a girl from the dead. Had he lied to me? Yes. But I couldn't hold it against him. He had to. It was his job. And due to his job, we couldn't be together.

When I left the shower, the mirror above the bathroom sink bore the refection of a girl. The image grimaced at the hollows under its eyes and the paleness of its cheeks, but then it smiled, pleased its lips were still plump and red, and that its irises glistened like sapphires. Its brows were thin and perfectly arched and its eyelashes long and full despite a one thousand year sleep of death. It was hard to believe that reflection was me.

Finally—underwear and bra. Both fit perfectly. The silky robe Ella left for me was luxurious and girly compared to my other robe and the plain tunic and pants I had been wearing. It was easy to put on and take off, comfortably slipping between my back and Standup's green cushion.

Several minutes passed as I walked around my room,

taking Standup for another test drive on the lowest setting, and challenging the strength of my muscles before I realized I was crying, not from the frustration at my pale, atrophied frame or for joy in having the artificial ability to walk — but for what would happen if I could escape from here. Could I be a brave girl in a brave new world?

When I returned to my room, breakfast was waiting for me along with a service bot that was busy changing my bed sheets. Steam rose from two deep-yellow yolks, the smell of sweet melons filled the air, and all I thought about was Michael again, and how hurt and disappointed he'd be if he came to my room to find I was gone.

As Standup lowered like a handheld telescope, I pressed a button on its right side to keep it at its minimal setting. My liberator rolled away and parked itself against the wall, leaving my back flat on the bed and my legs dangling. Within days — not weeks like Ella thought — I'd be able to walk using just the stim pack, and then I'd try to get the heck out of here. I couldn't think about Michael. I had to think about my own well-being.

If only there was a magical place called Tasma that I could run to, a place free from the plague's wrath and government control.

Chapter Nine

One last stretch and I was ready. My thigh muscle twitched as I lie on my back, pulling my knee into my chest. When I switched legs, I turned my head and gave Standup a wave good-bye before straightening my leg. Using my rubber friend at its lowest setting for two days tripled my mobility, and by day three, the stim pack became my new companion, pumping just enough electricity in my limbs to keep me stable as I marched around the bathroom, knowing no one would see my progress from there.

By the end of the week, Standup and its detachable pack were nothing more than a prop, as I kept it firmly against my back and paced my room with the apparatus in sleep mode. Finally it was time.

The black almond-shaped windows stared at me and I stared back, then I scanned the walls, searching for hidden obscuras, looking for the tiny dot of a lens or dime-sized bulge beneath the plaster to give away their locations, but the gray walls were unflawed, as smooth as glass. One swipe with my foot would deem the room "free," and one bound from my bed would take me to the switch embedded in the floor. I had to reach it before my act of defiance was discovered by spying eyes behind evil obscuras or blackened windows.

As Standup glistened under the starry lights of my room, I strained with all of my might and pushed up on first my elbows, then my knees with the balls of my feet pressed into the soft mattress of my bed. I made the leap, landing on all fours and reaching for the button with an outstretched hand. My heart beat hard, anticipating that my first grab for freedom would trigger a silent alarm, sending a brigade of armed bots to my hospital room, but the buzz from a bot gliding across the warm floor didn't follow.

Tiptoeing to the door, the scratching fabric of my white hospital clothes making the only sound, I cringed as the familiar *ding* sounded upon the opening of the door, unlocked for some reason I didn't know, or maybe my L-Band making it open, its programmer naively believing I could never accomplish an escape during the dead of night.

Taking a deep breath, I stretched my neck through the doorframe. The hall was unoccupied, not even by a JAN, which I speculated would recognize me through my L-Band and report my location.

At the end of the corridor, a wall shined with a steel-gray door — an A.G.-lift, the elevator, my next stop. In socked feet, I scurried rodent-like, my shoulder against the wall and jumped when the A.G.-lift opened its thick door with a magnified *ring* and suck of air. The door panel retracted and then slid back into place when I was safely inside.

"Um, lobby." But all was still. "Um, ground floor."

My words echoed against the lift's steel walls, walls without buttons or numbers to indicate the passing of floors. How did I make this thing work? The door opened, and I held my breath. A tiny bot shaped like a bell entered, humming and hugging the walls, sucking lint from the corners of the lift, and completely ignoring me. Thank God.

It vacuumed the floor in a succession of parallel sweeps, dodging my feet as I stepped over it and moved to the far wall. When it was done, the wall at my back vibrated, the door opened, and I emerged into a large, dimly lit room with a panel of windows and a pair of double doors to the east, the bot skirting past me to continue its cleaning job in the hall.

Where was I? I didn't care as long as the door looming in front of me led to further freedom. But would I be that lucky?

As I approached the window, my reflection appeared, followed by what was on the other side—the sky, dotted with stars, and the smile of a crescent moon, softened by a trail of wispy clouds. *Yes!* My body shook as I stepped forward and the heavy doors separated, releasing the gust of wind knocking on the other side. Catching the breeze, my hair danced across my eyes as I entered the chilly night air, rubbing my arms, taking quick steps, and ignoring the pain in my thighs as I broke into a solid run. Cranking my stiff arms and breathing hard, I pounded against the patterned concrete that was littered with tiny stones.

It didn't matter where I'd end up—alive or dead—I was free from GenH1 if only for a few seconds. But the seconds turned to minutes as I continued my escape away from the compound and onto a foreign street where movers hovered against the artificially lit sky at different altitudes of three to ten feet, their bullet-shaped noses and penetrating headlights piercing the cool air.

How could a world where its citizens were tethered to a central computer, and randomly viewed by strangers, be beautiful? But somehow it was. Despite the lack of trees and grass, I stood in tears and awe at the rivers of lights created by cars that flew against a backdrop of buildings reaching upward into infinity. When a spotlight above found my location, I squinted against the harsh light and drew in a deep breath.

I could run. I could end it now—throw myself into the path of a low-altitude mover, letting its metal nose plow into mine, ending my short reign as baby-maker. But I stood unblinking until a team of men in tight, black uniforms came up behind me.

"No," I screamed, dashing to the left and spinning to free myself from a hand reaching toward my arm.

There was time to make a dash and I took it, dodging a small mover and ducking beneath one with a little more altitude. With lungs craving oxygen, I jumped to the intersection and ran until I reached the other side of the street.

A row of uniform houses with perfectly manicured yards ran the length of the sidewalk. From each numbered front door, a small porch met a mover-width driveway that cut across a patch of synthetic grass to reach the curb. Equidistance from one another and identical from their slick roofs to their beige exteriors, they looked eerily familiar. I'd escaped into a real game of Ascendency, each home mirroring its occupants like fellow clones, its building plans used again and again to replicate the neighborhood.

Darting left, I sprinted down the sidewalk as the sound of footsteps at my heels increased. There were no trees to hide behind, no bushes in which to lay low and catch my breath, the landscape as sterile as a female clone. Obscruas on the light posts gave way to my location, and within seconds a bot-driven patrol mover appeared beside me, slowing to match my speed.

With a last burst of energy, I scrambled forward into the line of traffic, but this time my weak muscles didn't carry me to the other side of the street. I misjudged my capabilities.

My heart fluttered as a low-hoverment vehicle came toward me, its bumper meeting me at eye level. But my feet didn't move. I closed my eyes and held my breath, anticipating the pain. Dropping out of the way wasn't an option, was it?

I didn't want to be a mother—at least not the way they wanted me to.

The mover's lights obliterated my vision. This was it. The end.

"Remain where you are." It was the voice of a bot.

When I opened my eyes, it was as if time itself had stopped. Every mover within my view was frozen midair. Even those on parallel streets were at a standstill, including the members of GenH1 security who were as rigid as their accompanying bots.

I was approached from all sides, and within seconds someone pinned my hands behind my back with a palpable, electric band of light.

"No, let me go," I screamed and kicked, jerking left and

right to knock the security officers away with my shoulders. But they stood solid, their hold tight around my arms.

"I don't want to go back," I continued to shout as they led me back to a life of submission.

Despite almost being hit by a mover, seeing them for real soaring with almost inaudible purrs above the pavement, their sleek designs effortlessly slicing the wind, kept my heart rate from settling. My hair fluttered with each passing hoverbus. The night air, combined with the strange splendor of this regulated world, was intoxicating.

I slowed almost to a stop as a bovine-sized bot came around the corner, sucking bits of rock and debris from the opposite sidewalk, but the officer behind me pushed me along with a palm to my back. At that point, I dropped my head, watching my now-dirty socks doing little to protect the tender soles of my feet. But when we approached GenH1, I lifted my head and oddly found myself captivated by the grandeur of the building's modern architecture.

The lobby was empty, with the exception of a bot with a rubbery face and permanent smile stationed behind a long counter, and another bell-shaped one buzzing across the floor to collect lint and dust.

As the guards wound me through the halls of GenH1, the muscles in my legs became sore and stiff, making it hard not to drag my feet as we rounded the corner and ended at Dr. Little's office. He was the last person I wanted to see.

"We're not used to defiance," he said through a yawn after the door slid closed behind me. "You had us fooled, Miss Dannacher. You're stronger and more physically capable than you led us to believe. I don't like to be fooled, or awakened at three in the morning."

"I'm sorry I ruined your beauty sleep. You need all you can get," I smirked, twisting my hands against the electric cuffs.

"We can't afford to have anything happen to you. If you hadn't triggered a pedestrian warning system with your L-Band, you wouldn't be here with us today."

Oh, lucky me. "Can you at least take these cuffs off now? I won't run away again. I promise," I huffed as I crossed my fingers and bit my bottom lip; my only real promise was not to cry in front of Dr. Little.

He nodded, and in the next second, the electrified beam disappeared with a touch from one of the guards. I let my arms drop to my sides and sucked in a deep breath.

"No need to promise. You won't be leaving us again. The proper adjustments have been made to your L-Band. The tier four techs were careless. Not being privy to the project, they equated your condition to that of a comatose invalid and set your L-Band accordingly. They'll be punished with a decrease in pay."

Dr. Little rested his hands on his desk and interlocked his fingers, his eyes burning into mine.

"Are we done here?" I asked, shifting my gaze away from his. From over his shoulder, I saw a rectangular glass case about a foot-and-a-half tall, positioned vertically over a strange object centered on a wooden base. Chipped from gray stone, the object stood just over a foot tall. It didn't take me long to recognize what it was.

"I see that you're admiring Claus," he said.

"Claus?"

"That's what I like to call him. He's over eight — "

"Thousand years old. I know all about him."

"Then I'm sure you'd like to hold him. I rarely take him out of his home, but since you promised to never run away again," he said sarcastically, "I think I'll make an exception."

I didn't answer but watched as his fingers fumbled to lift the glass case and remove the object from his so-called home.

Claus was a fertility idol, a male fertility idol, which made it extremely rare. It was discovered in Germany shortly before I left 2022, hence Dr. Little's German name for him. Officially, he's known as the Man of Zschernitz, named for the town near which he was found.

Like the Woman of Willendorf, a world-famous female fertility idol unearthed in Willendorf, Austria, Claus was missing his feet and lacked a face, but his external reproductive organs were intact and their size highly exaggerated.

Trying to hide my excitement for the chance to hold such an ancient and rare artifact, I feigned a scowl, especially when he laughed with satisfaction before he handed it to me.

It was heavier and smoother than I imagined, and I ran my index finger across the top of the idol's head and tried to estimate its weight.

"So, what do you think of Claus?" He grinned.

"I think he's an archaeological treasure. Where'd you get him?" Dr. Little didn't deserve to own Claus.

"He was handed down through one of the original forefathers."

I lifted an eyebrow.

"Yes, Miss Dannacher, my great, great, great, great, great, great, great, great-grandfather was one of the original forefathers. He saved it from a museum in Region Two before the museum was abandoned and eventually destroyed. I like

Claus. He reminds me a lot of me," he sneered as he reached out to retrieve his precious idol and restore him to the safety of his case. Poor Claus and how pathetic—bragging about a having a famous ancestor, when he was merely related by chance and not by genes.

"Some cultures believed the mere handling of a fertility idol would increase a woman's chances of conceiving and bearing healthy children." His cheeky smile was enough to make me puke.

"Now can I go?" I said

"Oh, you're not getting off that easy, Miss Dannacher. The tier four techs aren't the only ones being punished. You're being punished, too. For the next four weeks, you'll be staying in one of our, let's just say, less accommodating hospital rooms, and your only visitors will be bots."

Punished? Was a month of isolation worth twenty minutes of fresh air and a real peek at this world? And what was this punishment designed to do—turn me into a complacent captive ready to beg my captors for mercy and willingly submit to their plan?

"Whatever," I said in my nastiest tone. "It was worth being away from you and this hospital. Can I go now?"

He stood, smiling like he had a secret he was ready to tell. "Not quite. Before you're taken to your holding cell, there's something I want you to see first."

I wasn't in the mood for show-and-tell, let alone spending any more time with the man than I had to. *Just take me to my cell, you jerk, so I can get my punishment over with.*

As if he could pass for a gentleman, he stood behind me, waiting for me to exit his office first and directing me to make a right turn by holding out his arm. A pair of guards accompanied us as we passed through the halls of GenH1, and I tried to make a mental note of each turn in case I found another opportunity for an escape in the future.

The muscles in my thighs burned, but I readjusted my pace every time Dr. Little synched with mine. From the corner of my eye, I could see he was slightly out of breath, his face red, and hear a small grunt when his arms swung heavily to increase his momentum as he tried to keep up with me.

"Where are we going?" I asked as my eyes darted left and right. I was half ready to sprint down the corridor with all of my might to enjoy a few last minutes of freedom before I was locked away from anything human.

"You'll see," he said between breaths. "We're almost there." He put out his hand to stop me in front of an A.G.-lift when we reached the end of the hall. We entered and then exited seconds later on a floor with white walls and a white floor, with a surface so shiny it reflected our images. His soft-soled shoes squeaked eerily.

"The prenatal ward," he announced as he pointed to a door labeled PNW One — a different door from the one he brought me to before. This wasn't the same floor.

"I don't need to see another one. Nothing you can do will make me cooperate."

"Oh, I wouldn't be so sure about that." He smirked.

The door slid opened noiselessly, courtesy of his L-Band, and the two of us entered, the guards remaining outside.

The smell of chemicals, an artificial yet organic pungent odor, made me want to pinch my noise, and even after my eyes adjusted to the dim light, I had trouble believing what I was seeing.

The long tables containing babies in artificial uteruses were identical to those in the first prenatal ward, with the exception of the letter "X," followed by a series of numbers on a label affixed to each jar's base

"X," I said under my breath, though Dr. Little could still hear me.

"The X chromosome. It contains over two thousand genes," he said. "Male or female, we all have one."

Several workers were present, three men and one woman, but they were missing the colorful smocks and instead wore fitted white uniforms, the expressions on their faces as indifferent as the bland, undecorated room. Without giving us so much as a nod, one of the men lifted a long, metal rod with a hooked end from its place on a rack, removed the lid from container X-36782, and proceeded to fish a foot-long fetus from its artificial uterus.

"Why is he doing it that way?" I gasped in a whisper as my heartbeat quickened and the muscles in my chest tightened.

"Why not? It does the job, doesn't it?" answered Dr. Little, drawing his hands behind his back.

"But it's—it's insensitive and disrespectful."

The head of the dead fetus lolled forward as it was raised from the cylindrical tank. Eyes, like black marbles covered by a veil of translucent gray skin remained closed, but its jaw, unhinged and tiny, and stick legs unlocked from its fetal position.

I shivered as the worker let the baby drop into a sack that bulged with what must have been at least a dozen or more dead baby clones. "I still don't understand why the success rate is so low. It shouldn't be—not with the technology of this century," I said, trying to hide my emotions by raising my voice from a whisper.

"Like we said before. It's the fault of the synthetic uterus. For an umbilical cord to form, the embryo needs to implant in the placenta, a difficult task considering these are made from engineered human tissue that's maintained through an artificial blood supply." He brought his arms around to his gut, interlinking his fingers and resting his hands below his chest.

As he spoke, I focused my attention on the slow rise and fall of his abdomen, choosing to ignore the fact that another gray fetus, X-87209, with paper-thin skin was being pulled from a tank in front of me.

"During the natural gestation process, one vein in the umbilical cord carries oxygen-rich blood and nutrients to the fetus, and two arteries return waste and deoxygenated blood from the fetus to the artificial placenta. We mimic this procedure, but maintaining a working placenta is a feat within itself."

I eyed the red, throbbing placentas affixed to the inside of each tank. A blood-red tube ran from the top of these slug-like objects, leading to the machinery below, while an umbilical cord of flesh at its center coiled and connected to each baby.

In the tank to my left, an embryo the size of my thumb was afloat, and from its blue color and the fact that its tiny umbilical cord was half detached from the blob of man-made placenta, it was obvious the fetus was dead. Within minutes, another worker scooped the tiny fish of a baby from its watery grave and flung it into a smaller sack that bulged with weight.

"Where are the tiny coffins?" I asked, looking past Dr. Little to the stark wall behind him.

"Come," he said. With a nod, he led me to the far corner of the room, and though my stomach twisted and each breath made the center of my forehead ache, I followed, stunned, and not wanting to believe the scene before me was a reality.

The stench increased as we walked, a sweet, chemical smell, mingling with something reminiscent of raw meat, like a coyote's fresh kill, something I'd smelled millions of times before in the desert on a dig.

One of the workers met us at a metal drawer flush with the wall. When he opened the drawer, the smell of flesh rose with a puff of smoke. I swallowed to keep from vomiting as the man emptied his sack, shaking the bag to rid it of the last tiny baby, it's long, spindly limbs crossing as it dropped into the drawer.

"The incinerator. There are too many to give them a proper burial. Such a shame. If only they had real uteruses in which to thrive." His tone was so sincere I almost forgot the man standing next to me, his brow dotted with perspiration, was Dr. Little.

"But I don't understand. Why is this room different from the other one you showed me?"

"All prenatal wards are like this," he answered, extending his arms. "It was my hope we could convince you to join the program willingly with the use of a mock PNW, but that little nudge of guilt obviously wasn't enough."

More guilt. That's what I felt, and that's why he was showing me the truth. Yes, I did wish they all had a real uterus, and why couldn't that be possible? What stopped them from using the clone women to fulfill this role?

To my right, an almond-shaped window similar to the one in my hospital room glowed with a soft blue light around its perimeter. The room on the other side was much brighter than the room we were in, and as I took a step toward it to peer inside, I was momentarily forced to squint.

MEDs with smooth silhouettes and telescope eyes bent over lab tables with needle-like left hands, poking into test tubes and petri dishes in an orchestrated robot dance for what I could only assume was the betterment of mankind—replicating the DNA of an ancient ancestor.

"But I'm not the only female on the planet with a uterus."

As the incinerator drawer slammed closed, I turned from the lab window and watched a spark shoot upward, bringing a smell like a lit cigarette to my nose. Flooded with nausea, I imagined the babies in various stages of growth catching fire as they hit the flames, babies who never had a chance, fetuses who didn't choose to be born under odds that were against their fate.

A worker in a gray uniform entered the prenatal ward from a door on the opposite side of the room. Screams escaped through the door's opening before it resealed, human-like screeches, yet there was something primal about them, something animalistic and filled with fear and pain. I winced as the door pinched closed, cutting off a curdled yelp that brought chills to the back of my neck, and Dr. Little stiffened, diverting his eyes to the floor.

"What's in that room?" I asked, knowing that its close proximity meant it must have had something to do with the prenatal ward and its lab.

"What's in that room doesn't concern you at the moment."

"Doesn't concern me?" I crossed my sore arms and balanced my weight between both of my legs, ignoring the ache in my thighs. "At this point, I think just about everything concerns me. You brought me this far. Take me to the end." The incinerator door opened for a third time, and the smell of burning flesh made me gulp and hold my breath.

"Very well." He held up his banded wrist, and when the door reopened, the cries resumed as if they had never stopped.

As we entered, I plugged my ears in a weak attempt to muffle the screeches of suffering, but it wasn't enough. My hands trembled against my head.

Cubicles as far as the eye could see lined the expansive room, each square of bright white harboring a creature that stood with a bent back, sat on its haunches, or paced in its enclosure, walking on all fours. Chimpanzees.

The screams increased as we approached, crackles, howls, and grunts coming from the throats of animals with pink lips pulled taunt across yellow teeth. I slowed my pace, letting Dr. Little take the lead.

"They won't attack. That would be impossible."

A chimp in the closest cell beat its chest wildly and shook its head, sending its ears into a flap and legs into a pump like it was ready to make a leap. It rapped the air with its knuckles when it was done and with a final knock hit the transparent, electrified door to its cubicle. A sizzle came, followed by the smell of burnt fur, and the chimp's cries, its call like an alarm that sent the other primates into a series of wails and vocalizations so loud they vibrated in my chest.

"What's wrong with him?"

"You mean her. They're all females."

There was a buzz almost as irritating as the chimps' screams. A black nozzle lowered from the ceiling of each cubicle, and seconds later, a steamy spray of hot water filled each cell, making each occupant howl and scurry in circles.

I took a step backward as the smell of feces and urine billowed through the room, followed by something that burned the inside of my nose.

"It's cruel," I shouted.

"Cruel?" he asked, surprised. "They're given the best of care. Their diets are carefully selected, and their cubicles cleaned and sterilized daily. Maintaining their health is our top priority."

"But why are they here in the first place? What are you using them for?" And then I knew. I didn't need his answer. A theory in my century was a reality one thousand and three years later. "These chimps are supplying the eggs. And once the monkey DNA is extracted and replaced with harvested human DNA, the egg is implanted in an artificial uterus."

"You are correct, Miss Dannacher. There's a 95 percent similarity between the DNA of humans and apes, but that remaining five percent prevents the embryo for living in utero for more than ten hours after implantation in the uterus of a female clone, making this our only option." He pointed to the closest chimp.

The cries of the animals rose as he spoke, and he adjusted his tone to shout above the caged creatures. "Our success rate with synthetic uteruses is only slightly better." He shook his head.

"What about the women who survived the plague?"

"Unfortunately, the plague left the internal organs scarred, resulting in underdeveloped ovaries."

A chimp to my left squawked and spun in its cell before stamping the ground and making a face at me so human, its forehead wrinkling with emotional pain, that I whimpered and stepped backward. "But it's so cruel. How can you do this to them? Isn't a happy, stress-free chimp more likely to produce healthier eggs?"

A chimp formed in my mind's eye, strapped to a table, half drugged, while some kind of MED with a speculum for a hand and a long needle committed the vile act of harvesting eggs from the chimp's ovaries.

Immediate disgust for the clones and their vile acts of desperation invaded my heart. To propagate at the expense of others, even if they were only animals, made me want to puke. The dead babies in the next room, the MEDs with their micro-injectors, the gravediggers defiling the tombs of my ancestors. Everything about this world made my head spin, and when I tried to obliterate the thoughts by blinking my eyes hard, I half expected to see Dr. Little grinning at me with the yellowed teeth of a primate.

"How can we do it?" he snapped. "It's easy, because there wasn't any other choice until now."

Until now?

He meant until me.

"During our research, we discovered that creating an atmosphere of so-called tension," he said, wiggling his fingers, "actually increases their reproductive abilities, their state of anxiety triggering an innate need to populate."

Maybe so, but it was still uncalled for.

We didn't exit the way we came by winding back through the rows of plastic uteruses. A door in the Primate Housing Unit led us into the hall and to the closest A.G.-lift on that floor. A set of guards walked to our rear, and I tried to focus on the clicking sound the buckles on their boots made instead of thinking about how each one of them was produced using the hollowed-out egg of a chimp.

I hated this place. I hated this world. I repeated this in my mind with each step, and almost said it aloud when Dr. Little left at the end of the next hall while I was marched to my new quarters, maybe something similar to what the chimps were living in.

As the guards led me through the corridors of GenH1, I tried to memorize each twist and turn down the halls, more determined than ever to make a future escape, but my adrenaline-spent body and mentally spent mind couldn't keep anything straight. The twisted faces of apes in pain hammered my thoughts.

My new hospital room was more than a brightly lit cube with an electric door. It was more like a twenty-first century prison cell with matte gray walls and exposed bathroom. A vessel and sink sat in one corner of the room, and in another corner, a showerhead protruded over a drain in the floor.

When the guards were gone, I tiptoed to the door and held out my wrist, but Dr. Little was right—my L-Band was properly adjusted and the door didn't open.

And I thought my old room was boring. Apparently a "less accommodating" hospital room also meant a "less accommodating" L-Band. No matter the command, my L-Band remained dormant, with its ghostly gray screen, and shouting demands at the hidden obscuras in the walls didn't bring forth any changes either.

On my first night of isolation, I sat on the bed, defeated, listening to the sound of my own breathing, until I recalled the desperate cries of the chimpanzees and their high-pitched yelps. Pressing my palms against the sides of my head only increased the intensity of the resounding grunts, and it wasn't until I stood and paced the room that the imagined vocalizations subsided.

In the past, my dreams were usually bizarre but benign, scenarios like flying under my own superpowers or discovering the fossil of a new dinosaur species. Babies screaming, their mouths full of teeth with tartar, their canines extended to a point, were the images that invaded my sleep. A few of the babies were pink and robust but most of them were spindly with gray, lucent skin. Sometimes the fetus had the head of an ape and the body of a human, or vice versa, and I'd hold it snug in a blanket, talking to it gently until I lifted its arm from the blanket, a hairy monkey arm with a monkey hand. Every dream ended with one of those ghastly babies, its gurgling and sweet coos rising in volume until they became an evil monkey scream.

The only time I felt at peace was when I thought about Michael and our kiss. Was he thinking about me, too, or had he shaken me from his mind, knowing the two of us could never be? We couldn't be together, but I yearned for his affection, driven with a desire for him to quit the program and steal me away from here. If only that was possible. The fact that he was derived from a blank ape egg didn't bother me.

Damn Dr. Little for showing me those dead babies and suffering chimpanzees. The level of guilt tugging at my soul rose with each passing day whenever I considered running away again or ending my life but retreated when I imagined myself barefoot and pregnant.

By the fifth night, I was ready to throw my dinner tray and bang my head against the wall, but then I heard a knock and gentle whisper.

"Cassie."

"Michael? Is that you?" I asked, searching the room and seeing no one. "Where are you?"

"Up here."

A set of fingers poked from a small vent positioned one foot below the ceiling. After a wiggle, the hand disappeared. "I tried to make your room free, but it was impossible—even with *my* clearance. Security's too tight when it comes to you."

"How did you—?"

"Bot closet on the other side of this room. Entered the wall through an electrical panel and squirmed my way through this vent."

"What about your band? They'll know you're here."

"Only if someone tries looking for me. It's a chance I'll take." After stacking both pillows at the head of my bed and standing on them, I was tall enough to see through the vent, and there was Michael, his face shaded by the alternating stripes of the grate. I moved close enough to feel his breath against my face when he spoke. "How are you?" he asked. A wrinkle of worry formed between his eyebrows.

"I'm fine, I guess, considering all that's happened. What happened to you?" I asked, after noticing a fresh scrape on the side of his face.

"It's nothing. The vent opening was too small, so I had to force my way through. But that doesn't matter. I had to see you."

"What if someone's listening to us?"

"They're not, or a SEC would be here by now. Besides, that doesn't matter. There's something I need to tell you." He licked his lips. "I'm so sorry. I didn't know it would be like this, what they'd do to you, or how I'd feel about you." The blood on his temple ran to his cheek. "My hands are tied, but I promise I'm going to do everything I can to make things right."

Make things right? Was that even possible? "How?" I asked, glancing down at my banded wrist.

"I'm not sure, but I'll think of a way. All I want is for you to be happy, and there are only two ways for that to happen: the program has to change, or you have to change. And asking you to change is something I've decided I won't do to you again—not now, especially not now." He shook his head and smeared the blood away before it hit the corner of his lip. Beads of sweat glistened on his forehead.

But what did he mean by not now? "Why? What's happened?"

"Nothing. I just want you to know that just like you, I'm a pawn in the presidents' plan. If circumstances change, if more truths are told, just remember that I was never the decision maker, please—please remember that." His eyes, unblinking, were so intense I sucked in my breath and held it until I spoke again.

"What kind of truths? What aren't they telling me?"

Michael glanced below him. "I need to go." As he stuck his fingers through the grate and I caught them with mine, my racing heart became palpable.

"No, please stay, just a bit longer," I begged.

"I can't. If I'm caught, they'll either limit our future time together or drop me from the program."

"But I need to know you're safe."

"I'll knock on your door once I'm back in the hall."

He left as quickly as he came, dropping below as my fingers reached through the vent for one last attempt at human contact before he was gone.

A human touch, a human voice, was something I needed while in lockdown, especially since they came from Michael, but at the same time, his visit made my emotions waver even more.

More truth? What the hell was he talking about?

Within minutes, there was a soft rap upon my door, and I smiled, knowing Michael was okay.

Minute, hours, days continued to pass. I was so angry at this inept world that at times I screamed at the top of my lungs, calling Dr. Little a liar and a bastard, and at other times I found myself crying at the thought of another dead fetus being fished from a vial.

To Dr. Little, I was a prenatal ward chimp, minus the need to enucleate the eggs. My daughters would be treated with the same level of controlled detachment, existing in the state of perpetual pregnancies forced upon us.

Forced—that was the problem. I'd gladly donate my eggs for the good of mankind, but the team's plan didn't end there.

Bots of all kinds continued to rotate in and out of my room, JANs to clean, SERVEs to deliver food, and MEDs to conduct simple medical exams, and each time, I hoped it was Michael taking the risk to sneak back into my room.

The disappointment made me uncooperative. When bots approached to change my sheets, I took my sweet time moving out of their way, and during showers, I stayed under the hot water for so long, it activated the automatic shutoff.

When it came to blood samples, I was even less than accommodating. "Why does Dr. Little want so many blood samples?" I demanded from the stoic bot as it held out its pin-concealed finger for the eighth day in a row.

"Routine samples are needed to gauge your recovery, Miss Dannacher," is all it would say. In the end, there was no use in putting up a fight, knowing a SEC was stationed outside my door.

The room's lighting never changed despite my voice commands, forcing me to gauge the time of day and the day of the week by the type and number of food deliveries. Surprisingly, I wasn't given a diet of bread and water. In fact, the cuisine was not only tastier in this wing of the hospital, the portions were larger, so large that after dinner all I wanted to do was sleep until morning. When I awoke weak and groggy, I'd circle the room in a half hour jog and follow that with push-ups, sit-ups, and stretches to keep up my strength and improve it.

One morning was marked with an even bigger, more appetizing breakfast, a bouquet of flowers with a magnolia blossom positioned at its center, and when a team of security guards returned me to my old room, Magnum was there to greet me, although I wished it was Michael.

"Hi, Cassie, how are you feeling?" he asked, concerned but smiling.

"Not bad, considering the fact that I was restricted from sunlight, fresh air, and leaving the building for four weeks. Oh wait, I'm restricted from those things when I'm in this room, too," I joked.

Magnum chuckled. "Actually, you were only there for

three weeks, thanks to Dr. Bennett."

"What do you mean?" My chest inflated with a big breath and smile.

"He couldn't talk Dr. Little into cutting your sentence, so Dr. Bennett contacted President Gifford himself and convinced the president to do it instead." His eyes were as wide as his smile. "That takes balls, going over Little's head like that," he added. "Dr. Little was ready to transfer Dr. Bennett to another hospital."

"But he didn't, right?" I asked, holding my hand against my chest.

"Nope. Gifford wouldn't let him—said Dr. Bennett was a key player in the program and they needed him here."

Whew! That was a relief.

"He was docked a month's worth of credits instead. Michael knew there'd be a consequence, but he didn't care, said he'd gladly lose a year's pay to shave a week off your punishment."

Poor Michael. I could have handled my full sentence.

Magnum dug into his right tunic pocket. "At least your L-Band will be functional again, and you'll also have this." He beamed, pulling out a folded Liaison.

"You're kidding. Even after what I did? Isn't Dr. Little afraid I'll try to use it to come up with an escape plan?"

"Not after Gifford insisted." A set of dimples erupted with a refreshed grin. "You can thank Dr. Bennett for that one, too. He told the president it would help you pass the time and might even quench your need to run away again, since it would give you a glimpse into the outside world."

Just like he said, Michael was looking out for me, trying to be on my side as much as he could. My insides warmed.

"It must be boring sitting in here all day. I can't blame you for what you did. I would have jumped out of a window by now."

"Yeah, you better not give my any more ideas." I laughed. "So, um, you didn't get in trouble because my L-Band was programmed wrong, did you?"

"Nope, that wasn't me. It was a tier four, but I think it was Dr. Little's fault," Magnum whispered. "To the tier fours, you're classified as being on life support—his doing."

"That's good. I would have felt really bad if it was your mistake, and they found out about it because of me. I just…I just had to get out of here. I need fresh air, trees, a pretty sunset."

"I know, but since that can't happen, maybe this will make it a little easier." He handed me the Liaison, and it popped opened against my palms. "Soon you'll be able to communicate and access information directly through your L-Band or your Liaison. I'm also here to fit you with an L-Bud, which will make things easier."

"That's great." But was it? It was just another device to tie me to their world.

"Dr. Bennett's only concern is making you happy. He also knows how miserable this must be for you. He doesn't blame you for running away either," he whispered. "Now let me show you how this works," he said, sitting down and inching his chair as close to the bed as he could without hitting his knees.

The Liaison and L-Bud were simple to use, and after ten minutes of tutorial, I knew I could probably figure the rest out on my own, but I wanted him to stay. He seemed so familiar to me, his appearance, his charm, and his endearing laugh, like someone I met in a dream.

"Magnum, do you ever wonder about who you were before?"

"What do you mean?" His dimples disappeared.

"You know, who your DNA came from."

"Does it matter?"

Like Ella, Magnum obviously never imagined the corpse of his ancestor, the DNA donor who lent the dried marrow of a thigh bone or tooth so he could stand there today, hundreds of years later, instructing me in the use of a Liaison.

I bit my lower lip. "No, I guess it doesn't matter. I just know that I'd want to know who I came from if I was a clone. I'd wonder how much in common I had with the original person. You know, if I ended up wearing my hair the same way, having the same taste in clothes, or even the same kind of job—stuff like that."

"Huh, I never really thought about it."

"Why not?"

"I don't know. Maybe because I don't want to feel like I have to live up to what my donor was, and what if he was a criminal? I wouldn't want to know that. I don't want my life predisposed in any way. I am who I am now—not who my DNA contributor was."

"But in a way, it would be just like trying to find out more information on a long-lost relative. Your donor is your only real relative. You could think of him as your biological brother, so I think it would be cool to know all about him."

"Yeah, maybe. I see your point." He scratched his chin and a dimple appeared in one cheek and then disappeared.

"Can you look it up if you want to?"

"Yeah, I guess I could. There probably aren't any restrictions because it's not information people usually try to access. I have clearances in anything genetic, but honestly, I'm not sure I want to know."

The feeling of familiarity, the déjà vu, with Magnum was hard to ignore. There was something familiar about his charisma and easy ways that I couldn't shake.

He cleared his throat. "Let me show you how to contact someone who's not in this building." He tapped on my Liaison. "Just in case you need to contact Ella or any of the other doctors at home."

"So you have top-secret clearance."

"And more. Don't tell, but I can override any restriction," he murmured.

"You're so bad."

"What can I say, I'm a rebel." He crossed his arms and leaned back as if his shoulders were against an invisible wall. He crossed one foot over the other as his knee jutted out to the side. He looked like an image on a billboard. It was just too perfect, the pose, the dimples, the charm. It was magnetic, making Magnum the perfect name for this small-statured man with a big personality. He laughed while tilting back his head.

Drunk on our laughter, I said, "Come on, let's look up your DNA donor. I want to know. Aren't you just the least bit curious?"

"I'm not sure."

He was still smiling, so I persisted. "Just think about it then."

"Okay, I promise that I'll at least think about." Magnum glanced at his L-Band. "Damn, I have to go. I forgot. Two units on the fifteenth floor need to be tech prepped and upgraded by noon."

"That's in twenty minutes. Will you have time to do it?"

"Probably not, but when I'm told to do something that involves Cassie Dorothy Dannacher, I drop everything else and do it. You're the number one priority around here now." He grinned and changed his pose to what was yet another billboard-type stance.

"Sorry I kept you so long with all of my questions, Magnum."

"I'm not."

"Then I'm not, either."

"You're a brave girl, Cassie. I'm glad you're back."

"Thanks. You're too cool, you know that?" I said.

"I don't know what that means, but it's good, right?" Magnum walked to the door and gave a half wave over his shoulder.

"Yeah, being cool is definitely a good thing."

Truths that still remained a mystery—that was definitely *not* cool.

Chapter Ten

"I still don't understand why Dr. Little is suddenly allowing me to leave my room." Since the answer was always no, I'd finally stopped asking.

"Who cares as long as you get to do it," said Ella. She stood in the doorway of my bathroom as I primped my hair in the mirror, brushing it smooth with my hand.

"And what was his reason?"

"To celebrate your recovery."

What was this, my reward for good behavior? I hadn't caused any problems since my isolation ended three days earlier. I didn't protest when another blood sample was taken by a MED. During my therapy sessions, I didn't pester Ella to take me to a window, and when Dr. Love came for a visit I didn't lecture her about how I still refused to fully participate. Why? Because I knew it wouldn't do any good—not because three weeks' worth of solitary confinement turned me into an ingratiating captive.

"Is Dr. Bennett going to be there?"

"No, but Magnum's coming."

That probably meant Michael didn't want to make it. Just because we couldn't take our relationship any further didn't mean we had to stay away each other. Was he purposely avoiding me?

"Are you sure you don't want to use Standup?" joked Ella. Standup was against the far wall, slumping like an unwanted mutt with its head down, waiting for its master to call its name.

"Nope, I don't need it anymore," I teased back. "Gumby's officially retired."

"Okay, we'll retire 'Gumby,' or whatever you call it. How do you like the clothes I picked out for you?"

She scanned my body two days prior with a sizing wand and sent the results to a clothing store called "Apparel Five." Twenty-four hours later, I was sent ten mix-and-match pieces tailored to my skinny frame, and two pairs of shoes that molded precisely to my feet.

"You look beautiful, Cassie."

"Thank you." Scrunching sections of my hair with my fingers and spraying it with something she brought me took my hair from flat to full and smelling like lilacs. A dime-sized amount of foundation, plus blush, eye shadow, mascara, and lip gloss, again brought by Ella, disguised the dark circles under my eyes and gave me a "tanned" complexion and lips the color of a fresh peach.

"So are you ready for your first authorized night out?" she asked as we crossed my room.

"Yeah, but I still wish we were going to the botanical garden instead."

"I know. I tried to change Dr. Little's mind, but he's still doesn't want you leaving the building. You're lucky he's letting you leave your hospital room. Come on, let's go."

Leaving my room for the third time was almost as momentous as the night of my escape attempt. My sore feet shook as I stepped through the sliding door and entered a hallway I had only seen in short glimpses.

Ah, freedom once again. But not truly, I thought, glancing down at my L-Banded wrist. This definitely wasn't 2022, now that I could take my time and see it properly. The brightly lit, taupe walls of the hall were adorned with abstract paintings and recessed monitors that glowed in the same taupe color when they weren't flashing advertisements or weather updates.

"That's the A.G.-lift I took when I ran away."

"Oh, no wonder why the guards in the lobby didn't intercept you before you left the hospital. That lift is reserved for bots."

After two turns we entered a corridor packed with uniformed employees bustling like busy bees that were happy in their hive, collectively working at the same tempo or pulse, like they were sharing one heartbeat.

"Most of the employees live here," she said. "Including me. That's why GenH1 has its own restaurant."

Half of the wall to my right was a large, single pane of glass from the ceiling to the floor. Two buildings loomed across the courtyard, bold and alien against the blue sky as wisps of white clouds turned pink with the setting sun. Natural light—yes. Finally! Vitamin D, here I come.

"We're here." Ella clapped as we approached an indoor marquee that read, "GenH1 Bon Appetite." Not very original.

Magnum beat us. He was already at our table, sipping an artificial beer. "Thanks for inviting me to join you two for dinner."

"You're welcome," I said, giving him a hug.

"You look great, Cassie." His eyes made a typical, guy-type scan of my body. He tried to be nonchalant, but it was way too noticeable and made me blush.

"Oh, and by the way," he added, "you can call me James B. Dean if you like, but just for tonight." He settled back into the chair next to me.

Before I could respond, a waitress took our drink order and returned minutes later with a Ninja cocktail for Ella, a soda for me, and another beer for Magnum.

"So, um, what were you saying earlier? You said I could call you what?"

"James B. Dean."

"What made you say that name?"

"You did."

"Me?" I asked, half choking on a sip of my soda. Ella sucked her Ninja cocktail through a neon-pink straw.

"Yeah, after I left your room the other day, I started to think about my DNA donor, how he was my only true relative, so I looked him up. The only information in the archive was the name on my ancestor's tombstone, and that name was James B. Dean."

"What else did you find out about him?" I asked.

"Just his name. That's all I know."

"What about a year? Did it have a birthdate and date of death?" James B. Dean. I knew that name. He was a famous actor during the 1950s. Oh my God! Could it be him?

"Yeah, I think he was born in 1930-something and died in 1950-something. He wasn't very old. I figured it out. He was only twenty-four. It makes me wonder what he died from. I hope it wasn't a genetic medical issue." He frowned.

"I can't believe this," I said, taking three deep breaths and placing a hand on each side of his face. His skin was warm and stubble-free. "Why didn't I realize this before? No wonder why you seemed so familiar to me. Don't worry, your donor didn't die from a medical issue."

"Did you know him?" whispered Ella across the table, her eyes wide.

"No, I didn't, not personally." My grandfather introduced me to him one stormy night when we sat together on the couch and watched the movie *Giant*. I complained about the movie being in black and white but stopped the minute Dean appeared on the screen. He was so cute!

When the movie was over, my grandfather continued our marathon with a second Dean film, *Rebel Without a Cause*, and I watched it, completely mesmerized by the hot, young actor. It wasn't until after the movie ended that my grandfather told me Dean died in a car crash at the age of twenty-four.

I spoke, my words slow and controlled. "I didn't know him, but I knew of him. He grew up in Indiana, but he moved to Los Angeles. He was—"

"No, Cassie, don't." Magnum wrapped his fingers around my wrists. "That's all I want to know. His name is enough. He died so young, and oddly enough, it makes me kinda sad. I really don't want the details."

"Okay." I said, bringing my arms around his body until we were snuggling shoulder to shoulder. I could feel his chest expand with each deep breath. I imagined him in Levi's, a white T-shirt, and a black leather jacket, a rebel without a cause, his hair slicked back with gel. Out of context, uniformed, his hair free of grease, and in the thirty-first century, I couldn't place the resemblance until now.

He rested his head against mine. "Are you okay?"

"Yes. I'm sorry. I just needed to do that," I answered, pulling away.

"Remember, I'm not him. I'm a different person with my own soul. It wasn't me who died at twenty-four. I'll be twenty-six next month. I already have him beat." Magnum laughed and brought his hand around to stroke my hair.

"I know." He was a different person, but with the exception of a different hairstyle, I could see James Dean in a way that no one else who was born after 1955 ever could.

"Well, I'm never going to look up my donor. No way," said Ella with a pouty smile. "I don't care who she was."

She tilted her head back and inched forward. Her eyes closed slightly, but her mouth remained opened and smiling before she took another long sip of her cocktail and released her straw, leaving it crunched and indented with tooth marks.

"Even though I don't like knowing my donor died so young, I'm still glad I did it. It made me think about how vulnerable we really are. How dependent we are upon the dead, robbing their bones of DNA." Magnum took a long gulp of beer. "The whole thing is pretty pathetic when you think about it. Maybe the human race wasn't meant to survive the plague in the first place."

"What are you talking about? Life is way too precious to think that way," Ella interrupted, stirring the ice in her glass with her straw. "And now that Cassie's here?"

"Yeah, now that she's here, the pilfering is going to continue." He looked to his left and right and dropped his voice to a whisper. "This time stealing eggs from young girls—beginning with her." Ella crossed her arms and glared. "And don't forget, they're also going to force them to give birth—again and again."

Touché! Magnum was definitely on my side. I couldn't say the same for Ella, who was making this awkward moment even more uncomfortable by staring at the ceiling. "Thank you for understanding," was all I could say.

"Cassie, honey, now don't take this the wrong way," Ella finally said, after crunching on a piece of ice, "but as much as I don't like the idea of anyone being forced to do something he or she does not want to do, there are times when it's necessary to give someone a little nudge when it comes to having that person decide to do the right thing."

"A nudge?" he asked, shaking his head through a sarcastic laugh. "How about a push?"

"It's just hard for me to understand why you don't want to have a baby." She twisted the egg ring on her finger. "I mean, if I ever had the chance to give birth, I'd take it in a heartbeat, no matter the circumstances and no questions asked, especially if it meant saving the human race. I'd do anything to be in your shoes."

I believed her, and I couldn't blame her. Every female soap opera character had an inner longing to procreate naturally, clutching their flat bellies, their eyes brimming with tears as the newborn clone of their choice was plucked from a plastic uterus and handed to them by a MED.

"Please don't be mad at me for feeling that way," Ella begged just before the waitress arrived with a tray of food.

"I'm not mad at you." But was she secretly mad at me because of the way I felt?

She leaned toward me for a long hug and whispered, "Thank you," in my ear before she let go and eyed the plate of food in the center of the table.

"I'm seventeen. I have a long life ahead of me," I added, "and I should be the one who decides what to do with it."

We ate our appetizers, oddly shaped mushrooms smothered in a savory orange sauce, and downed small glasses of smooth, cold soup referred to as soup shooters. Magnum tapped his foot, Ella became giddy, continuing to laugh for no apparent reason, unless it was a failed attempt to lighten the mood, and I sat in silence with a movie star to my left and a woman to my right who wanted to be me.

"Hey, you two go out and dance." She giggled as the restaurant lights dimmed and the volume of the background music increased.

"No, no, you two go out there," I said.

He groaned. "I don't dance." He tilted back in his chair, and I pictured him with a cigarette hanging out of his mouth.

"Yeah, right. Mr. Cool is too cool to dance? Go on," I urged.

He lowered his chair to the floor and stood with hunched shoulders. "Okay, I'll dance, but you have to dance with me, Cassie."

"Yeah, go on. It can be part of your physical therapy," said Ella. She gave his lower leg a push with the tip of her pointed-toe shoe.

"But I've never danced with a guy before," I shouted above the music as he took my hand and led me to a small clearing on the dance floor.

What could I do other than resort to imitating the moves of the other women around me? There was more upper-body movement and less grinding than I remembered. Apparently "dirty dancing" was dead, and I was glad.

Magnum kept to the beat, but his movements were not fully extended. He was only half dancing, trying to appear nonchalant and detached from the other men who, in probably his mind, looked like buffoons.

"So do you really think I'm cool, whatever that means?" he said when the music slowed.

"Absolutely."

"No one has ever called me that before."

"That's because no one uses that word anymore—at least I haven't heard anyone use it here, not even the people on the entertainment channels. How do woman usually describe you?"

He smiled, embarrassed. "Oh, I don't know. Usually I'm told that I'm cute."

"Well, you're more than that. You're cute, and you're cool," I teased as he gave me a twirl.

Here I was dancing with James Dean. Magnum was charming and charismatic, fun and fascinating. The thought gave me a good set of chills and made me forget about being a mother in the near future.

"So, um, how are you handling things anyway? Are you doing okay?"

The music slowed. He pulled me against his body, and like the other couples, I brought my arms around his neck as he drew his arms about my waist.

"No, not really. I know I don't have a choice, and I know I can't change things," I whispered in his ear. "But at the same time, I can't accept my fate. I don't want to be a mother, especially under these circumstances, even if it means no more dead fetuses and no more tortured chimps."

"Whoa, you know about that?"

"Yup, I saw it for myself. It broke my heart," I said, letting out a soft sigh.

"I do what I can to avoid both rooms. If there's ever a technical issue I send one of my techs, but Dr. Bennett, he goes in the chimp room all the time."

I stiffened. "Why? Is he the one who has to harvest...?"

"No, that's a bot's job. Dr. Bennett feels sorry for them, but instead of ignoring their existence like many of us try to do, he brings them special treats, things they don't get in their regular meals."

"Aw, that's so sweet." I wished Michael was here now, his arms tight around my waist, his hands pressing my back, his lips light against my neck.

"So were you telling Ella the truth when you told her you weren't mad at her? I'd be a little mad if I was you."

"No, I'm not mad." Not at her. How could I be?

"You know, she's not the only one who'd jump at the chance at being you. I think any woman would."

"At least you understand how I feel."

"That's because I've spent a lot of time thinking about your situation. If I got married today and my wife and I decided to have a child, we'd show up at the GenH1 maternity ward, and twenty minutes later leave with a baby in our arms. Even though that baby wouldn't be tied to either one of us genetically, at least I'd have a choice as to whether I wanted a baby in the first place, and if so, who the mother of my child would be." His forehead touched mine.

"That's not going to happen for you."

He was right, but it was something I didn't want to think about. I rested my chin on his shoulder and pressed my cheek against his neck. If I could pick the father of my child, would adjusting to my role here be easier, or would it make things more complicated? My stomach knotted.

Colored spotlights from above bounced between two mirrored walls, one on each side of the dance floor, pulsing in time with the music. From over Magnum's shoulder, I watched the clones' mirror images dance, turning in small, slow circles as they held one another. Like their reflections, they were copies of another human, distant echoes from the past, something that was still so hard for me to believe.

"I'm sorry this is happening to you. If I could stop it, I would," he said, his soft breath on my neck.

"Knowing that means a lot to me. Thank you."

When the song ended, he gave me an extra-long embrace before we cut across the dance floor toward Ella.

"Cassie," said Ella as we sat down. "Dr. Little called. He wants you to report to his office when you're done eating."

"Why?"

"He said the celebration wasn't going to end here. Apparently it's going to continue in his office."

"What's he talking about?"

"I'm not sure," she said, shaking her head.

Magnum snatched a straw from an empty glass, chewed the end like a toothpick, and chucked it across the dance floor.

Chapter Eleven

Two security guards were waiting for me outside the restaurant, and as we turned into a corridor leading to an A.G.-lift, the three of us were joined by a SEC. A rush of panic filled my core, tempting me to rip my arm from the security guard's grip and sprint away from them down the hall.

"Welcome, Miss Dannacher," said Dr. Little when I entered his office. "Thank you for agreeing to see me tonight."

Did I have a choice? He motioned to one of the chairs on the other side of his desk, and I sat down, my nerves on fire. "So, what are we celebrating?" I asked as blasé as I could and looked over his shoulder at Claus rather than making direct eye contact with him.

"Something special, something very, very special. Something that should make you very, very happy. Making you happy and keeping you that way are very important to me." The fervor in his eyes made me cringe.

Yeah, right. Then let me go. "Really, you could have fooled me. Don't forget that I spent three weeks in solitary confinement."

"That was for your own good. We couldn't have you trying to run away or consider hurting yourself again, now could we?" He smiled. "I can only hope it gave you time to think about how well you've been treated since your awakening. We gave you back your life—something that was impossible in your century—and in doing so, healed all of your injuries. We've provided you with food, clothing, a warm bed, and medical care."

All of which were true, yet hard to appreciate considering why they brought me back to life in the first place. I didn't get *my* old life back, but they did give me life.

"You can never give me what I really want."

"That may be true, but we have given you something."

"What?"

"Let me show you rather than tell you," he said, setting his Liaison in front of me and giving it a tap. The black screen flickered and an image appeared, something alien-looking, something pink with an enlarged head and tiny limbs bent at their knees and elbows.

"Why are you showing me this?"

"Congratulations, Miss Dannacher. You've just completed your first trimester." He grinned. I held my breath as I studied the image again, a fetus about the size of a domino floating in a fluid-filled sac of flesh. "It's a girl, of course, due to our gender selection method."

"There's no way. I don't understand?"

"What is there to understand? This image was taken last night by a MED while you slept. As of today, you're twelve weeks into your pregnancy. In approximately twenty-six weeks, you'll be giving birth to a healthy baby girl. This is your baby," he said, pushing his Liaison closer to me.

"I don't believe you." I gasped, pushing it back, and remembering the soft *ding* I thought I heard in the middle of the night. "I haven't been throwing up every morning for the last three months." I'd been nauseous from time to time, but I was sure that was due to anxiety and being dead for one thousand and three years.

"Only 75 percent of pregnant woman suffer from morning sickness during the first trimester, and of that 75, 25 percent experience occasional nausea without vomiting. Think about the symptoms: fatigue, nausea, dizziness, an increase in appetite."

I'd experienced all of those things, but weren't they signs of my recovery, symptoms born from my mental struggle to get a grip on this world?

"You could've gotten this picture from anywhere. There's no proof that it's from me," I shouted, folding my arms hard across my chest and giving the desk leg a kick.

He pointed to the picture on the screen. "It is your baby, Miss Dannacher, and if you don't believe me, I'll call in a MED right now for another scan, so you can see the image being taken for yourself."

This is what Michael was talking about—a truth being told.

My head grew light, and for a moment I thought I was going to faint. The pink, thumb-sized fetus blurred as my eyes welled, but I sucked in my trembling lower lip, determined not to let a tear fall.

"You've made these last three months rather difficult for

all of us. Eighty percent of all miscarriages occur in the first trimester. After the stunt you pulled three weeks ago, we had to do everything we could to keep you and your baby from harm, which included moving you to the isolation ward and checking your hormone levels regularly."

It all made sense, but I didn't want to believe it. I couldn't believe it. Three months? I'd only been awake for one.

"When? When did you do this to me?"

"Two months before you were awakened."

"Y-you had no right to-to violate me like that," I stammered. "I was unconscious. I couldn't give you my permission."

"What rights? You were a ward of the region. The president made the decision for you."

"But why? Why do it before I was awakened? And why didn't you just—"

"Just what? Take one of your eggs, fertilize it in the lab, and pop it into an artificial uterus or a waiting surrogate?"

That was my question, although that wouldn't have made what they did to me any better. Touching my body without my consent, invading my private places, and impregnating me using who-knew-what from someone I didn't know. The words curdled in my throat as I tried to answer yes, and my hands shook as I balled my hands into fists.

"Like we explained to you before—the artificial uterus has not been perfected. Whether the donor of the egg is a human or a primate, the odds are against its survival. We can't afford losing, or should I say, wasting any of your precious eggs."

With the word "precious," Dr. Little's dry lips curled, and his eyes gleamed. He deserved a kick in the groin. "In the twenty-first century, the surrogacy success rate was 39 percent. One thousand years later, we suspect that number won't be any different, since our women already require hormone therapy. Surrogacy is our next best option, but right now, you are our first and best."

"If only you had asked," I said, not that it would have made any difference. I imagined myself unconscious and naked on an exam table, a MED with a syringe-like hand ending my chastity.

"At the time, we weren't sure an awakening was even possible. It wasn't until after the conception that our team found a way to bring you into consciousness. And to be quite honest, Miss Dannacher, Dr. Pickford and I voted against it." He leaned back into a stretch. "We wanted to keep you in stasis before, during, and after each pregnancy. We expected you'd be reluctant and difficult to manage, but I was outnumbered, the others insisting it would be healthful to the growing fetus and an act of injustice if we didn't."

Michael wanted me awake. And Michael had known I was pregnant this whole time.

"In the end, President Gifford made the call. He has plans for you, Miss Dannacher. You are a symbol of fertility and hope for this world. Your happiness is also one of *his* top priorities."

A poster child for their program—and now that I was pregnant, I could never be happy.

"So, they all know I'm...? Everyone's known this whole time?" I asked, my body sick and trembling.

"Of course."

No wonder Magnum was so pissed off.

"Everyone who has contact with you needs to be privy

to your rare condition," he continued. "This is a top secret program. The public can't know about you—at least not yet."

"Why?"

"Ultimately it was our president's decision not to tell the people. So far we've kept them sheltered from our predicament. If they knew the truth, he suspects riots and protests if we can't deliver what we promised, a scene from 2425 before our forefather's regained control of the world and rebuilt our population."

"But you should have told me. From the very beginning, I should have known!" Michael should have told me, regardless.

"The team was ordered not to tell you. There are two very good reasons why we waited. First of all, we wanted you past your first trimester, and secondly, we thought easing you into the project slowly would make you a willing participant by the end of your twelfth week, and you'd take the news in stride. Apparently we were wrong."

"Yes, you were wrong," I said, holding my tears.

"I suppose so." He stood and nodded to the guards. "But we had to tell you now. You'll start noticing changes in your body in a matter of weeks."

While pushing up from the chair, I looked down at my stomach. It wasn't sunken like it was when I first awakened, but I was too thin before. Over the last few weeks I'd gained weight, but it was needed weight, muscle weight. Could there really be a baby inside me? I crumpled at the thought.

"So what's going to happen now, now that I know?"

"Well, first of all, tomorrow you'll be meeting the father of your unborn child."

My knees buckled, and the taller of the two security

guards caught me at my waist, holding me until I was stable. The father of my baby. They wanted me to meet him? Why?

"Who…?"

"That question will be answered tomorrow. In the meantime, remember that everything you do has a direct impact upon the baby you're carrying. Every choice you make is no longer just about you, it's about you and your child." He winked and gave a nod to the security guards, and after one of the guards took my arm to lead me into the hall, Dr. Little called, "Don't you forget that," as the door slid closed.

He was right. It was no longer just about me, it was about me and the pink little being he showed me on his Liaison. Every decision I made was a decision for both of us. To kill myself meant taking an innocent life with me. A hunger strike meant starving my baby, too. Now that I was pregnant, a roll of the dice meant two playing pieces were moved in a game I didn't want to play.

A hot shower left me physically and mentally numb, my legs unsteady, my arms weak. In the mirror, I tried to find the face of a young, independent woman, but the face of a depressed, seventeen-year-old girl stared back at me instead. I was pregnant and stuck in a world of restrictions.

What if I had thrown myself into a high-speed mover? Two lives would have been lost instead of one. What if I had a miscarriage? Even though I was three months in, it could still happen. And then what would they do—make me conceive all over again?

Ella and Dr. Love were in my room when I returned from the bathroom. "Cassie, honey, how are you doing?" asked Ella.

But I couldn't answer. My body trembled. My throat

tightened. Ella wrapped her arms around me, and I couldn't stop my tears.

"Everything's going to be okay. We're all going to help you through this. It'll be easier now that you know."

"I wish I'd known sooner," I sobbed, letting her go.

"We wanted to tell you," said Dr. Love. "But we had to do what was best for you and the baby. I hope you're not upset with us for that."

Ella brushed a tear from my cheek. "It was so hard to go along with Dr. Little's plan and not tell you the real reason why he wanted us to go out and celebrate. I had to bite my tongue more than once, and poor Magnum. He was on edge all night, knowing what was going to happen after dinner."

"No, I understand." And I did to an extent.

When it came to Michael, I couldn't and didn't. He'd had plenty of times to tell me after he made the room free, giving me a secret to use to my advantage. He also could have told me the night he snuck into my isolation cell. But now it was too late. I had one choice: I had to play their game, and I had to play by their rules.

"It's late, sweetie. You need to get some rest and keep up your strength for that baby of yours. It's a miracle, Cassie, and absolute miracle," she said, giving me another hug.

Dr. Love gave my shoulder a light squeeze, and said, "Sleep tight," as they walked out the door.

Yeah, right. Sleep tight. That night, I lay in bed and thought about miracles—the miracle that I was alive and the miracle of life itself. Maybe I was there for a reason, one beyond my control, and one that would bring a miracle to this desperate world. But what about my baby? Right from birth, she'd inherit my problems. Could I let that happen?

Chapter Twelve

"His name is Travel Lee Carson III." Dr. Little's wrinkled jowls shook, and I shivered. Meeting the father of my child made me more nervous than I thought I would be.

The third? Apparently clones kept the old traditions. It wasn't about bloodlines and biological relations anymore. It was all about being related by marriage and adoptions. Preserving last names and titles gave them a past even though they didn't really have one. I'd seen it one too many times in the soaps.

"Why do I have to meet him?" I asked, rubbing my wet palms against the tops of my thighs.

"He wants to meet you. He and Dr. Bennett will be here any minute," said Dr. Little, glancing at his L-Band.

"So, Dr. Bennett is going to be here, too?"

"He is."

Oh gosh. Talk about awkward. Michael was the last person I wanted to see. The pulse in my neck pounded as my anger toward him mixed with my anxiety.

"Last night, I told you that one of my top priorities is to make you happy. I think giving you something from your world will make you happy." He smiled, and his cheeks puckered, pulling his wrinkles.

What could he possibly give me from my world? Claus?

The door to my right slid open. He stood, and I did the same, following his cue. A guy entered first, smiling nervously. Michael came next, his head down, his hands in his pockets.

"Cassie, I'd like to introduce you to Travel Lee Carson III," said Dr. Little. "The biological father of your child."

Biological father—the words plunged through my heart, my soul, and just as I semi-recovered with a deep breath, that pang of familiarity that I felt with Magnum ran through my body in a wave that made me gasp. Travel Lee Carson III looked very familiar. My cheeks burned as I studied his profile, his straight, perfectly proportioned nose, and his sideburns trimmed and neatly slanted at the bottoms.

"Hello," he said, offering a hand for me to shake.

Our eyes locked, and I sucked in a short breath, my hand falling away from his. I stumbled backward, grabbing the arm of my chair to steady myself before lowering slowly to my seat.

"Are you okay?" he asked.

"Yeah, I'm fine," I said, looking from Travel to Michael for a silent explanation, but Michael's eyes were on the floor, his lips tight as he sat down in the chair farthest away from me. As Travel took the chair at my right and our eye contact resumed, an eerie, cold prickle ran up my spine, because Travel Lee Carson III was none other than the clone of my first crush, David Casper. This had to be more than just a coincidence.

Travel's gaze in my direction was almost palpable, momentarily sending me back to my last day at Central when David and I said our good-byes, and he gave me my first kiss.

Brown eyes, deep brown wavy hair that hit at his shoulders, and a parade of light freckles that ran across his cheek, over his nose, and down the other cheek. Broad shoulders, a small waist, and a distinct jawline. Travel and David were identical down to the way they wore their hair.

And just like David, his features were boyish but rugged, and there was a youthful recklessness about him, like he would accept any dare and make any bet. But there were two differences: this version of David was older by two if not three years, and though the tone of his voice was the same, his accent was weak, marked by just a touch of the Australian drawl I loved. When David died, he must have been buried back in his home country.

For a moment, he made my insides tingle, my skin goose pimple, and my heart quicken, but I knew what I immediately felt for him was superficial, born from the fact that he looked like David.

Magnum said that clones were different people with their own souls, but how true was this? Could Travel and David have more in common besides their looks? This clone struck me differently than Magnum. James Dean was simply a pinup from an era gone by, the era of hula hoops, poodle skirts, and car hops. Dean's image was immortalized in merchandise and movies. Over time, he slowly lost his individual identity until he was just an icon, a mascot of the

Hollywood glamour days.

I never knew James Dean, but I knew David Casper. For this reason, it was different with Travel. Magnum was Magnum, but when I looked at Travel, I saw David.

He was it—my present from the past? But how did Dr. Little know about David? Did Travel know I knew him before, in the form of a guy who was intelligent and sincere, someone who had almost become my boyfriend? Did Travel know he was selected to be the donor simply because Dr. Little wanted to anchor me to this world with a familiar face from 2022? And this was supposed to make me happy?

I was pregnant with this guy's child.

My sweaty palms met the arms of the chair as I caught my breath and crossed my legs, first one way and then another. I tried to appear calm, my thoughts collected, when in truth, my insides twisted. The reality of my pregnancy and the father of that child gnawed away at my core.

"As of tomorrow, Travel will be calling GenH1 home," said Dr. Little. "His belongings are being moved to an employee housing unit on the fifteenth floor, the first floor above the hospital. Another unit on that floor has been reserved for you.

"I made that request. I hope you don't mind," said Travel. Travel's cheeks were pink like mine probably were, flushed with anticipation and a bit of fear.

And then I looked at Michael. His cheeks were pale and taut, appearing oily in the dim lights of Dr. Little's office. Michael still hadn't looked at me, and I was totally okay with that. I had some choice words ready for him, but now was not the time.

"I'd like us to become friends and raise our daughter together," said Travel as he nervously wrung his hands in his lap.

Raise a baby with someone he didn't even know?

I gulped, and an empty spot grew in the pit of my stomach. "Um, actually, I haven't had a lot of time to think about this. I haven't decided what I want to do. I'm not sure I want to be a mother. I haven't—"

"Please raise our baby with me. I want us to be like a real family." He blinked anxiously, and I remembered the seventeen-year-old boy who took my hand and said, "Cassie, I think we could be more than just friends. What do you think?"

That was the day I planned to tell David the bad news. My mom was on a flight back to the States, and I'd be back in Arizona in less than two weeks, preparing for a dig. He let go of my hand when I told him we'd probably never see each other again. And with his gaze fixed on the horizon, he said slowly, "Oh, then I guess there isn't any point." I locked myself in my room that night and cried in my pillow, refusing to answer when my grandfather knocked on my door.

"We're stuck here at GenH1, so we might as well make the best of it." He laughed.

"We're stuck here?" I said, raising my voice.

"Travel," Dr. Little interrupted. "Cassie's commitments to the project haven't been fully discussed with her yet. But I have her contract right here. It's identical to yours. Cassie, all we need is your final approval," he said, as if I even had a choice. What a phony.

He set his Liaison in front of me. "Cassie, you and Travel are invaluable to us. We can't risk losing either one of you, so we need to keep you at GenH1 for your safety, health, and well-being. This program is also highly classified. We can't risk a security breach."

"So I can never leave this building?"

"You can't leave the GenH1 compound—at least not until it is deemed safe. It's for your own protection"

"And when will that be?"

"That date has not yet been determined, but the time will come. It's all here in the contract."

While Dr. Little spoke, he kept his fingers interlocked and his hands on the table, but every so often he'd smile from one side of his mouth, look at me, and then nod toward the table behind him like he and I had some kind of inside joke about Claus. It made me sick.

"Travel understands," he continued, "that at times, being part of this process will be, let's say, an inconvenience, but he also understands that the outcomes exceed the cost of his independence during all phases of the program. We're currently in Phase I. Phase II begins our surrogacy program, during Phase III—"

"How many phases are there and how long will each phase last?"

"There are currently seven phases. Each phase is dependent upon the last, and there are many factors involved, making it difficult to establish an accurate timeline, but at some point you'll be allowed to leave the compound. And at that point in time, we have no objection to you starting a career or even getting married to whom you choose."

"So basically I'll be a prisoner here until you decide I'm not."

"Miss Dannacher, you have to understand that—"

"What is there to understand? I was impregnated against my will, and now I'm being forced to stay here until you see fit." My volume half doubled.

Travel drew in a deep breath. Raising my voice made him uncomfortable to say the least, since his outlook on the program and mine were in sharp contrast.

"It's not like you don't have any choices. Like I've told you before, your budget is unlimited, and you'll have full access of the GenH1 compound."

"Then I want to move into my housing unit today. And I want permission to explore the GenH1 compound and visit the botanical garden any time that I want."

"Done," said Dr. Little. "You know your happiness is of the utmost importance. We just need you to sign the contract."

"Can I please have a few minutes to talk to Cassie alone," interrupted Travel.

Dr. Little and Michael stood abruptly and walked to the door. Michael kept his head lowered, his hands in his pockets, but that didn't stop me from glaring at the two men until the door slid closed behind them.

Travel bent forward until his face was a mere three inches from mine. He took my stiff hands in both of his, cupping them lovingly like we'd known each other for years rather than a few minutes. His eyes glistened, and though their intensity was at odds with our situation, since I was a mere stranger, something about them put me at ease.

"Cassie, right now inside of you, our joined DNA is producing a child whose body is unique. Not a reinvention of an ancestor's bone marrow, but a living, breathing piece of you and me combined, connecting us in a way I never thought was possible for a man and a woman."

His words were melodic, his breath well-seasoned with

peppermint, but my hands remained rigid in his with the thought of a baby—his baby—inside of me.

"We're creating a new, one-of-a-kind life from our own DNA, proving that the preservation of mankind through reproduction can still exist even with clones. It is such an honor to participate in this mission to save the world, but I need to do it with you at my side. I want you next to me, hand in hand, through all phases of the program. Can you do this for me?" His voice was desperate, his breathing quick, making me almost pull away.

By his side? He didn't know me, and I didn't even know him, though I did feel some kind of strange connection. His mannerisms, his gestures, the way he pushed his hair behind his ear and tilted his head to one side when he was listening intently—all of that was David.

I didn't grow up in an infertile world, a world where the prospect of having a biological child was unconceivable until now. I'd never be able to understand any clone's unending yearn for this type of bond with another human being. For him, this link to me was almost as strong as marriage, and who was I to ruin this thought for him? He wasn't the one who'd forced me to become pregnant.

"I'll try," I whispered. Right now he wasn't Travel. Right now he was David. My hand relaxed in his.

"This might be hard for you to believe, but I feel like I've known you for months. I saw you before you were awakened. I asked to see you. I never expected that the woman destined to be the mother of my child would be the most beautiful girl I've ever seen. After that day, you were all I could think about."

The lighting above formed soft shadows across his face as

a lamp at the back of the room cast an aura of bright light at the base of his head and shoulders. Wow, he was hot—totally, indiscriminately hot. His strong, tall build, asymmetrical, manly facial features, and raw unbridled sexiness made my heart beat just like it did for David Casper.

"When they told me you were pregnant," he continued, "I wished so badly you were awake, so we could share the news together and celebrate."

"So you know I was inseminated before I was conscious?" I said, pulling my hand from his.

"Yes, and I know you feel deceived. I'm sure I would, too, if I were you, but I also know those feelings wouldn't last because I'd understand that what they did was for the greater good of the world."

With his finger, he gave Dr. Little's Liaison a push until it was directly in front of me. "Please sign the contract. I understand why you're reluctant, but I trust Dr. Little. I trust the team. This contract will protect your rights."

What a joke. Protect my rights? Those contracts were nothing more than a couple of props to make the project appear ethical. Travel wasn't the one who was violated. He wasn't the one who was misled. He was a willing participant.

The contract was shorter than I expected. I read through each provision I was required to follow, such as refraining from activities that could jeopardize the baby's safety or mine and remaining within the confines of the GenH1 compound. Each phase of the program was outlined along with my required participation and an understanding that the projected timeline was subject to change. There was nothing there that I didn't already know or had been told.

"Okay, I'll sign it."

Travel guided my thumb to a rectangular box on Dr. Little's Liaison, and I pressed down harder than necessary, nicking the screen with my thumbnail.

"Thank you," he said, squeezing my hand.

The door slid open. Michael and Dr. Little entered, Michael still keeping his gaze on the floor. "So," said Dr. Little. "I see that you've approved the contract." He pretended to lift a champagne glass. "Gentlemen, and lady," he said with a smile in my direction and a nod at Claus, "a toast to the Van Winkle Project."

From under the table, Travel set his hand on mine, and I repeated these words in my head: *the Van Winkle Project, VWP*. But there was one big difference between Rip Van Winkle and me. He didn't wake up after one thousand years to find that he had been betrayed by the entire world.

Chapter Thirteen

"Cassie, your living unit is down here. It's a two bedroom, two bath apartment with a living room and eat-in kitchen." Kale stood near the end of the hall next to an open door, waving both arms in the air.

"Oh, this is really nice," I said, entering a living room that sparkled with metallic fabrics of gray and smoky blue, and a big vase of flowers in the center of the coffee table. "Finally, I have a window." The screen was down, blocking my view of the outside world, but enough light pierced through the weave of fabric to light the entire room.

Kale's tour included a refrigeration and freezing unit stocked with food, a closet in the master bedroom full of clothes my size, equipped with a voice-activated rotating rack, and a master bathroom with toiletries in the cabinets and a therapeutic shower similar to the one I had in my hospital room.

"Well, if you have any questions, call me, or Travel can

also help you," she said before ordering the bathroom light to turn off. "He's just down the hall."

"Okay. Thank you."

"Oh, and one more thing," she added as we re-entered the kitchen. "Remember, you can't leave this floor without permission or an escort."

"I know," I said sarcastically. "I read it in the contract."

I walked Kale to the door, and a *ding* rang through the house when it closed behind her.

The kitchen was full of unrecognizable foreign machines that roasted, brewed, mixed, and crushed. One press of a button produced a perfectly brewed, caffeine-free vanilla latte. Another gave me a cold glass of carbonated lemonade. An appliance the size of a coffeemaker sliced a carrot into perfect coins, and the only thing I had to do was toss it into the bin on top and close the lid.

She told me I could make my own meals or have meals delivered by a bot. Bot delivery would definitely be easier. At my command, Liaison One displayed a menu on the closest monitor, and I scanned the items, knowing I could order anything I wanted.

No expense had been spared, only my freedom. And that freedom was replaced with a responsibility I didn't want— raising a child, and in time, saving mankind. Was it a burden I could carry alone, or did I need someone like Travel to help me bear some of the weight, balance the worry, and ease me into the acceptance of my fate?

I strolled to the living room, stood in front of the window, and retracted the blind with the touch of a button. The sun was high, creating shadows against the compound's buildings as clouds skated across the bright-blue sky. Below, tiny dots of people made their trek through the compound's square, making their way in and out of a society I hardly knew and probably never would.

One man cut across the concrete, leaving the compound, and I remembered myself there on the night of my escape, my arms cranking and legs burning in a cold sprint to run away to anywhere but here. I could have died that night, and in doing so, taken a tiny life with me—one I didn't know existed until yesterday. Here I was—pregnant and a stranger in a strange land. Dr. Little gave me one thing from my world—David Casper, my almost boyfriend—but was he or anyone else going to be enough to make me appreciate this world and my fate?

David had created quite a whirlwind his first week at Central. Girls were left whispering and giggling in his wake. He was invited to every party, and he couldn't make it through the quad without being tugged on by someone who had to tell him his Australian accent was cool. But when it came to spending time with someone, he wanted to spend it with me.

A *ding* rang through my apartment, and on my L-Band I saw Travel standing in the hall.

"Hi," I said as I opened the door with a tap.

"Hi. I, um, just wanted to see what you thought of your apartment."

"I like it. How's yours?" I asked as we walked into the living room.

"Identical to this one. Like clones." He laughed. "Except for the view, since I'm on the other side of the building. I actually think yours is better. You'll have to check mine out sometime."

"Yeah, I'll have to do that. So, have a seat," I said, pointing to the couch. "Would you like something to drink? I figured out how to make lattes and fizzes."

"No, I'm fine. Thanks."

I sat down next to him, hoping my close proximity wouldn't make my half of the conversation any more awkward than it already was.

"So, I was told that you spent a lot of time traveling with your mom."

"Yeah."

"What was she…a paleo-something?"

"A paleontologist."

"And what exactly is a paleontologist?"

"Someone who digs up dinosaur bones and studies them. I used to help her. You can learn a lot from just a single bone."

"Like what?"

"Well, first we establish the species, age, and size of the dinosaur, and then we try to figure out how the dinosaur lived. You know, what it ate, how it reproduced—sometimes a whole life story can be told with one bone. We can also determine if the dinosaur was injured and died from its wound or survived and lived beyond its injury just by studying the bone growth."

"I came from one bone." His voice was almost a whisper.

"I know," I whispered back, hanging my head.

"Where did the flowers come from? I don't have a bouquet in my living room."

"Then I'm pretty sure they're from Ella, my physical therapist. She sent flowers to my hospital room, too. I think they're from GenH1's botanical garden. I love flowers, especially magnolias."

"I'll have to remember that." He smiled and pushed a chunk of hair behind his ear like David used to do. "It looks like we had the same buyer," he said, smoothing his shirt with his hand. We were dressed alike: white T-shirts and jeans.

"Didn't you bring your own clothes?"

"No, I guess I should have. They told me a wardrobe had been provided for my convenience, and it's not like I'll be going anywhere anyway, right?" His tone bordered on being flirtatious, and I fought not to flirt back, trying to think of him as Travel instead of David.

"So, how are you feeling?" he asked, eyeing my stomach.

"I feel fine. And she's fine," I said, tugging the hem of my tunic. "I'm just tired, and when I'm tired, I start thinking about my life—what it used to be and where it's going—especially now."

"I do that, too—start thinking about my life, asking myself 'What if this' and 'What if that,' and thinking about all of the mistakes I made in my past. I have a lot of regrets. What about you? Any regrets?"

Regrets? I had plenty. I regretted leaving Central and going back to Arizona with my mom. I regretted getting into that helicopter on the night it crashed and I died.

"Well, I wish I could have spent more time with my grandfather. I didn't grow up with a father, so he was like a father to me. I lived with him for one semester of my junior year. Every weekend, we'd make popcorn, watch old movies, and talk about life. I miss him a lot. There's a lot from my century that I miss."

"You're so amazing. To think you survived over one

thousand years to end up here, just in the nick of time, with the ability to reproduce and save the world. It's still so hard for me to believe."

"You are giving me way too much credit. It all has to do with chance, luck, and the new technology. I didn't ask for any of this. I didn't give consent to be frozen and stored. It's all a coincidence."

"I believe everyone is here for a greater purpose, and this is yours. And now I know mine." He placed his free hand on top of mine. "I have faith this will work."

A *ding-ding* rang through the living room as Ella's face appeared on my L-Band. "I forgot that I have a physical therapy session," I said, standing and smoothing my T-shirt.

Ella didn't say anything other than "Hello, Mr. Carson" when she and Travel passed each other at my door, but as soon as the door slid shut and he left, she asked with two bats of her eyes, "So, what was Travel doing here?"

"Oh, just checking out my apartment."

"So is that what you called it in the twenty-first century?"

"What do you mean?"

"You know what I mean. I saw the way he looked at you when he left. He is the father of your baby after all."

"But that doesn't mean we have to be more than just friends."

"Well, if I were you, I'd think about it. That guy's a cutie-pie." She bubbled with laughter. "If he was ten years older, I'd be fighting you for him. I'm ready to put a wedding ring on this finger." She held up her hand and wiggled her fingers. The egg ring glistened. "Hey, I have a surprise for you."

"What?" This better be a good one.

"Today your therapy session consists of a trip to the

botanical building."

"Yes!" I screamed.

"But a SEC has to come with us. It's waiting in the hall. Dr. Little doesn't want anything to happen to you."

My vision tunneled as we made our way to the East Wing, and I soon forgot that I was being followed by a SEC bot with active weapons, and focused on how many turns we made and which halls led the way out of this place. My ride in the A.G.-lift was the only thing eclipsed by my eagerness to see grass, trees, dirt, and rocks.

"This is it," she announced as a glass double door in front of us slid open.

"Finally, fresh air and sunshine," I said, taking a breath so deeply that I was momentarily light-headed.

The sky was blue, etched with a rip of clouds just above the roof of the wood-slatted botanical building. A star of sunlight burst through its uppermost slats as the sun slowly made its way to the brink of noon.

"It's so beautiful." The lath building curved like a Quonset hut at each end, but its center rose upward into an octagonal dome that was topped by an impressively carved fleur-de-lis. To its right was the Magnolia Café, an unimpressive building in comparison.

"Really? You think this old building is beautiful?"

"Yeah, of course. Oh, and there's my magnolia tree." I rushed up to its trunk to give it a big hug. Ella giggled and the SEC bot, which was now within two feet of me, stood at attention with cold eyes and an even colder rubbery smile.

"What's that?" I asked, releasing my botanical friend. A hundred yards behind the botanical garden, a dull, chain-link type fence, at least eight feet tall, wrapped a rectangular plot of land of at least ten acres. Thigh-high grass ran the inside length of the fence, making it impossible to see the ground.

"The remains of some kind of old factory. A factory built before the plague."

Tall buildings spread across the concrete landscape, their windows flashing in the afternoon sun. The patch of bleak land, unused and neglected, was out of place and an eyesore.

"Why is it still here? I'm surprised the whole thing hasn't been torn down."

"I'm not sure, something about the land being unusable. It contains some kind of pit."

The wind shifted, and an odd odor filled my nostrils. She wrinkled her nose.

"The botanical building was supposed to be part of the Great Demolition after the Great Plague Migration, but one of the forefathers fought for its preservation and removed it from the list," she continued. "Apparently he took refuge in this building while recuperating. Now it's a registered landmark, one of only a few in the region, but like I said before, no one ever comes here, except for him." She pointed at GROW as it came around the corner of the building, holding a pair of clippers.

"Have you ever been inside?"

"Nope."

"Well then, let's go."

Between the lath, green leaves sparkled like jewels: emeralds, peridots, and jade. The building's thick wooden door hung in its frame the old-fashioned way on two hinges. Ella nearly broke a sweat as she first pulled, then pushed, upon the heavy door and complained about either breaking a nail or getting a splinter, but she insisted on doing the honors. Apparently she wasn't used to natural wood products.

"This is fabulous." I eyed the rows of neatly trimmed plants and flowers. "Oh, and here's a ginkgo." I darted toward a raised bed of shrubbery.

"A what?" She cocked her head and her hips.

"A ginkgo. This is a ginkgo biloba, a deciduous seed fern. It's known as the living fossil. They flourished during the Jurassic period. They've been around for over two hundred and seventy million years. My mom's team found fossilized ginkgo in Utah. See how its leaves are shaped? It splits into two distinct lobes," I said as I stroked one of its waxy leaves.

"Yeah, um, that's great. I guess." Ella inspected her manicure.

"Hey, what's that?" My attention shifted to a planter made from crude, brown bricks.

"Um, I'm not sure. I'll ask Liaison One."

While she made her query via her L-Bud, I ran my hand along the planter's edge, noting bits of dried plant debris encased within the hard sand and clay.

"It's the remains of an adobe building built by the indige-something people."

"Indigenous."

"Yeah, indigenous people in the eighteenth century. When this area was being leveled for the botanical building's construction before the plague, part of the ancient structure was uncovered. The architect decided to use one of its remaining walls as a planter since the bricks were made from organic material."

"Wow. This is such a find. You have no idea. These bricks

must be over thirteen hundred years old. I'm going to excavate this site, set up my own dig. This is so amazing."

"Yeah, I guess that's pretty amazing," she said, disinterested. To a clone, they were obviously nothing more than rectangular cubes of dried mud.

But then her hands slipped from her waist to her stomach. "Oh no!" she screamed, dropping to her knees.

"What's wrong?"

"I'm not sure. Help me up." Her breathing was heavy, and she winced repeatedly, holding her pelvis as I pulled her onto her feet.

"Who should I call?"

Ella grabbed my shoulder, and I brought my arm around her waist.

"No one. Not yet. Just get me back into GenH1." Her red lips stretched into a grimace as she doubled over and supported her gut with her forearm. "No, no, please, no. This can't be happening." She sank to her knees, almost taking me with her.

"I've called for a MED, and I've notified Dr. Little," said the SEC in the same inconsequential tone it used to say hello.

Ella wailed, long sobs that made her shoulders quake. "Dr. Leo. I need Dr. Leo," she cried while trying to catch her breath.

"Who's Dr. Leo? What's happening to you?" I asked, kneeling next to her.

"It's not me. It's…it's the baby."

The baby? What baby? Everything spun a swirl of brown and green. The adobe bricks blurred. The ginkgos became indistinguishable, and I dropped to the ground beside her.

Chapter Fourteen

Where was I? Blinking against the light from the window, I rose from the couch to find Michael sitting next to me.

"What happened?" I asked, sitting up against the cushion. "How's my…"

"You fainted, but don't worry, you and" — he broke eye contact — "you and your baby are fine." To my left stood a MED, its panel pulsing with colored light, tracking my vital signs.

"How's Ella?"

"She's fine, too, considering — "

"Considering the fact she just had a miscarriage?" I snapped.

He turned from me and walked to the window. It must have been a Saturday. It was easy to lose track of the days. He wore loose-fitting jeans, a white button-up shirt, and casual black leather shoes. The curtains were open, revealing a bright, blue sky with cottony clouds. The tops of the distant buildings gleamed like copper mountains in the morning sun, and Michael, his eyes fixed upon the panoramic view, looked like a college boy in a frat house.

"Are there more surrogates, or was she the only one?" I fumed.

"She was the only one. The surrogate phase of the project hasn't officially started. We needed to test a new insemination process we designed for the surrogates and Ella volunteered. Since she lives here in one of the employee housing units, it made it convenient for us to track her progress. Like you, she hasn't been allowed to leave the compound since her conception."

"How far along was she?" I asked, my tone hard and indignant.

"Not far. Six weeks." His tone was the opposite of mine—slow, controlled, and apologetic.

I stormed to the other side of the window and stood, my arms folded against my chest, my body angled away from his, and as I did so, a shiver traveled the length of my spine. "Who was the father?" I demanded. "Travel?"

"No, her donor was randomly selected. The plan is for half siblings, not full."

"And my eggs—when did you take them? I didn't read anything about that in the contract I signed." Not that I had any faith in the contract to begin with.

"I know. That contract was drawn up after your awakening. Your eggs were collected prior to your awakening. We had to perform the procedure while you were still in stasis. What if you had died during your awakening? We couldn't risk losing you or your eggs," he continued. "So far, Ella is the only one we've insem—"

"And I'm supposed to believe that?" I shouted. "For all I know, this hospital already has a wing full of surrogates ready to give birth to my babies."

"That's not true," he said, coming up to my side. "If it was, I'd tell you." He wrapped his hand around my upper arm and gave it a squeeze.

"Yeah, right." I sniffed, yanking my arm from his grip. "Just like you 'told' me you were a bunch of clones, that my fertility was going to save the human race, and that I was already three months pregnant." My eyes watered, I was so angry. "You kept all of those things from me. You should have told me everything from the beginning. You lied to me."

"Withholding information is not the same as lying. I only lied when I had to." His brow furrowed when he spoke, and as the clouds moved away from the sun, a ray of light drifted across his face, making the gold specks in his eyes sparkle even more. "Please don't be mad at me. My hands were tied; I've told you that before."

Truths untold. "How can I not be? You guys played me like a fool—including you."

"Please, try not to see it that way."

"This whole time I've been refusing to get pregnant, I was pregnant all along, and when I said I wouldn't give up my eggs, you already had them and Ella was pregnant. Someone I saw every day."

"Don't be mad at her for taking the opportunity she was given. Any clone would have jumped at the chance. It hasn't been easy for her either."

"I'm not mad at her."

"Then try to understand why everything we did was

necessary."

"To an extent, I do. I understand why the team waited to tell me you were clones and that it was my duty to replenish the world with fertile females. But when it comes to impregnating me without my knowledge and implanting one of my eggs in a surrogate without my permission—that's unforgiveable!"

"If I could have told you without the team finding out, I would have."

"You had several opportunities to tell me when my hospital room was free, and you didn't take them. You could have told me the night you came to my isolation room." He tried to take my arm again, but I twisted away.

"I was afraid you'd say or do something that'd let the team know I'd told you the truth. That night I wanted you to know there was more, more I wanted to tell you but couldn't. But I promise you now that I'll never lie to you again."

Yeah, right. "For all I know, you're lying right now—giving Dr. Little and Dr. Pickford a little show."

"No one's watching us. I made this room temporarily free. I meant what I said." He lowered his voice and met my eyes with a gaze so intense I drew away from him and turned toward the window. When he set his hand on my shoulder, I jerked away.

"You know how I feel about you. For the sake of the program and for the sake of my own heart, I've tried to push those feelings away, but it's been impossible," he said, replacing his hands as I crossed my arms.

His grip on my shoulders tightened as he searched my eyes for emotions that matched his own, but before I could sever our gaze his lips were against mine, hot and hard as his palms slid to my upper arms. My need for his comfort and love eclipsed my raw anger. My lips parted and my arms fell loosely to my sides, accepting his kiss.

When his hands shifted to my back, drawing me closer, his kisses filled with desperation. I told myself to stop, but with my next breath, the woodsy smell of his cologne lulled my rage.

I forced myself to remember what he'd done to me. That he was one of them.

"No," I shouted, pushing away. "Things are different now. I don't want to be with you."

Michael took a step backward and brushed the hair above his forehead back into place.

The smooth wrinkles in his brow were exaggerated by the glare of the sun through the window. Clouds blew across the sky, shifting the light patterns in the room, projecting a broad beam of sun across his eyes. The blue of his irises glistened, contrasting sharply with his taut skin. His gaze told me he was hurt by my words and actions, but he'd never suffer as much as I would.

Michael had restarted my heart and filled my lungs with air, bringing me back from the deepest possible sleep, the tip of death. He was the first thing I saw. He was the first touch I felt, but at the time, he didn't awaken me out of love, he did it because I was the epitome of their life-is-precious mentality. He knew all of their plans from the beginning and wouldn't tell me, leaving me awakened but still in the dark. He'd betrayed me to the program, and I'd never forget that.

"Michael, please leave," I said, turning my back. "I want to be alone, and I don't want to see you again unless I have to."

Chapter Fifteen

"How's Ella?" I asked Dr. Little the next day after my presence was requested in his office. Claus wasn't on the shelf behind him. Today Claus and his glass home were positioned at the front and middle of his desk, and I couldn't help but stare at it and smirk with the realization that I was sitting across from two figures with hearts of stone.

"She's disappointed, as can be imagined," he said, "but physically, she's going to be just fine. We still have high hopes for our surrogate program, despite one minor setback."

"And you should have told me she was pregnant." I said, leaning across the table.

He folded his arms against his middle. "When it comes to the surrogate program, we were in a trial phase with one volunteer. Why burden you with that knowledge? One of my primary goals is to keep you happy." He smiled and nodded at Claus.

"Well, I'm not." My knee hit the underside of his desk,

giving Claus a little shake.

"There are plenty of reasons to be happy." He moved Claus to a shelf on his right. "We're willing to meet all of your needs and wants, within the terms of the contract, of course. Our budget is unlimited. I've also given you someone from your past. Clone or not, Travel is a familiar face. We were lucky. He was cloned nineteen years ago, making him the perfect age to be a father and a friend, and he was living right here in this division."

Nineteen. That was too young to be a father. I was too young to be a mother. I set my palm against my stomach. And how convenient was that? He was already living in this division? Maybe too convenient. "By the way, how did you know about—"

From under the desk, he brought out a yearbook and placed it on the table, already opened to the page with a photo of David and me. "This was in your cryonic chamber."

The photo was taken the day before David Casper asked to be my boyfriend, the day before I had to tell him I was moving away, and the day staffers were going around the quad at lunch, snapping pictures for the yearbook. Someone shouted "smile" in our direction, and before I knew what was happening, David grabbed me by the waist and pulled me into his side. In the photo, we were both laughing and looking into each other's eyes.

My grandfather knew how much I'd valued that one semester of real school. He must have gotten his hands on a yearbook and put it in my chamber.

"Does Travel know?"

"No. You can tell him if you like. It won't affect the program."

"How do you know he won't be mad, knowing he was selected just because I knew his DNA donor?"

"I'm 100 percent sure that trivial fact won't bother him. He has the opportunity to be a father—a real father. Nothing will pull him away from that opportunity."

"Ah, it's time for another visitor." As he looked up from his L-Band, the door opened and a middle-aged man entered with two security guards.

"Miss Dannacher, let me introduce you to the president of our region, President William Gifford." He stood and shook the president's hand.

"Hello," I said, unimpressed.

"It's a pleasure and an honor to see you again." He smiled.

Again? And then I remembered what I'd been told. He was behind one of the almond-shaped windows during my awakening.

"Thank you, I guess."

"Dr. Little tells me that you don't quite understand the significance of the opportunity that's been given to you. The public will come to know you as a proud representative of the Van Winkle Project."

Proud? "I thought the public wasn't supposed to know about me."

"Not now, but once the project is grounded and in its third year, you'll come to be known as our savior, our giver of life. You'll be an inspiration to all as you are to us right now."

Give me a break. "How can I be an inspiration if I'm trapped at GenH1?"

"Through interviews, speeches, and weekly reports via

Liaison One. Within weeks, you'll be a household name."
His arrogant tone made me sick as he leaned across the desk
with a haughty smile.

As if they could buy my happiness with unlimited
credits and fame—yeah, right. Yup, that's why they wanted
me happy—so I could lead a team of surrogates and all of
my children into a life of false freedom while honoring our
humble region. Three years wouldn't be enough time to
convince me to do that.

"You've wasted your time. I'll never willingly help you
lead a pack of women into a government-controlled baby
mill."

"You're making a big mistake."

"That's your opinion," I snipped. "Are we done?"

"We're done," he said, giving me, and then Claus, a wink.

"It's been a pleasure to see you again," said the president,
who stood when I did.

Dr. Little and Gifford followed me to the hall. The SEC
followed me as I walked briskly, anxious to get as far away
from the two men as possible, but when I turned at the end
of the hall and heard them speaking, I stopped. The SEC, as
dumb as a rock, waited while I pretended to tie my shoes.

"VW-1 has caused enough problems," said the president.
"I don't think she'll change." VW-1? That's what they call me
behind my back?

"Neither do I," said Dr. Little. "And VW-4 will end up
having the same attitude as her mother."

"No doubt. But that doesn't matter, as long as our clock
to extinction stops ticking."

"What about the other two presidents? Do they know?"

"Still in the dark," said Gifford smugly, "but once we

jump to part two of our program, that won't matter either." Part two? The contract detailed seven phases. I didn't read anything about a part two, and I'd never heard a part two mentioned by anyone on the team. "Whether she's a willing participant or not, this will be the most influential region in the world."

"She doesn't want power. She wants freedom."

"But she understands her power over us," said President Gifford.

"Not to worry. We'll have more control after the exchange."

What exchange? Were they planning to move me to a different location? As I retied my shoe for the fourth time, the echo of footsteps bounced up the hall and around the corner. An A.G.-lift opened at my right, and I made my escape, the SEC in tow. The lift's door closed just before Dr. Little and President Gifford turned the corner.

Whew! That was close.

When I approached my apartment door still flustered and full of questions, Travel was in the hall with a SEC at his side.

"Hey, have you been to the hospital's gift shop yet?" he asked when he saw me. "They actually have some cool stuff in there." He held a small, pink bag, fastened with a white bow.

"No, I haven't. I'll have to go there sometime. What did you get?"

"Something for you."

"For me?" I asked, surprised.

"For you." He smiled, presenting the small bag.

A set of quick footsteps sounded from around the corner of the hall. It was Michael. He stopped when he saw us and diverted his eyes to the ground. Under his arm, he carried a box labeled "Ascendancy." Did he honestly think he would win me over with a board game? I'd told him to stay away from me.

I couldn't control the fact that I still cared for him, and thinking about being in his arms set my insides on fire, but at the same time, I couldn't forgive him for his deceptions and "untold truths."

"Oh, I'm sorry," he said, shifting his gaze to the shiny gift bag.

"Hey, Dr. Bennett," said Travel with a cheery voice I knew I couldn't replicate.

"Travel." Michael's shoulders fell. "I, um, got off on the wrong floor. I'm supposed to be…" He gave his L-Band a fake glance. "Anyway, I better go."

"See ya," said Travel, still holding out the bag, oblivious to the thick tension in the air. "Will you open it now?" he asked after Michael disappeared.

"Sure," I said, leading him into my apartment.

"Come on. Open it," he urged when we entered the living room and sat down.

"You know you didn't have to get me anything. What's this for?" As I set the box in my lap, I hoped he didn't notice my shaking hands. Darn you, Michael, for showing up like that.

"You'll see."

The bow fell away from the bag with a soft tug. Within a fold of pink tissue paper shined an opulent lacquered box. "What is it?"

"Just open it." Travel spoke and smiled softly. "It's for good luck during your pregnancy."

Inside was a gold ring with a small golden egg at the top. The egg had a frosty, matte finish and the setting, inlaid with a circle of tiny white gems, sparkled around the golden egg like a nest for a pair of royal birds.

"The egg is a symbol for fertility. A lot of women wear them as a means to perpetuate the hope that one day we'll be able to, you know, but you can already do that, so I thought...you know..." He stuttered.

He thought wrong, but there was no way I'd refuse it and hurt his feelings. And wearing it could possibly fool Dr. Little into believing I'd suddenly become complacent. Ella and Dr. Love would probably like the gesture, too, equating it to a sign of respect toward all clone women and their unfortunate malady.

My gaze shifted from the ring to my stomach. Did my belly look less flat today? Maybe. It was hard to tell. She was only about four inches long at this point, so I couldn't expect my belly to have a bulge or that I could feel her moving inside me. But as much as I didn't want to be pregnant, I found myself spending much of each day wondering if she was okay or if I'd end up miscarrying like Ella.

The crystals surrounding the tiny egg glistened as I brushed my finger across the top of the ring. Like Ella said, it was the only egg they had. The thought took me back to the prenatal ward and the man with the hooked tool removing dead babies. The cry of a chimp in pain followed as it sat on its haunches and swayed back and forth in its cubicle. A mighty dose of guilt came next, led by the possible truth that I was being selfish with my eggs and my body.

My cage took up an entire city block, and my baby was firmly attached to a real placenta. Shouldn't I be happy?

"Thank you. I love it," I lied, slipping the sad reminder of my fate on my finger and then giving him a hug.

The warmth of the back of his neck against my arms and his soft breath upon my shoulder reminded me of David. I pretended it was him and didn't want to let go.

"So, did you hear about Ella?" I asked, using the question to break my hold.

"Yeah. Dr. Little told me about it this afternoon. He said you didn't know she was pregnant until it happened."

"No, I didn't know. Did you?"

"Nope, not until Dr. Little told me about the miscarriage."

"They should have told us."

Travel's reaction was basically no reaction with the exception of placing a hand on my shoulder. "You're right. They should have told us, but on the other hand, the next phase does include a surrogate program. It's not like we didn't know it was going to eventually happen."

"That's not the point. They kept information from us. How are we supposed to trust them if they're not honest with us?"

"I trust them."

"Well, I don't. I don't think I ever will." I blinked away a tear.

"Come on, Cass. It will be okay," he whispered, his voice soft and melodic. Pulling me into a loose hug, his chin resting on my shoulder, he proceeded to sing me a song of hope, a song of love, a lullaby paying tribute to the gift of life while I stared at the egg ring on my finger. Singing me a song was something I could never image David Casper doing.

"That was beautiful, Travel," I said as we parted.

"My mom used to sing that song to me when I was little.

She died last year from liver and kidney failure right here in this hospital. Her last transplants didn't take."

"Oh, I'm so sorry. What about your father? Does he live near here?"

"Not anymore. He died when I was twelve." Travel dropped his head.

"From what?"

"Bad genes. You name it—he had it. He was sick for a really long time, so sick that when my parents applied for a second child, they were almost denied because of my father's health."

"So you have a—"

"Brother. His name is Trail. He doesn't live in this region. He's in Region Three, Sector Nine. That's where we were born and raised."

"Region Three, Sector Nine. That has to be Australia. I recognize your accent."

"I don't have an accent."

"Yeah, you do." I smiled, walking to the couch and sitting down.

"After my father died, I was really depressed," he said, taking a seat across from me. "I hated the world and got into a lot of trouble at home and at school. I should have been there for Trail. I should have been the responsible older brother, but I wasn't. He had a hard time growing up under my bad reputation. Anyway, once Mom died, we just kind of stopped calling each other. I should call him, though. He's probably pretty lonely. He's not married and doesn't have any kids. The last I heard, his dog was his best friend."

No bloodlines, no bond. For the pre-plague world, genetic lines established royalty and leadership. They designated heirs and guided wills. They predicted appearance, intelligence, and athletic ability. A pregnant woman wondered if her baby was going to have her own delicate features or get stuck with Uncle Bob's large nose. Everything was different for a clone, but now that I was here, Travel was going to experience those things.

As much as I loathed what was happening to me, I was happy for him.

Chapter Sixteen

My belly looked a little bigger today. This morning, Dr. Stanley Leo, the project's official ob-gyn, told me I was in my fourteenth week and then spent the next two hours educating me on the stages of pregnancy, labor, and delivery.

Other than an increase in my appetite, I still didn't feel any different. Knowing there was a little being inside of me wasn't enough to seal the hollow pit in my stomach from missing my world and knowing the duty I was supposed to fulfill during my second chance at life.

Though in the last two weeks I'd appeared more complacent, my role as a brood mare accepted, inside I was burning for justice and trying to kindle a love for the baby I didn't want. The only thing I could do was accept my responsibility to my unborn child and try to be a good mother during and then after my pregnancy. I had to keep myself as physically healthy and emotionally intact as possible—if not for me, than for my baby.

As the days passed, Travel and I spent a fair amount of

time together hanging out in each other's apartments, eating meals we ordered from Bon Appetite or listening to music, and every day, we'd take an A.G.-lift to the GenH1 Café.

"Ready?" he asked one early morning through a yawn.

"Ready."

Still a bit groggy, he leaned against the inside of the lift and crossed his arms.

"After you." He gestured.

The café was crowded as always, but we managed to find a small table in the center of the room and place our order within minutes. "Caramel berry latte and a caffeine-free mocha," repeated the SERVE.

While we waited for our coffees, he leaned his elbow on the table, rested his head in his palm, and a strand of his wavy hair fell across his nose to dance in time with his silent breathing.

Our drinks arrived, but Travel didn't stir, and when I moved his latte closer so he could smell it, he remained still while the rising stream left a damp spot on his cheek.

"Wake up," I said playfully, scooping a dab of whipped cream from my coffee and dotting it on the end of his nose.

His eyes jerked opened, and he sat up. "Hey, what are you doing?" He laughed, grabbed a napkin, and before I could dodge it, a smear of whipped cream met its target on the point of my chin.

"You brat," I said, giving him a happy punch on the shoulder.

"Hey, you started it."

The hard scrape of chair legs broke my laughter, and when I turned, I saw Michael, alone, pushing up from a table in the corner. His eyes shifted from mine, his face like stone, and he turned his body sideways to avoid our table and exit out an opposite door.

Outside of the brief meeting in the hall, it was the first time I'd seen him since our argument in my apartment. His cold stare and jealous eyes rekindled my anger. I didn't expect him to be waiting outside the café for me.

"Can I talk to you for a minute?" he asked, catching my upper arm with his hand. Travel, standing there oblivious with a welcoming grin on his face, was the only thing that kept me from jerking my arm away and shouting "no."

"Alone?" he added, and let go of me.

"Sure, um, I'll catch up with you later," I said to Travel, smiling to hide my nerves.

"What do you want?" I asked sternly after we walked to an empty corner in the hospital's atrium.

"I need to talk to you. I need to tell you how sorry I am."

"I know you're sorry," I snapped. "And that doesn't change anything."

He shook his head. "You have no idea how I feel about you, do you?"

I didn't answer. "Seeing you two together kills me. I can't stand it." The arch of his eyebrows disappeared and his forehead wrinkled.

"Then you shouldn't have impregnated me with his baby," I said in a cold whisper.

"That's something I wanted *before* you were awakened, not something I want now. You're making a family with him. Do you really think I want that?"

His misty eyes stopped me from rolling mine, but at the same time, his words worked their way into my heart.

"I'm not ready to talk about this. I don't know if I'll ever be. Right now I need to focus on her," I said, dropping my eyes to my stomach. "Please, I need to go."

I walked forward, but he took a sidestep, blocking me, his shoulder at my chest. On his next breath, we were touching. "Not yet, please. Just give me a chance," he said softly. He set one hand against the side of my face. His gentle touch was enough to slow the momentum of my anger. "Please," he urged.

"I—" But his lips stopped my words.

"No," I said, backing away. "You can't keep doing this to me. Please, just leave me alone. There's nothing more to talk about."

From the corner of my eye, I saw his head drop as I dashed away to find Travel in his apartment.

I enjoyed spending time with Travel, but most of the time all I wanted was to be alone exploring in the botanical garden. The garden rescued me from the artificial light of my apartment, and the ridiculous, government-produced sitcoms he liked to watch with me. Working on my "dig" kept my mind focused on a specific task and kept away memories of my family and friends from the twenty-first century.

There was only one thing it couldn't do—make myself temporarily forget there was a little person growing inside of me, especially when I'd sit to take a break and find myself relaxing with my palms against the barely noticeable bulge of my stomach.

One afternoon when I couldn't stand to watch one more episode of "Life is Precious," I grabbed a sweatshirt and headed to the botanical garden for some special me time. It was the perfect day to dig. The sun was high in the sky, poking its warm rays into the building and as the wind picked up, it whistled through the building's slats like a whimsical chorus of birds.

"Hi, Cassie," came a voice when I was in the middle of exposing another layer of adobe.

"Hey, I never expected to see you here."

"Why?" asked Magnum. His biceps flexed as he set down a large cardboard box.

"Because no one ever comes here. I invited Ella once, but she said being here would make her relive what happened to her all over again. Dr. Love, Kale, and Travel keep telling me they want to see my dig, but so far my only company has been these two." I pointed to the SEC and GROW, who was pulling weeds from a hanging planter.

"Well, I like it here. I mean, I've never seen a stubby little palm like that one before."

"Oh yeah, that's a sago palm, although it really isn't a palm. It's in the cycad family, cycas revoluta. Cycads flourished through the Jurassic and Cretaceous periods."

"Wow, that's cool." He laughed. "Did I use the word correctly?"

"Yeah, cycads are cool. At least they are to me."

"I brought you something." Kicking the box with his toe, he popped open the lid. He lifted a small pickax out of the box and handed it to me, followed by a camping shovel and a thick-bristled paintbrush.

"Where did you get these?" I asked, fingering the tip of the pickax.

"You know me. I have my ways." He smiled and his face dimpled.

"Now, you do know that I'm *not* allowed to have these, right? Dr. Little doesn't want me to overexert myself before, during, or even after my pregnancy. GROW wouldn't even lend me a hand trowel, and yesterday when I tried to break into the tool shed, that stupid SEC stopped me and even told him about it. So basically, I've had to resort to what I can find in my kitchen." I lifted a dull spoon.

"You won't have to worry about a SEC taking away any of these tools. I've changed their codes. Bots recognize objects through the item's engrained code rather than sensory means such as shape, size, and color. To that SEC and GROW over there, that pickax is an L-Pen, and that shovel is a fork—two items you're allowed to have." His dimples grew.

"Thank you so much. You're awesome," I said, tossing the pickax to the ground and throwing my arms around his neck and shoulders.

"You're welcome." We held on to each other for so long that letting go was a little awkward.

"Show me what you do out here all day."

Pulling him by the hand, I led him to my makeshift "dig," a twelve by eight section of earth with four rows of stacked brick sticking out from it.

"These bricks are handmade from sand, clay, and straw. They were shaped using a frame and then set out to dry in the sun. This is part of a wall from a small dwelling, and look what I've found," I said, picking up a piece of broken pottery. "It's from a clay pot. I'm hoping to find the rest of it. It's a good thing this building was constructed before obscuras were mandatory, or I wouldn't have gotten this far with the excavation."

"Don't worry. It'll be a while before Dr. Little finds out what you're doing. He sent the order for a technology upgrade the day you requested unlimited access to this building, but I keep finding reasons to put it off. You know how busy I am." He grinned.

"Thanks. I really appreciate that."

He found a spot next to me on a patch of fresh dirt and watched as I tried out my new tool by hacking away at the base of the adobe brick.

"I'm so glad you're here and that we're friends. You're like the brother I never had."

"Thanks. Like a brother, I'll always be there for you, you know that, right?"

"Yeah, I do." That was Magnum, true blue and always with a trick up his sleeve.

He lifted the empty box, folding and flattening it until it was easily held in one hand.

"Thanks again for the equipment," I called out as he made his way to the door.

"No problem. That's what brothers do." Through the lath, I watched him trot back into GenH1 and disappear behind a sliding door.

He was cute, cool, dashing, and daring. He was James Dean, but my love for him was sisterly, built on a foundation of trust and respect for one another.

I was so lonely. I wanted somebody. I needed somebody to love and love me back, but at this point, Michael couldn't be that person—not with all of his deceptions. Even if we made up, it was against protocol.

I sank to my knees and used the brush Magnum brought me to sweep the dirt away from a piece of adobe.

"Hey, Cass," came a voice from over my shoulder. It was Travel.

"What are you doing here?" I teased.

"What do you mean?"

"Every time I ask you if you want to join me, you come up with some kind of lame excuse why you can't," I said, giving his arm a playful punch.

"Oh." He laughed. "Actually, I've wanted to come every time, but I know you come here when you want to be alone, so, you know, I wanted to give you that space."

"Thanks, that's really sweet of you."

He smiled like he was embarrassed by my compliment.

"So, um, what's made today any different?"

"Today I have something for you, something for your dig." From behind his back, he produced a small shovel and pickax made from kitchen utensils. "I converted the laser burner on my stove into a welder and cutter, so I could machine and then connect the parts. Then I turned one of JAN's spare rotary brushes into a grinder and smoothed all of the rough edges. Since they're made from objects you're allowed to have, the bots won't recognize them and take them away."

"That's amazing. How did you know how to do that?"

"I was going to school to be a mechanical engineer before I joined the project."

Travel's life of clone normalcy, a life full of goals and dreams, was taken away from him, too. But at least his was replaced with something he wanted.

I took the pickax first and examined every detail, how each weld was ground flush to its counterpart, how much care was taken to shape the pick at both ends.

"These are incredible. This must have taken you forever to make."

"Not quite." He chuckled. "But it did take…" His smile died as he peeked over my shoulder. "Oh, I guess you already have real tools."

Magnum's presents were visible despite a camouflage of dust and dirt. "Yeah, um, Magnum came across those somewhere and brought them to me…" He dropped his head. "But they're actually too big for most jobs. These will be perfect for tight areas. This was so thoughtful of you. I'm trying to reconstruct the remains of a clay jar that I found. These tools will help me do that."

But the flicker of happiness didn't return to his eyes. I set down the pick and pushed his fallen hair away from his forehead. "The fact that you made them makes them even more special." I pulled him in for a deep hug. Surrounded by conifers, ginkgophytes, and ferns, we held each other until my eyes were moist, and I drew away. "You're a good friend. I'm glad you're my baby's father," I said. And I was.

All smells bothered me, but the smell that offended my pregnant body the most was the one coming from that old factory behind the botanical garden.

• • •

With a gust of wind on an afternoon a week later, the building's slats rattled, and the strange odor wafted by me again, sharp and pungent, a combination of motor oil and something else, something familiar, but I couldn't place it. After I uncovered another square foot of my dig, the smell re-entered the building on a billowing breeze and lingered. Ella said that place contained some kind of pit, and with that memory, I recognized the dull stench—something like a house being reroofed on a hot summer's day. Tar. A pit of tar?

My heart hoppity-hopped as I pulled my Liaison from my back pocket and hit the screen with my fingertips, bringing up a map of the area to the east of the botanical garden. Another series of taps produced an identical map from my century. A last hit superimposed one map upon the other.

Oh my God! No wonder why it was still there. It was a natural phenomenon impossible to destroy.

I dropped my pickax and stood, wiping my hands on the butt of my jeans. I had to see it. Why not? It was part of the compound. I was allowed anywhere in the compound as long as a bot followed. My SEC escort turned toward me, and its glass eyes flashed.

The sun was high in the sky. I shaded my eyes with my hand and glared at the long, metal fence. Yup, if the gate was locked, I could easily give it a climb, even in my forth month.

Sweat formed as I strode forward, picking up into a light jog the closer I got. Catching a strong whiff of oily tar, I coughed and met the fence.

The enclosed land was riddled with several large pits, one as big as a medium-sized pond. A thick grate of thatched wire stretched across each ditch like the lid of a pot as the tar below bubbled, a black stew of dust, twigs, and dead leaves.

La Brea Tar Pits, something I'd studied back in 2022, but had never seen due to my mother's work schedule. Who'd guess that here, in the heart of L.A., mammoths, mastodons, dire wolves, and the saber-toothed cat, met their demise in a well of sticky asphalt.

The SEC followed as I walked the perimeter of the fence,

eyeing the ooze below the grates, before finding the gate. My L-Band wouldn't open it, but it didn't matter. Hanging loosely at its hinge, it was ajar from its frame just enough for me to squeeze through. Knowing the bot would sound a silent alarm because we were separated, I held the wobbly gate as the SEC pushed through behind me.

Dashing from pit to pit, I hoped to see a fragment of bone or wolf fang poking through a bubbling pool. But I knew the fossils had settled deep within the littered pitch and despite their cold boil, a treasure from the past would never push to the surface on its own.

One pit was different from the others, the mass of asphalt pooling at only one end of the basin, while the rest lay exposed, dirt and chunks of solidified tar encapsulating forty-thousand-year-old bones. I wanted a piece.

The integrity of this pit was compromised. One of the bolts anchoring the cover to a cement block was broken, and when I tried to curl the mesh aside, it bit into my palms but rolled away, creating an opening big enough for me to slide through.

"Stay here," I announced to the bot. "I'm going to be right there—just twenty-five to thirty feet below you." But would it comply or report me to Little? At that point, I didn't care.

The pit was wider at the top than at the bottom, giving me a slope that was easy to hike as I climbed downward, edging the tips of my shoes into crevices and gripping patches of hardened tar with my fingertips. The smells made my nose itch, half tempting me to loosen my grip and give it a scratch.

"Damn it!" At the bottom, the earth gave way under

my right foot, and I fell backward, landing on my rear but bracing myself with my palms. Nothing hurt, but I felt like a fool, and awkwardly stood to brush off my pants. "I'm fine," I yelled up at the bot.

The thick blob of tar bubbled, and stubby mounds jetting up from the blackness oozed tar from their centers. Several bowling ball-sized clumps of hardened tar lay at the pool's edge. With curious fingers, I studied the exterior of the closest one. A scatter of fossils was visible—bits of bone fragments and petrified plant material—things I could chisel loose back at GenH1.

But carrying it back up the pit would be difficult, so I spent the next few minutes examining each piece, weighing them in my hand.

It was hot—not hot enough to give me a headache, but while I sprinted from one specimen to the next, examining each one, a dull pain washed across my forehead, and when I stood, the pit spun. Whoa! Overcome by my light-headedness, I stumbled but steadied myself before I fell.

What in the world was happening to me? And then I remembered something from my research.

Methane gas, odorless and colorless, a miner's worst enemy and now mine, exploded from the oily goo, and I, too intent on finding a fossil, forgot about the dangers.

Semi-trapped by the pit's steep walls, the methane collected, creating a pocket of deadly gas in the area in which I stood. The rock of tar I held slipped from my fingers, and I staggered toward the pit's wall, but tumbled backward instead as I lost my balance.

"No!"

The warm, thick pitch engulfed my body as I sank first to

my knees and then up to my waist. A hard kick with my legs was futile, since they hardly moved, and I lunged forward, reaching toward a bulge of hardened asphalt, aiming my hand at its volcano-like peak.

"Be calm. Be calm. Don't struggle. It will only make it worse," I told myself as my fingers slipped away and my body dropped another inch into the goo. The pain in my head and the pounding of my heart synced, pulsing as I tried to catch my breath against the pressure of dense tar enveloping my chest. As I took short, methane-laden breaths, my eyes fluttered and my light-headedness increased.

"Cassie," a voice shouted from above.

"Michael?"

He stood at the edge of the pit, leaning forward with his hands on his thighs and breathing heavily.

"I'm coming down there. Try not to move."

I closed my eyes, and when I opened them again, Michael was at the edge of the pool. "Grab my hand," he cried, stretching his toward mine.

"I-I can't. You're too far," I yelled, holding my arm out for him. He inched forward, letting one foot sink into the goop. "No, don't come in here. You'll get stuck, too."

Ignoring my words, he leaned forward and his leg sunk to his thigh. "Almost there," he called between breaths.

"Don't do it. It's no use. You have to get out of here. The methane gas will…"

His other foot slipped forward until the toe of his shoe hit the tar. "Gotcha," he said as his hand met mine. "Just another inch."

My fingers desperately clawed for his palm, and I gasped for air.

"That's it. Now hold on," he coached as our grip locked.

He turned sideways and took a step. My body, trapped in the ooze, barely moved, but with his next yank and step, I rose up to my waist. When his tar-laden leg met the shore, he gave a powerful pull, gritting his teeth. My foot came down on something hard, and as I straightened my leg, I rose far enough for Michael to catch me at the waist and draw me to safety.

"Come on, we have to hurry." He was breathing heavily, and two veins stood prominently against his forehead. My legs went limp, and he draped my arm around his shoulders. The back of his neck was sweaty and hot, his face bright red.

When he brought me to my feet, my swirling head dropped to his shoulder, and the sick smell of tar was replaced by the sweet spice of his cologne.

"I can't carry you. You have to climb back up on your own, but I'll be right behind you," he said. "I won't let you fall."

Excluding my arms, everything below my shoulders was covered with tar. When we reached the bank, he set his hands at my back, pushed through the goo, and gave me a light nudge in front of him.

"One hand, one foot, one hand, one foot," he urged gently in my ear. At one point when my strength gave, he grabbed me by the back of my thighs, and with arms trembling, pushed me upward.

When we reached the top, I stuck my hands through the web of the wire cover to regain my balance, and with a final shove from below, wiggled myself through the pit's cover, my lower body so heavy with tar, I thought I'd break at the waist.

Michael came next through the bent wire, snagging the

front of his tar-stained uniform and giving his chin a nasty scratch.

"Deep breaths, in and out," he chanted. "Yup, just like that." He wiped his hands on his pants, but the sticky tar wouldn't budge.

"How did you know I was here?" I asked, trying to catch my breath.

"Your band went through an upgrade last week. Any change in elevation alerts the team in case you fall." My band was smudged, but Michael's was barely visible under the asphalt.

"Thank you," I said slowly.

"Are you okay?"

"Yeah, I'm feeling better. Do you think…?" I look down at my tar-soaked body.

"I'm sure she's fine. The tar won't affect her, and you weren't exposed to the methane long enough for it to be an issue either." He smiled.

"I was so stupid. I should never have—"

From over Michael's shoulder, I saw Dr. Little coming through the gate on a hoverscooter, followed by two SECs and a MED.

"What's going on here?" he shouted when his scooter came to a stop and settled to the ground.

"Just a little tar. It's nothing," I said, regaining some composure. "I was exploring and fell in the pit, but Michael—"

"This area is off limits, hence the fence." He shook his head and MED came up beside me to take my vitals. "We can't trust you. We never could and we never will, and for that reason, and for your own safety, you'll no longer be allowed to leave—"

"But—"

"All systems normal," reported the bot.

"No buts. Those pits are dangerous. You could have gotten yourself killed. If Dr. Bennett didn't get here when he did then—"

"Simon," interrupted Michael, putting up his hand. "You've got this all wrong. You see, I'm the one who brought her here." From the corner of my eye, I saw Michael square his shoulders. "I wanted her to see something that survived her century. She was with me the whole time. She was never in any danger whatsoever."

"You? You're responsible for this?" The wrinkles in his neck shook as he jabbed an angry finger.

"Yes, and I don't see why that's a problem." He lifted his chin. "You gave her permission to explore the compound, and this is part of it."

"You, take her back to her apartment," sneered Dr. Little, pointing to the nearest SEC. "And you, Dr. Bennett," he continued with a glare that could freeze tar, "you come with me to my office so we can have a little chat about your role here."

From over his shoulder, Michael gave me a thumbs-up and a smile as he walked away.

• • •

My work in the botanical garden continued, but only because of Michael.

By the end of my second trimester, I uncovered another adobe wall and was close to completing the clay jar, which over the last three months had become my latest obsession.

Unfortunately, Dr. Little found out about my use of a real pickax and shovel when he made a visit to the botanical garden after hours to see what I'd been up to. My tools were confiscated, and Dr. Leo, my gyno, gave me a lecture about not doing anything too strenuous, something that could jeopardize my pregnancy. I was still allowed to visit my sanctuary while I could hide my pregnancy with oversized tunics, but I wasn't allowed to dig.

My daily retreat now consisted of throwing a towel on the ground, lying down, and staring at the blue sky between the lath. But one day, I dared to pick up one of my old tools, a dusty spoon, and chip away at the dirt delicately, hoping to find another piece of clay pot, knowing this small exertion wouldn't hurt me or my baby.

And that's when I noticed my "dig" wasn't the way I last left it. A small section of earth was disturbed, a small hole dug and crudely refilled. A bot didn't do it. On my orders, GROW never touched my dig. If I was in 2022, I'd blame it on a rabbit or a squirrel, but the bots in 3025 made this structure varmint free.

On my next trip, I found the smear of a footprint in the soft earth. With one arm supporting my pooch of a belly, I came down on my knees to examine the wide width, suspecting Dr. Little of invading my territory again. The thought made me ill, but I dared not accuse him for fear of being banned from the botanical garden again.

Or maybe it was Travel. The impression was from a man's shoe and though distorted from the shift in sand, it was large enough to belong to him.

At the start of my third trimester, Dr. Little planned to order my immediate sequester, the bloom of my belly becoming too big to hide and a threat to exposing the project to anyone who was not part of the VWP team. With that in mind, I spent most of the days before that time in the botanical garden, sitting in front of my dig in a funk of unrest. It was also my eighteenth birthday.

"Now what?" I asked myself when I detected another section of earth that was disturbed by someone other than me. Raking my fingers through the soft dirt loosened a set of stones. Tossing them aside, I sifted what remained until I saw something glistening to my right.

A piece of clay pot lay in plain view like a gold coin from antiquity, centered on a brick of adobe, sparkling as the sunlight flashed through the lath. Examining it closely, I let my finger run over its jagged edge before placing it in my pocket. But why was it here in plain view? Someone had to have left it there.

If only I had enough time to find every last piece before I was banned from the botanical garden altogether. But with a baby on the way, restoring my clay pot had to wait.

Chapter Seventeen

Whose hand exhumed the ancient prize I was unsure, or maybe I had done it myself, setting it upon the wall of hardened mud, forgetting it was there, due to the toll of the pregnancy upon my torn soul. I wasn't sure, but I kept it with me at all times, a reminder of my dig, thumbing it in my pocket.

And as I did so, two faces emerged in my mind's eye — my mother and my grandfather. My baby would never know the two most important people in my life.

While I was confined to my apartment, a fresh magnolia blossom was sent to my apartment each morning, courtesy of GROW and at Travel's request. "I'm counting down the days with these," he said on the third delivery day.

"To what?" I asked, setting the blossom in a large, flat, wide-rimmed crystal bowl of water to join the other two.

"To your delivery date."

"Oh, that's so sweet, but I think I'll need a bigger bowl."

I laughed, cradling my arm under my belly.

The bowl sat next to my clay pot, which was still in a state of restoration, held together with a chemical adhesive. One-sixth of the bowl was missing. I continued to keep that chip of pottery like a shiny new penny in my pocket, a good luck token to help me through my pregnancy.

It was still so strange, feeling and knowing that a baby was actually growing inside of me. So strange, in fact, that on several mornings, I'd wake up in disbelief until a little kick from the human life I was carrying knocked me back into reality. By midday, Travel's smile was usually enough to put me in a better mood and make me forget my old life again.

Maternity clothes didn't exist, so I resorted to extra-large T-shirts and pants with elastic waists until one afternoon when Ella, Dr. Love, and Magnum brought me a wardrobe from Apparel Five, modified by a TAILOR bot.

"These are great," I said, holding up a pair of jeans. "Thank you so much!"

"There's no need to thank us. We'd do anything for, you. And you, too," said Magnum, pressing his hand against my belly and hoping to feel a kick.

While they thought of my baby as a mini miracle, Travel regarded me as something more than human, someone to be worshipped and praised. To him I was a China doll, delicate and vulnerable, susceptible to illness. Fortunately, I found his ignorance amusing rather than annoying.

"How often do you think these rooms are free?" I asked him one evening while a team of bots filled the spare room in my apartment with baby furniture.

"Who knows? Honestly, I don't really care, and when they are watching us, I'd rather not know. Neither one of us has anything to hide, right?" He was as disillusioned as any clone.

"I just have a feeling that the obscuras in the walls are on all the time in this apartment."

"I doubt it, but if they are, they're just doing it for your own safety and protection. They can't let anything happen to you. You're their golden girl. That's why he's here now," he said, pointing to the MED, or bodyguard, as I liked to call it, standing against the wall, watching me with eyes that didn't blink.

With one hand bracing my sore back, I lowered down onto the couch, and he joined me, clutching a pillow to wedge behind me. Cuddling up close, he pushed the pillow into place as I leaned forward. "Are you comfortable in there?" he asked my stomach.

"Hey, what about me? I'm the one with swollen feet and an aching back."

"I'm sorry. How are you? Are you comfortable?"

But the sincerity in his tone wasn't enough to fend off my agitation.

"As comfortable as a walking incubator can be," I retorted, resting my crossed arms on my fat belly.

"You're not a walking incubator," he said.

"Yes, I am. That's what I am to them. To all of them—Dr. Little, Dr. Pickford, the president—even to me."

"You can't think that way."

"Why not? Because it's not good for the baby?" I said sarcastically. Pushing up from the couch, I stood and cut across the living room to stand at the window.

He came up beside me. "Do you love our baby?"

"Of course I love her," I said, offended.

"Really? Because sometimes I think—"

"Think what? That I resent her for making me fat and miserable, especially when I didn't want to be pregnant in the first place?" I blurted, turning to confront him.

"Don't be mad at me, but yeah, sometimes I think that. You don't talk about her all the time like I do."

He was right. He could go on for hours, talking about what she'd look like, how she'd probably be born with a full head of hair because he was and how her eyes would be brown like his instead of blue like mine because the brown gene is more dominant.

"Why would I when I don't want to be pregnant?" I shouted.

And that's when I could no longer hold my pent-up tears. A flood of additional guilt erupted as well, the shame of spending my nights in bed, thinking about a miscarriage even though the image of dead fetuses was still so fresh in my mind.

Travel held me while I cried, my shoulders shaking uncontrollably, and when I settled down enough to speak I said, "I don't resent our baby. How can I? She's a victim in this program just like me. I didn't have a choice and neither will she. I don't resent her. I resent the project for forcing this on all of us."

"They didn't force it on me. I volunteered. I'm happy here with you. I want to be a father. I want to be a family."

"Haven't you ever asked yourself why they chose you?"

"Of course, and they told me. I was randomly selected from a group of healthy eighteen- to twenty-year-old males living in this division." He pushed a strand of hair behind his ear, smiling naively, and my "I told you so" mentality dwindled.

"Yes, that's right." I sighed. "You were randomly selected."

I let him believe that. Why tell him the truth? I carried enough lies and deception for the both of us.

"Look. I am happy. I'm happy that we're friends." I swallowed hard. "I'll love her when I see her, and I'll be a good mother to her no matter what."

"Then let's give her a name. Let's name her now. Giving her a name will help you think of her as a person and not a thing."

"Okay, I guess I can do that," I said, although I knew it probably wouldn't make a difference.

"I know. Why don't we name her after your mother?"

"Victoria, are you kidding? My mother hated her name. She didn't like it when people called her Vicki."

"Then we'll never call her Vicki, and we'll make sure no one else does, either. I think Victoria is a beautiful name."

"Then let's use your mother's name for her middle name."

"Victoria Layne Carson. Yeah, I like that."

"So do I. It's perfect," I said as the late-morning sun radiated though the apartment's east-facing windows, creating patches of white light on the carpet and furniture.

"Hi, Victoria. I'm your father," he said, kneeling until he was eye level with my belly. "And this is your mother," he added. With a light touch, he guided my hand to my basketball of a stomach. Victoria kicked, giving me a boot with more oomph than ever before, and I drew my hand away, struck by the cold reality that there was really a baby inside me.

"Oh, did she kick? I missed it. Maybe she'll do it again." He pressed both hands against my middle.

Two weeks before my due date, Dr. Leo came to my apartment to give another lecture on the labor and delivery process and scan my belly with an instrument that transmitted the pictures of the baby to the monitor in my living room. Travel watched in nervous anticipation as the screen flickered to produce the live image while I closed my eyes and didn't open them until he said, "There's my girl."

And there she was, Baby Victoria. Her little legs and arms were long and thin with what I imagined was pink and satiny-soft skin like a pair of ballet slippers. Her delicate lips were pursed together like a tiny rosebud, and the top of her head was crowned with a brown fluff of hair that reminded me of spun sugar.

Now she was real. There was no turning back—not that I ever could.

With a voice command, Dr. Leo made the picture enlarge and refocus on the baby's face. Then he rotated the image so she was head-up instead of head-down. The curve of her face and slightly pointed chin were reminiscent of mine, but the slight angle of her eyes and ear shape were Travel's.

"Hey, she has my eyebrows," he said. "She's so beautiful, absolutely beautiful. Just look at her. I love her so much."

Did I love her now, a baby I've never held and never heard? It was still hard to believe that the domed contents of my belly contained a baby. But there she was on a full-color, 4-D monitor in my living room, moving in real time, alive and well unlike the babies who ended up suffering and dying in their plastic chambers.

My being here, Victoria's being here, would eventually

end the use of the artificial uteruses and the need to enslave chimpanzees, but at whose expense? Ours! Two walking baby-makers instead of one, forced to live the lives we didn't chose for ourselves, the two of us the only people in the world who could understand the pain of being valued and used for only one purpose.

It was up to me to give her the support she'd need to maintain some semblance of happiness and fragment of hope while we fulfilled our womanly duties to the world.

"Yes, she is beautiful, and I love her," I said confidently as Travel took my hand and gave it a squeeze.

"Well, I have all the images I need," said Dr. Leo as he pushed a button on the sonogram. Victoria's picture flickered and disappeared but a poke against my insides from a tiny elbow or toe reminded me that she was still inside me safe and sound until her delivery, which was something I didn't want displayed on every monitor in GenH1.

"Dr. Leo," I said before he left. "I know you're going to be the one to deliver Victoria, but who else is going to be in the delivery room helping you or watching?" Watching—I cringed when I said the word. The less people who saw me indisposed and half naked, the better.

"Dr. Love and Dr. Bennett, of course. They've been an integral part of your care from the beginning. It's only appropriate they witness this miracle," Dr. Bennett said. That was going to be too awkward.

"Who else?" interrupted Travel.

"A pediatrician and a tier two assistant. The rest of the team, including Ella, will watch from the observation lounge."

"What about me? I'm her father."

"I'm sure you're on the list. Don't worry."

And Travel, too. Of course he'd be there. Victoria was his baby. We were close, great friends, but I still didn't want him to see me in any less-then-discrete situations either.

When Dr. Leo was gone, Travel pressed his cheek against my belly and closed his eyes. I could feel his warm breath through my thin shirt, blowing rhythmically in soft whispers of air that echoed his heartbeat.

"I have to be there. There's no way I'd miss her birth," he said, and his words trailed into a lullaby.

The simple lyrics coupled with his great singing voice wove a spell of enchantment. His song soothed me, each note massaging my heart, as I admired the guy whose chromosomes combined and twisted with mine to form the DNA strands that made Baby Victoria unique and blood related to both of us.

After he ended his lullaby, his voice trickled to a whisper. He pressed his lips against my middle and made a smacking sound, kissing the baby through a layer of fabric, flesh, muscle, and the uterine wall.

He scratched his chin. He hadn't shaved that morning, and now his lower face was rough with a shadow of stubble, making him savagely handsome. He pushed his hair behind one ear, revealing more of his defined jaw.

"I'll get us something to drink," he said, walking into the kitchen.

"Oh no." A pain emerged deep in my belly. It twisted and turned like a fist, wringing and pulling at my insides. I didn't mean to cry out, but a sound escaped from my throat, a sound laced with agony.

"What's wrong?" he asked, running from the kitchen.

"I don't know. I think—" I gasped, strapping my arms across my abdomen as if the pressure could suppress the uncontrollable ache. Another deluge of pain flowed through my nervous system, burning from my middle to my extremities. "I think I'm going into labor."

His eyes spilled with tears. "What do we do?"

"Call Dr. Leo. Tell him that I'm having contractions."

He tapped his L-Banded wrist and shouted, "It's time. Cassie's going into labor right now. Hurry!"

"It's okay." I laughed despite the pain building in my gut as I braced myself for another contraction. "He doesn't have to rush. I could be in labor for hours. My contractions are at least five minutes apart. Maybe more. We have time. Don't worry," I said as I staggered down the hall and changed into the hospital robe Dr. Love gave me weeks ago in anticipation for this day. And now the day had come. My hands shook as I clasped the gown closed, and my heartbeat quickened.

Travel ran to the door as I returned.

"It's Dr. Leo, Dr. Love, and a bot, and they brought the transplant capsule," he said, looking at his wrist, his voice quavering.

"Great," I groaned. I took a practice ride in a capsule designed for organ transplant patients months before I started showing. It was exactly 2.3 minutes, a time calculated by the technicians who modified the sphere for my use, so no one would see a pregnant lady riding through the halls of GenH1 on a hoverchair. He took deep breaths between each word as he commanded the front door to unlock and open. "Come in. Hurry."

"Everything's going to be just fine, Travel. This is the day we've all been waiting for. Life is so precious," said Dr. Love when she entered, her terrific smile full of fire.

Ugh. I was so tired of that phrase, but how could I do anything less than say, "Yes, it is," when she squinted, releasing tears.

"You're a strong girl. You can do this," she added, patting my back while I was hunched over and experiencing another contraction.

Dr. Leo directed the transplant capsule to a spot in the living room. It hovered noiselessly before lowering to the ground. When it hit, its entrance panel opened automatically, anticipating its passenger. Travel held my hand as I entered the capsule and didn't let go until the door started to shut, enclosing me and baby-to-be in a protective mechanical cocoon. Just as the lid clicked, I saw the kitchen counter top in the distance, littered with six wilted magnolia blossoms that wouldn't fit in the crystal bowl.

Inside, the capsule was dark, cold, and uncomfortable. It made me claustrophobic and nauseous, especially when I thought about what it would have been like for me if I had been conscious instead of brain dead in my cryonic chamber in an abandoned warehouse.

"I'm right here, Cass. Everything's going to be okay, right Dr. Leo?" said Travel, his words cracking through the transplant capsule's speaker.

"Yes, Travel. We'll take good care of her." Dr. Leo tried to give me a doctor-type, reassuring smile, but his quivering lips and trembling hands told me he was more nervous and anxious about this birth than me. It was the first time I'd seen any true emotion from him.

Through the capsule window, I noticed that Travel's cheeks were wet with tears, tears he didn't bother to wipe away. I placed my hand against the thick, cold glass and met his.

"Don't worry," I said as another contraction burned in my abdomen.

Dr. Love patted the top of the transplant capsule above the spot where my head rested against a pillow. Each pat produced an echoing thud like a heartbeat, and for a second I thought the sound was the beating of my own heart. Nothing could chip away Dr. Love's smile. It was frozen solid against her teeth, along with the wrinkles of worry and excitement trapped between her eyebrows, her expression reminding me of the first time I uncovered the bone of a Ceratosaurus.

And today will be the first time a baby will be birthed by a human female since the plague. From inside my robe pocket, for good luck, I fingered the mysterious piece of pottery.

In less than a minute, we were in an A.G.-lift that delivered us to the lab floor where the team stood waiting, prepared and positioned for this monumental event. And there was Michael with his hands in his uniform pockets, staring at the floor.

"Did I miss anything?" asked Ella, frazzled, her composure teetering. She flicked her hair off her shoulders with the back of her hands, her chest and breasts rising noticeably as she tried to catch her breath. With a big hug and a clap against his back, she greeted Travel, but Dr. Little and Dr. Pickford barely gave him a nod.

"No, you haven't missed anything," said Dr. Leo as my capsule popped open. "There's a spot reserved for you in the observation lounge."

Struck with another contraction, I tightened my muscles

and arched my back. My hands balled into fists. I closed my eyes and struck the sides of the transplant capsule again and again, somehow managing to hold off a scream.

Dr. Leo and Dr. Love each took an arm, lifted me from the crypt, and positioned me on the long-awaited birthing bed.

"Where's Travel?" I asked. "He was just here."

No one answered me, but as I scanned the room, I saw Claus in his container, positioned on a counter at the back of the room. Claus's head and torso were barely visible due to the glare of the overhead lights, but his lower half was in clear view, reminding me of my virginity.

My uterus contracted just as Dr. Love pushed another pillow behind my back. I rounded my shoulders, bent my knees violently, and sucked in a deep breath. A team member I didn't recognize rushed forward with an IV, but hesitated when he reached my arm, studying me like I was a glass figurine ready to shatter into splintered fragments.

"Rynne, it's okay," said Dr. Bennett, coming forward for the first time.

Rynne slipped the IV needle into the biggest vein on the top of my hand.

Instead of receiving a traditional epidural, an impulse-regulator patch was affixed to my spine just above my tailbone. Within seconds my body relaxed, my breathing eased, and my legs became numb and felt heavy.

"Where's Travel?" I asked again as Dr. Love dabbed a damp cloth on my forehead.

"Dr. Little?" Dr. Love's voice was stern, her eyebrows tight and her smile gone.

"Okay, let him in," he said without taking his eyes away

from his Liaison.

Travel circumvented the team when he entered, choosing a route that brought him closer to Michael and Dr. Leo than Dr. Little. When he passed, Dr. Little sneered and his nostrils flared like he caught an unpleasant odor in the air, and I wondered why he was so rude.

At my side, Travel kissed the top of my free hand and pressed it against the side of his face.

"Watch," I said, pointing to the monitor next to my bed. "I'm having a contraction right now, and I can't even feel it." A red line rose to a jagged peak and fell. "And that's our baby's heartbeat," I said as a blue dot pulsed on the screen. "When I was born, my mother was in labor for seventeen hours."

Dr. Leo set down his Liaison and washed and gloved his hands. "I have a feeling this baby won't take that long. We've already given you something to speed up your contractions and aid in dilation."

Another doctor, who Michael referred to as Dr. Clayton Hatch, a pediatrician specializing in neonatology, watched the monitor with his arms crossed and his lips drawn into his mouth like he was sucking a sour piece of candy. How could a neonatologist witnessing his first live birth be so unemotional and detached?

"This room isn't 'free' is it, Dr. Leo?"

"No, Miss Dannacher. A historical event is about to occur, a medical phenomenon that less than a year ago we could only dream about. All three presidents are watching from secured locations in their perspective regions."

For an hour, maybe two, Travel and I watched the lines on the monitor explode into a peak that reached the upper edge of the screen and drop again when the pressure I felt in my abdomen subsided. He never left the room despite Dr. Hatch's insistence that it would "be a while."

At the fourth hour, there was a small cry followed by a much louder wail as Dr. Leo lifted Baby Victoria into the air, and everything at the moment became real.

I was a mother, a mother with a responsibility greater than I could fathom, but one I was fated to fulfill. My legacy was now Victoria's. I couldn't give her the life I wanted, but I could give her my love and support while we fulfilled our duties to the world — mother, daughter, and future daughters banded together, an exclusive team, sharing each other's burdens and our dreams.

"Give her to me! I want to hold her!" I shouted, while Travel gasped, "Oh my God. She's so beautiful."

"Let me have her!" I screamed.

"Are you ready to see your mommy?" Dr. Leo asked as he lowered Victoria onto my lap.

The achy heaviness of my lower half, the fatigue in my upper, and the uncomfortable awkwardness of knowing I was under the watchful eyes of obscuras dwindled with the sudden rush of love I felt for my baby girl.

"And here's your daddy," I said through tears as Victoria blinked and choked out a small cry.

"Wait," said Dr. Little, emerging from the observation room. "She needs to be examined first. We need to follow protocol. Give her back to Dr. Leo."

Dr. Bennett positioned himself between Dr. Little and my hospital bed. "The examination can wait, Simon. She can see her baby first."

Travel sat down on the edge of the bed and stroked our

baby's cheek with a touch so light, it barely brushed her skin. "She's so amazing, Cassie."

"And she's ours," I said, blinking away a set of happy tears.

Victoria lay in the cozy crook of my arm, with the rest of her body snug against my chest. "She has a chin like my grandfather's."

"And like my father's," said Travel, even though it was due to coincidence and not genetics when it came to his dad.

Her pointed chin was cleft like a tiny thumbprint left in pink clay. Baby Victoria yawned and blinked, and Travel and I laughed together as we watched her tiny tongue move against her gums.

Dr. Little tapped Dr. Leo on the shoulder. "That's enough. It's time."

"Cassie, we need to take her now. We'll bring her back after her bath and examination. You'll have plenty of time to see her today," said Dr. Leo.

"Dr. Hatch," Dr. Little demanded, "do your job."

Dr. Hatch snatched Victoria away before I could press my lips against her cheek.

"Hey," said Travel.

"Don't worry. She won't be gone for very long." Dr. Hatch held Victoria with two hands, one under her neck and the other under her knees. She cried and twisted in his grip.

"Dr. Leo, are you going to go with her?"

"No, it's not part of the protocol plan. My job is done for now." He stepped to the end of the bed. "Clayton examines and bathes all the clones once they're birthed. He'll do the same for Victoria."

"Go with him, please," I begged.

"I can't. Don't worry, Cassie. Dr. Hatch is an excellent neonatologist. He's extremely dedicated. He's the first parent of every clone birthed at this hospital, and he's very proud to have that honor. Your baby's in good hands. He's just going to run some tests and give her a complete physical examination. He'll be back with your baby in less than half an hour."

Ella left the observation room and joined Dr. Love and Travel at my bedside where Travel stroked my hand and periodically kissed my forehead while we all waited for baby Victoria's return. Ella and Dr. Love praised Victoria's beauty, my strength, and Travel's bravery for not passing out, while Michael leaned against the wall deep in thought.

Minutes later, Dr. Hatch returned with my bundle of joy, squeaky clean, wrapped in a pink blanket and a matching knit cap on her head.

He reached over Travel, nudging him aside with his shoulder to set Victoria in my arms. "You smell so good." I sniffed while Victoria blinked from the bright lights of the delivery room. "Are you ready to hold her, Travel?"

"Yeah, I think so." He readied his arms. With love in his smile and passion in his eyes, he cradled Victoria delicately.

Victoria blinked twice more and yawned. Her tiny lips closed like a flower above her pointed chin, a plump and rounded pointed chin.

"Wait, this baby isn't Victoria!" I shouted.

Travel peered deeply into the baby's face. "She's right. This isn't our baby! What did you do with her?"

The tiny infant in Travel's arms was missing the distinctive cleft in her pointed chin. She had the same eye and hair color. Her skin was pink and brand new, but it was not the child I delivered. Travel set the imposter baby on the bed. It hiccupped twice and cried, its face turning red. The exchange Dr. Little and President Gifford had talked about—this was it!

Michael turned until his shoulders were square with Dr. Hatch's. "What's going on, Clayton?"

"This is your fault, Michael," interrupted Dr. Little. "Travel shouldn't have been allowed in the delivery room in the first place, and you shouldn't have intervened when I told Cassie to give the baby to Dr. Hatch. You should have followed the plan, and then we wouldn't be having this little problem!"

"Where's Cassie's baby, Simon?"

He didn't answer.

"Stan," Michael shouted. "Do you know what's going on?"

"I have no idea what's happening," Dr. Leo answered, shaking his head and backing away as Dr. Hatch approached him with balled fists.

Dr. Little turned to face me, resting his folded arms on his gut. From behind him, Claus's house caught the light, reflecting a wide beam of white that flashed as he spoke.

"This is also your fault, Miss Dannacher. If only you'd been a willing participant from the start. But you refused, and while you've been at GenH1 you've done nothing but show us your wild temper, contempt for authority figures, and disregard for human life."

I tried to lift from the bed, but my legs, like lead, wouldn't budge. And when I tried to pull the IV from my wrist a MED grabbed my hand.

Dr. Little added, "While we've continued to treat you

with the utmost respect, your best interests and the interests of your baby have continued to be our main concerns. And as such, we can't jeopardize your daughter's safety by allowing you to raise her—even in your apartment at GenH1. She needs to be monitored twenty-four hours a day, protected from accidents and illness. I'm sorry, Miss Dannacher, but you've proved to be too unstable. This is for your baby's own good."

Respect? They didn't respect me—they only respected what my body could do. "You son of a—" As I wrenched my arm from the MED's iron grip, Travel grabbed Dr. Little by his uniform collar and pushed him against the far wall. "Give us our baby now!" he shouted, raising his fist and readying it to take aim.

"Let go of me. Let go now or you will regret it!" barked the doctor. "Dr. Hatch, do your job. Follow the plan."

As Dr. Hatch came to the other side of my bed, Michael stepped in front of him, his jaw tight.

"Move out of my way and help Simon, Dr. Bennett. You know what will happen to you if you don't," Dr. Hatch sneered.

His posture remaining strong and defiant, Michael stepped aside and pulled at Travel's arm. "Let him down. There's nothing we can do. Dr. Little is in charge of the lab, and Dr. Pickford is the head of this department. Their authority is beyond Dr. Leo's and mine. Dr. Little has already called security. If you hit him, they will arrest you."

But Dr. Little's raised arms were no match against Travel's angry fist, a fist that rocketed against the side of the doctor's face less than a second later. There was a grunt from Dr. Little, screams from Ella, Dr. Love, and me, and then another explosive punch from Travel, which brought Dr. Little to his knees.

A security team rushed into the room before Travel could deliver the next blow. Three uniformed men took him to the ground after receiving their own series of desperate punches from their assailant.

I tried to yell, "Let him go. Leave us alone," but my words were thick and distorted, delivered by a dry mouth and lips that barely moved. But why? Then I saw the reason: Dr. Hatch stood over my bed, making adjustments to the machine hovering above my head, pushing buttons after adding a vial of clear liquid to one of the machine's compartments.

Reaching out to push him away, my limp body folded at the waist and refused to move. "What are you doing to me," I tried to yell as my eyelids drooped.

"I'm so sorry, Cassie. I didn't know. I swear. You have to believe me," were the last words I heard. The words came from Michael, an angry and confused Michael, while he was escorted from the delivery room behind Travel, who bore a bloody lip and a puffy cheek from his gallant battle with the security team.

Chapter Eighteen

At my request, my private recovery room was not barren and void of sunlight like the hospital room where I was "awakened" a little less than a year ago. Instead, its walls were the color of butter and bedecked with wall-mounted monitors, displaying works by eighteenth and nineteenth century artists that rotated every hour. During the day, the skylight in the ceiling was milky-white, but at nightfall, it cleared to reveal the stars. The request was made during my third trimester when I thought Victoria was mine to raise.

My baby girl. With her, I was no longer genetically disconnected to this foreign world. I had a daughter, and with her birth an instinctive, unconditional love for her blossomed inside me; something I'd never felt before.

With that love, I was ready to share, understand, and help her through her future disappointments and pain. She'd need me, but it was more than that. I needed her, too.

Two overstuffed chairs and a rocker were tucked neatly

into the corners like scolded dogs, while a table to my left held a bouquet of flowers, including one magnolia blossom, their stems packed into a clear, beveled vase containing blue-colored water. But none of it mattered anymore.

This was the day of a fertile female's birth, and in a way, another awakening that would help bring the clones' dark fate into the light of hope. But now it was tainted, blemished by avarice and mistrust. We had all been deceived: Travel, Michael, me, Dr. Leo, even Ella, and Dr. Love. During the labor-room pandemonium, their faces told me they had not been privy to Dr. Little's and Dr. Pickford's vile sham.

In sharp contrast to the passive clones, my prenatal behavior was more than appalling: a botched escape, suicide attempt, and even the throwing of a cheap coffee cup against the wall were signs of mental illness and instability to the docile, non-violent clones. I was a rule breaker, my need for independence dictating my every move rather than the "life is precious" motto adhered to by the clones. Now I was paying for it with the price of my baby, and my once hard, round stomach, now gelatinous and deflated, was a malevolent reminder of my sad fate, Victoria's sad fate, and Travel's sad fate.

I ran my hand around my back and found that the pain-inhibiting patch was still in place, but it was ticking slower than before, keeping me minimally paralyzed. One pick at the edge of the patch with my fingernail allowed me to rip it away, leaving a spot of raw, sticky skin that burned as if I was leaning against a candle flame, but the IV needle came out easily and painlessly, barely leaving a mark in my skin.

Walking was difficult. My legs were still a bit numb, but I managed to make my way across the room to discover a

SEC stationed outside my door, so I retreated back to my bed, using my arm to support my aching breasts.

My first visitor was a MED to take a blood sample. My second visitor was Michael. He put his finger to his lips before I spoke, grabbed my wrist, and slipped a metal disk under my L-Band before I could pull away.

"Now we can talk," he said before pulling a chair up to my bed and sitting with his knees apart. "Please, trust me, Cassie."

"What did you put under my L-Band?" I asked.

"Something to jam the signal. They think I'm here to fill your head with lies. I'm supposed to tell you that I approve of what's happened, and although most of the team members were previously unaware of the situation, we understand it now and support it." He glanced warily from side to side. "But I'm really here to tell you everything I know and help you and Travel any way that I can."

I was too mentally and physically drained to harbor any resentment for him. My last bit of anger toward him had fizzled, but that didn't mean I completely trusted him. Unfortunately, at this point, he was my only hope, a link to the team.

"What happened to Travel?"

"He's been arrested, so to speak, not by the Region One Police, but by GenH1 security. He's been placed in a containment cell and all of his rights have been suspended. He didn't go without another fight, though. He took down two security guards and a bot in the hall. He also threatened to tell the public about the program, which isn't part of the plan—at least not yet."

"How long do you think they're going to keep him

there?"

"I'm not sure." He clenched his jaw and spoke slowly between short breaths. "I asked them to let him go back to his apartment, but they refused. They don't want you two conspiring together. They think he's too dangerous, too emotionally unstable—just like you."

"What happened to Dr. Leo?"

"He's been reassigned to a hospital in another division. He's a good doctor, but he's a follower, not a leader. He'll keep his mouth shut, try to pretend like none of this ever happened, and go on with his life."

"And Ella and Dr. Love?"

"They're still here at GenH1. They signed verbal-restraint contracts promising not to disclose what happened in the delivery room, just like Dr. Leo and I did, but when I looked in their eyes, I could tell they did it just to save their jobs. Their hatred for Dr. Little and what he did runs deep."

"I can't believe this is happening."

"I don't know what to say, other than that I'm sorry. I'm so, so sorry. I should have suspected something. I should have protected you. I..." His voice was low, and he slowly shook his head back and forth as he spoke like he was trying to shake away his disbelief and disappointment with the program. He buried his head in his hands. "I should have fought harder for your rights, especially when you were still unconscious and had zero control over your situation."

"It wouldn't have helped. You would have become a nuisance and reassigned to another hospital. Besides, I have zero control now. What the heck am I going to do?" I asked, my words trailing into a defeated whimper.

"There's nothing you can do."

"But I have to get Victoria back. I want my baby." I sobbed. There was no way I was going to let someone else raise her. "And Travel, I have to help him, too."

"Even if you could do those things—then what?" He focused his gaze on me, intense, like he was seeking the answer to some unasked question.

"Then I'll…oh, what's the use," I blurted, throwing up my hands. "You're right. Even if I could break out of this hellhole, where would I go? There's no place where they couldn't find me."

He sat up quickly as if attached to a loaded spring. "Yes, there is," he said confidently and with renewed enthusiasm. He squared his shoulders and crossed his arms.

"Where?"

"I can't tell you—not yet." He took both of my hands in his. "But I can tell you this. I'm going to help you. We will find Victoria, free Travel, and then I'll take the four of us somewhere safe. But the first thing I need to do is continue to convince the team that I'm still part of their game, that I'm still loyal to the Van Winkle Project." He licked his lips and glanced at his muted L-Band.

"Maybe we shouldn't be talking about this. Not here. Not now," I said, scanning the walls. Are you sure this room is completely free?"

"I'm sure."

"How do you know? We can't trust them. Pushing a button on the floor may not be enough."

"I agree. That's why I had a little help in that department." His smile told me who.

"Magnum?"

"Yup. Ella ignored her contract and told him everything.

Within minutes he contacted me under a secure channel and told me that if I required any of his special services to let him know. He's made adjustments remotely to this room and gave me the L-Band inhibitors. He assured me that our conversation would be free." I noticed his eyes were red and eyelids a bit puffy. "He thinks the world of you and I trust him. I know he'll help us do this. He gave me full access to the Van Winkle files, and I secretly downloaded everything I could within the time I was given."

"What did you find out?"

"Part two of the plan is to keep VW-4 and her future VW siblings in a controlled environment under their care twenty-four hours a day, so they can prepare them for their future duties. The VWs will be given the best care, but for their own safety, under enforced limitations."

VWs, a name used to dehumanize us in the minds of the genetics team. As much as they valued our reproductive abilities, they still saw us as foreigners.

"What kind of limitations?"

"GenH1 will be their one and only home. They'll never be allowed to leave the building and have a normal life. Their only job will be to procreate."

That's what we'd be—a set of slaves under the will of the team—that was my job and now Victoria's when she hit puberty. I knew it! What happened to being treated fairly and with the utmost respect?

"Your daughter and your daughter's daughters will have no concept of time or reality. They'll live their life in a lab instead of having a home with a real mother and father. They'll never be allowed to fall in love and have families of their own."

"I can't let that happen. I can't," I cried, banging my fists against my mattress.

"I know. That's why I'm here to help you," said Michael, placing his hand on my rigid shoulder.

"I want your help, I do. I'm not sure I can do it alone. But it's too dangerous. Who knows what they'll do to you if they find out."

"Cassie." Michael sighed softly. "This is something I want to do. Something I need to do. When it comes to me, I don't care about the consequences. Everything's changed. It wasn't supposed to be like this. And…and you know how I feel about you."

When his eyes seared into mine, I understood his sincerity, for he didn't just describe the future life for my children and me, he just described his own upbringing. Just like Baby Victoria, he was brought to life for one purpose, raised by the team, and nurtured through a list of rules and regulations.

"And there's something else I found in the files. Gifford plans to renege on his contract with the other regions. He's not going to supply them with fertile females."

Ah, so that's what the other presidents, Tupolev and Lung, were in the dark about.

"We have to stop Gifford by telling the other presidents what he plans to do. And then maybe they'll help us," I exclaimed as the numbness subsided in my legs.

"But they could turn against us, be just as bad as Gifford."

"Maybe, but that's a chance we have to take."

"That'll be more difficult than you think. Not very many people have access to the presidents. I sure don't, and those who do probably wouldn't believe us. We need to find

Victoria and Travel and get out of here first before we can do anything else."

Victoria's sweet face appeared in my mind, her eyes blinking against the ceiling lights, her pink lips pursed like a tiny flower, before the image was replaced by President Gifford with his smug smile and nose in the air.

My heart wilted. "Do you think we can really pull this off?"

"I do because we know people who will help us."

"Then we're going to need maps of this entire region, maps that indicate the placement of every obscura. Do you think Magnum can get those for us?"

"I'm sure he can."

"And the Van Winkle files. We're going to need a complete copy, too, if we're going to convince Shen-Lung and Tupolev that Gifford plans to railroad them."

"I'll see if Magnum can get them for us, and I'll also tell Rynne, my new assistant, about our plans. His loyalty lies with me, not the program. I'll make sure he gets an inhibitor. He's been assigned to the eighteenth floor, so he has access to Travel. As for Dr. Hatch, I've lost all respect for that man. I never thought he'd turn on anyone like this. In the past, he's always done what's best for his patients instead of what's best for GenH1."

Michael glanced at his L-Band. "I need to go before the team becomes suspicious. Remember to take out the disk after I'm gone, and keep it with you at all times so you can replace it when necessary." He stood and took my hand in his. "And until we can work out a plan, you need to do what the rest of us are doing: pretend you'll follow the Van Winkle Project."

"Thank you. Thank you for helping me," I said, grabbing Michael's wrist as he stood.

"There isn't anything I wouldn't do for you." He gave my hand a squeeze, and for a moment his smile eased my sad heart as I pulled him in for a long hug.

A sweet warmth seeped into my chest as he held me, taking me back to our last kiss.

As he left my room with a final wave, I removed the disk from under my L-Band and put it in my robe pocket next to the good-luck chip of pottery from my dig.

Chapter Nineteen

Dr. Little cruised into my room, his hands behind his back while he whistled an upbeat tune.

"And how are we feeling this morning, Miss Dannacher?" he asked in the same melody he just whistled.

"Just peachy," I scowled, "for someone who gave birth less than forty-eight hours ago."

"Now, now, things are not as bad as they seem."

"Not as bad as they seem? You took my baby. You lied to me, and you tried to trick me."

"And you shouldn't have been allowed to hold your child immediately after she was born. Then you would've accepted the clone baby as your own, and we wouldn't be in this little predicament."

"There's one thing a clone can never understand. A mother knows her own child. Your plan would have never worked anyway."

"I'm not so sure of that."

"So what's going to happen to me now?"

Dr. Little stepped forward and sat down in the chair next to my hospital bed. He tapped his trimmed fingernails on the table next to my bed in the same beat of the song he whistled upon entering. "Your job and the job of all future surrogates will be to give birth to fertile females who'll be reared by a team of experts and prepared for their future responsibilities as birth mothers."

"Where's my baby now?"

"She's safe. She's receiving the best care possible. We won't do anything to compromise her well-being. That's why she's under the care of a GenH1 team of professionals."

"Can I see her?

"No. But you will see the others when you give birth—that is, before they're taken away."

Pretending to go along with the program was more difficult than I thought it would be. "I'm not having any more babies, especially now."

"But you have to. It's part of the plan." He smiled. "Insemination will occur against your will, but we don't want it to come to that, do we? Everyone else on the team has accepted the plan. You need to do the same."

"What about Travel? Where is he?"

"The team is still having trouble convincing him that we did the right thing. He's currently in isolation, but he'll be moved back into his apartment by this afternoon." He was lying. I wasn't fooled by his sick words and fake charm. "He's confined on the eighteenth floor for the time being."

There was a *ding* and Dr. Pickford entered, his forehead shining and his eyes blinking wildly. "Sorry I'm late." He threw an apologetic, yet worried look at Dr. Little. Dr.

Little's brow wrinkled like he could read Pickford's mind, their personalities as synced to each other as their Liaisons, making me continually wonder whether or not the two men had been brothers in the past.

Anger swelled over the edge of my heart like a flood, throwing the team's lies and deception like trash along a riverbank of disgust. "You can both go to hell."

"That's no way to talk to the men who are in charge of your future," said Little, interlocking his fingers and resting them on his gut.

"You mean the men who are going to help Gifford make this the most influential region in the world," I sneered, remembering the conversation I overheard in the hall. "What are you going to do? Deny them of fertile females?"

He chuckled. "Good guess. You've continued to prove you're smarter than you look."

Screw you! "When can I be discharged? I want to go home." Home. This wasn't my home. My home was a world full of hunger, disease, and other unpleasant conditions, but at least there we were free—free to love whom we wanted, free to have children with whomever we wanted, and free to keep them.

The seven deadly sins did not die with the plague, they just went into hibernation, waiting for the right moment to return, for Pandora's Box, my cryonic chamber to reopen.

I was their Excalibur, the missing link to their salvation, and once President William Gifford had me under his jurisdiction, he couldn't resist plucking an apple from the tree of knowledge and taking a bite. Travel and I were their Adam and Eve, but this was no Eden. There was no place like home, and clicking my heels together wouldn't help.

"You can return to your apartment today if you like. It's important that you return to a routine of normalcy."

"Then I'd like to go now. I want to be there when Travel's brought back."

"I'll make the arrangements." Dr. Little tapped his L-Band.

"Actually, you won't be seeing Travel, Miss Dannacher," interrupted Dr. Pickford. "I just came from his cell. That's why I was late. You see, um, he just asked for my permission to leave the program."

"What?" Dr. Little appeared genuinely shocked, but Pickford had to be lying. Travel would never leave me—at least not like this.

"Yes, I'm afraid so," continued Dr. Pickford in a fake fatherly tone and a curled lip. "He asked for amnesty and the right to leave the project. He promised to sign a contract guaranteeing his silence, and I agreed, promising to compensate him for his contribution to the program thus far. He plans to leave the region immediately."

"The region?" I tried to sound surprised.

"Yes, he needs time to think. He's going to visit his brother in Region Three and then move to a non-disclosed location."

"I don't believe it," I countered.

"Oh, believe it. You will not be seeing Mr. Carson ever again, but don't look so sad. You still have friends. You have us."

Oddly enough, Dr. Little sat there appearing as stunned me. He didn't say another word as my plan of escape expanded into a plan that included not only Gifford but the demise of Dr. Pickford and Dr. Little.

"The arrangements have been made," Dr. Little announced as he looked up from his L-Band. "You may go back to your apartment."

The two men stood in sync, and as they left my room I heard Pickford say, "You're needed on the eighteenth floor."

Putting on the same pants I wore when I arrived in the delivery room gave me little warmth in a room chilled with deception and fear. The waistband snapped into place, readjusting to my slightly smaller size, but the front panel sagged and wrinkled, missing what it had stretched out to hold.

Kale and a SEC met me in the hall. She smiled and nodded, her cheeks puffing up like she was holding her breath.

"Cassie, it's so nice to see you again." She laced her stubby fingers together and gave me a slight bow.

"Thank you" was the only thing I could say.

My nose and cheeks felt oily, and the clean shirt against my sweat-caked skin felt as unnatural and awkward as leaving the hospital room without my baby. I was so sore from giving birth that my first steps were like that of an old woman, hobbling in pain, making anyone who saw Kale and me walking side by side think I was doing a cruel imitation of her stride.

I focused on the audible rhythm of her walking and tried not to think about Travel, who was suffering somewhere within the walls of GenH1, but it was impossible. With each blink, my lashes batted tears down both cheeks.

"A MED's going to be stationed in your room with orders to dispense a limited amount of pain reliever to you at your request. It'll also record the times in which the pills have been given and once their effect has expired, it will ask you if you need another dose."

"So, it's going to stay in my apartment?"

"Yes, it's customary during any home-recovery period."

"Great," I scoffed. I decided once again that I hated bots, all bots. They were spies, ready to report and record my every move once I was home. At least I was free of the SEC watching my every move. It was relieved of its duties now that I wasn't with child.

Kale laughed. "Think of it like a piece of furniture, a piece of furniture that's there to help you."

MEDs were not as human-looking as the RELAX units, but they were engineered to pacify and appease, ease and relieve. That literally was their motto. The heads of MEDs were capped with short, synthetic hair that was glossy enough to be mistaken for curls of metal string. When they spoke, their vinyl faces stretched in ways that human skin never could, and despite their realistic, faux irises, the dead look in their eyes made it clear that there wasn't a brain of flesh mounted behind their plastic eye sockets.

"It's only for a few days, and then the MED will be relieved of its duties."

When we reached my apartment, she put her hands on her hips and said between breaths, "We should have taken a two-occupancy hoverchair." She placed her hand on my back and divided her weight between both legs, taking a stance that reminded me of a rooted tree.

"No, I needed to walk. Walking helps me think."

"And you have a lot to think about." She patted my shoulder. "I've been thinking about things, too, and there's something I want you to know—your baby has given me and this world new hope." Kale's globular face and globular words were so nurturing and motherly that for a moment I actually smiled.

"Now my children, and their children," she continued, "will live in a world full of optimism instead of fear. Without you and Victoria, we'd be hit with another plague, the plague of anarchy. That's our fate if we lose you: anarchy and then extinction."

"I know, but—"

"I understand how you must be feeling right now, but in time, your heart will heal. I believe that, and you need to believe that, too."

But she didn't understand. She was incapable of understanding, limited by her inability to procreate. I knew right then that I couldn't trust her.

"Thank you. I feel better now," I lied.

"If you need anything, you give me a call."

After a brief hug, she wobbled down the hall, and I entered my apartment and flopped down on the bed.

Chapter Twenty

"So, what brings you here?" I asked Dr. Little as I stood in my doorway later that day.

"Many, many, many things," he said. "Can I come in?"

"I guess. You don't have Claus with you, do you, or is he stuffed in your pocket? Because he's not welcome here."

"Rest assured, he's not here." The doctor laughed and his gut shook.

He complimented me on my quick recovery, and I told him I missed Travel and wanted to see him. He praised me for my contribution to the world, and I told him I missed Victoria and wanted her back. Both of my controlled rants were met with nods, and a, "Yes, I understand how you must be feeling right now, but we are not able to fulfill your requests."

"Then why are you here?"

"Unfortunately the nature of my visit is to deliver some bad news."

Bad news? What could be worse than what I'd already experienced?

"I regret to say that…" He paused and shook his head. "That Travel is no longer with us."

My stomach dropped. "What do you mean no longer with us? I know he left the program. You already told me that."

"What I mean is that Travel is dead. Such a waste, such a waste."

"What? I don't believe you." I spoke in a harsh whisper. He had to be lying. This was another part of their game, another deception used to break my spirit and keep me tame in the world of clones.

Dr. Little was composed, well-rehearsed. His shoulders lifted and dropped back into place as if he were giving a salute instead of a one-sentence eulogy. With a stiff neck and eyes that didn't blink, he said, "Oh, but you must believe. You see, he never made it to Region Three. The private mover in which he was riding malfunctioned. First it exceeded its hoverment, and then it collided with an unmanned supply transport. He died on impact. There was nothing anyone could do to save him."

Travel dead, and I would never see him again? Yes, it was a lie. I twisted my egg ring around and around on my finger until it created a deep, pink groove in my skin, but the little egg nested on the crown of the ring did not budge. It would never break. It was infinitely intact, a solid reminder of my fertility.

"There will be a funeral," he said as a lump of belief rose in my throat. "We'll give you all of the details after the arrangements have been made."

"No. I can't believe this. Are you sure it was him?" I choked through a sob.

Dr. Little's left cheek twitched under his left eye. He rubbed the spot with his hand and then spoke. "Yes, there is no mistake. It was him. Would you like to see the body?"

"Yes, I would." I choked again.

"A viewing can be arranged. His body arrived here at GenH1 an hour ago. I'll see what I can do." Dr. Little tapped his L-Band and mumbled. "Dr. Bennett would also like to speak with you. He's on his way here. He's concerned about your well-being, considering what's happened."

"Good. I want to talk to him, but please leave. I want to talk to him alone," I cried.

Dr. Little's only reaction was a smirk. The only thing that man lived by was his L-Band. He had a passion for orderliness, authority, and control—not for his employees or his patient's mental welfare.

When Michael appeared on the monitor, Dr. Little waited for him to enter my apartment before he slipped through the door, giving him a quick handshake and me a bow like he was actually sorry about leaving me in a state of grief.

"Is it true? Tell me the truth," I said after we made our conversation free by tricking our L-Bands. "Please, tell me he was lying."

"I wish I could. But, yes, it's true."

Travel left the program, which meant he left Victoria and me, too, something I never thought he'd do. My heart melted. As my legs buckled, Michael caught me in his arms, bringing me to the floor to sob against his chest. As he held me, I shuddered, short spasms in a hiccup-like rhythm.

"But I'm here for you, Cassie. I will always be here for

you," he said softly, smoothing my hair with his hand. I'll keep you safe. I'll take you and Victoria away from here. I care more for you than anything else on this planet."

"No, it's too risky," I said, pulling away. "I've already lost Travel. I'll have to leave on my own."

"I won't let you do that. I could never leave you." He held my head in his hands, his watery eyes filled with sorrow and affection.

"You can't come with me."

"And I can't let anything bad happen to you. You mean too much to me. You still have no idea how much, do you?" He blinked and swallowed hard, and I shook my head no. "Before Victoria was born, I used to visit a very special place every evening before I left GenH1 for the night. Do you know what that place was?"

"No," I said, my lips trembling.

"It was the botanical garden—your botanical garden. I went there after work before I went home. I sat in the same spot where you sat each day. I held your tools in my hand and dreamed we were there together. I kept track of your dig, watching for changes and counting the number of pottery pieces you unearthed each day." He dug into his pants pocket and pulled out something small, something flat, but curved with jagged edges.

"You found a piece of pottery," I said, holding out my palm.

"After Simon first took away your tools, I brought my own and continued digging for you. When your visits ended altogether, he ordered GROW to restore the garden to its previous condition. So that night, I went for the last time, and by the light of GROW's spotter, I found what I hoped was the last piece."

"So my dig is gone?"

"It's gone. I'm sorry."

My head hurt. My stomach ached like I was bedridden on the fourteenth floor all over again, but the piece of hard clay against my palm kept me grounded as the shock of Travel's death sunk into my heart and became real.

"I'll take you and Victoria away from here," Michael repeated. "I'll never leave you."

"Not even if you had a choice like Travel did?" I asked, pulling away from Michael and wiping my cheeks.

"Actually, there's more to that story if you're ready to hear it. He didn't die in a hover accident. He never planned to quit the program and start a new life in Region Three. He…he committed suicide."

Suicide? That was even worse. "How do you know for sure?"

"My assistant Rynne called me this morning. He told me to meet him on the eighteenth floor. He said he couldn't tell my why, that I just needed to see it for myself."

"What did you see?" I sniffled.

"Travel, dead, his containment cell secured by a net of laser-electric beams. He held his wrists against the current until they burned, blistered, and bled. He bled out before anyone noticed."

"Nobody was watching him?"

"An obscura was on him all night, but by the time a random check was made, it was too late."

"But he would have never taken his own life. If he did, they must have told him something that left him without any hope."

"They didn't just tell him something, they showed him something: his reclone. It was still lying on a gurney on the other side of the electric fence when I got there."

"But I thought you couldn't clone a clone."

"Oh, it can be done. It just doesn't work, at least not yet. They usually die in infancy. But Travel's reclone was different. In less than twenty-four hours, Simon's crew grew his twin from an embryo, to fetus, to infant, to child, to teenager, the cells dividing so quickly, it produced even more debilitating side effects. Steroids gave the clone's useless muscles bulk, and someone cut and styled its hair to match Travel's, but it never received a brain impulse. The poor bastard never had a chance."

"But why did they clone Travel in the first place? What were they planning to do with it?" I pulled a pillow from the couch and hugged it hard against my chest.

"President Gifford gave the order to keep Travel incarcerated for life, something they didn't want you or anyone outside the program to know about. They planned to give his clone injuries indicative of a hover accident and tell you and his friends and family that he was killed while on his way to visit his brother in Region Three. Then they could show you the body, give him a grand funeral, and it would be all over, no questions asked, while the real Travel remained here, forgotten in a cell."

"So, they showed Travel his clone?" How could those doctors be so cruel?

"Yup. First they told him he was going to remain incarcerated for life. Then they showed him the clone and told him their plan as an added threat. It was obviously too much for him to live with."

"But he didn't have to kill himself. We would have found a way to make things right."

"He didn't know that. He didn't think he had any options."

"Suicide is never an option. Never, no matter what. Life is precious." As much as I was tired of hearing that repeated every day, the clones' motto was true, and for a moment, I was angry at Travel for giving up on life.

"And now it's my job to falsify his death certificate and Clayton's job to get rid of the reclone. Travel's suicide has actually made their cover-up easier."

"I have to find Victoria and get out of here. Now that I know what the doctors are capable of, there's no telling what they'll do."

Chapter Twenty-One

The next morning, I awoke to the sound of footsteps, and for a moment, I thought it was Travel striding down the hall, taking long but quick steps, manly and coordinated like he always had a rock beat in his head. Sometimes he'd sneak into my apartment and order breakfast, so when I finally awoke, two sunny-side-up eggs would be smiling up at me.

The light stomping on soft carpeting took me back to reality. It was a MED ready to dispense a dose of painkillers that I'd refused to take. I was still sore from giving birth, but that was a pain I could bear. I gave it a scowl and plopped down on the couch. This particular MED was not gender specific, but it wore the colors of GenH1, blue and maroon.

"Tell me, MED. What are your specific duties in regards to me?"

"I am to track your medication intake. Dispense medication at the designated times. Meter your level of pain. Offer physical and medical aide. Alert the appropriate authorities if you need assistance."

I walked to the far wall and stood close enough to activate the closet door. It slid open. "Stand in here, MED. I'm going to take a nap. If I need you, I'll call for you."

It walked straight into the closet without question, and the constant expression on its rubbery face didn't change.

Within minutes, I heard the closet door slide open. MED walked down the hall and stopped at my doorway. "Cassie, it is time for your medication."

"MED, I'm not in that much pain. I don't need it. You can go back to the closet," I said, throwing a blanket over my shoulders.

Again, the bot did not move.

"Go back to the closet," I shouted, jumping from my bed, giving the bot a hard kick, and upsetting one of the dispensers. The dispenser hit the floor and shattered, littering the carpet with an explosion of little white pills. "I hate you, you stupid bot." Two more kicks sent the bot in a tumble. Straddling the bot with my legs, I gave its rubber face two blows with my fists before wrapping my fingers around its neck and rapping the back of its head against the floor until its wig shook free. I abhorred what it represented, the future—this future.

"I hate you. I hate all of you. I hate this world. I want my world. I want my mom. I want my old life back," I screamed, scooping out one of the bot's eyes with my fingers. It popped out easily. I threw it as hard as I could, producing a marble-sized impression in the far wall.

By the time Michael and a security team arrived, the bot was the epitome of naked with its clothes and rubber flesh stripped from its body, exposing an array of mechanics and flashing lights.

"Be gentle with her," Michael shouted to a guard as one of them ripped me from the bot. "Let her go."

"I-I don't know what to say," I said, dropping to my knees. "I…"

"It's okay." He turned to the guards. "You can go now. She'll be fine. I'll take care of the situation from here. Her unexplained violence is a reaction to one of her medications. I've seen this happen several times before."

The security team left without questioning his diagnosis or authority.

My cracked fists bled and two of my knuckles turned blue. "I guess their faces are harder than they look," I cried through a smile.

"Let's go in the bathroom so I can wash and bandage your hands." In the bathroom, he produced his L-Band inhibitor from a pocket and wedged it in place. "Just in case," he said as I did the same with my mine. "Now tell me what happened?"

"I just lost it. That stupid bot wouldn't listen to me. I told it to stand in the closet in the living room, and it wouldn't do it. I think it's a spy."

"All I can say is it's a good thing that bot was a MED and not a SEC. SEC bots are programmed to protect themselves, even it means injuring a human. The only thing that MED could do was send out a distress signal."

Michael lifted me and sat me on the bathroom counter, then wrapped his arms around my waist and pressed the side of his face against my breasts. My heartbeat slowed almost immediately.

"You're a lot stronger than you look. You sure did a number on that thing." His laugh made me smile. "What did you do? Pretend that thing was Simon?"

"Yeah, maybe," I joked back. "But honestly, I'm just emotionally beyond what I can normally handle right now. What will Dr. Little do to me for this?"

"He won't do anything. MED bots are nothing special, and besides, it did give me a good excuse to come see you," he said, giving me a squeeze.

"Were you able to find out anything about Victoria?" I asked as he held my fists under the running faucet and then dried them with a towel.

"Yeah, with Magnum's help, I was able to locate her. It's not going to be easy, but we should be able to get her out of here."

"And go where—you still haven't told me." From the cabinet behind me, I produced a can of bandage foam. Michael gave my knuckles a thin spray, the white foam sealing each cut before changing color to match my skin.

"Region Three, Sector Nine will be our first stop. Travel's brother lives there. It's considered a low-security territory. The population is small, and is still quite isolated from the other sectors. From there, we'll fly to Sector Ten, where they will be less likely to look for us, and with Magnum's help, our communications and movements will be untraceable."

"And from there?"

"From there we go to our final destination." He licked his lips. "But I can't tell you the name of it—not yet. It's for your own protection. You can't know about this special place until we're almost there, and Magnum, well, he can never know about it."

"Why?"

"In case they augment his brain or yours and find out about our final destination."

My head spun. "But what makes this place any different from Sector Ten?"

"It offers us one thing the regions can't: freedom."

Freedom? I didn't think that was possible in this world.

"Are you sure that will work?"

"I'm sure," said Michael with a reassuring smile. "Besides, if we do get caught, you'll be detained, but that's all. They won't do anything to you that could be detrimental to your physical well-being."

"But what about you? What would they do to you?"

"What they'd do to me doesn't matter." He spoke with confidence and control.

"Simon will be here soon to escort you to see Travel's body. Just please, whatever you do, hold your anger toward him. We can't do anything to let them know that you know the truth. And remember, clones aren't prone to violence. We're raised to be passive and peaceful, which equates to compliance. If you were one of us, you would have been arrested and given psychological counseling for the rest of your life for destroying that bot."

"Don't worry. I don't have enough energy left to destroy another bot, let alone Dr. Simon Little. I'll just have to dream about doing it instead." We both laughed as he helped me down from the counter.

"Thank you," I said, giving him a hug. He stroked my hair, and as I closed my eyes, I felt his warm lips against my cheek. Turning my head brought his mouth to mine. It was a delicate, closed mouth kiss, but it awakened my soul all the same, and my suppressed feeling for Michael bubbled back into my heart.

After Michael left, I lay on my bed and flexed my

aching muscles. Though still tingly after Michael's kiss, the adrenaline rush I experienced while mutilating the bot left me weak and my limbs sore. My mind also raced with questions, and I couldn't stop thinking about Victoria and how much we needed each other.

A *ding* interrupted those thoughts and quickly replaced them with another. Did I have the mental strength to do what I was supposed to do next?

Dr. Little arrived just when the muscles in my legs stopped shaking. "We can go now," he said at the door. "A SEC will meet us at the end of the hall. When you return you will find a new MED in your apartment, a model fifty-six, no artificial skin, only metal. Try not to destroy this one." He winked.

I didn't wink back. "Don't worry. I might."

"Oh, and by the way, I'm not afraid of you, Miss Dannacher."

"That's too bad. You should be," I said. This time I winked.

As we walked toward the morgue, Dr. Little raised his eyebrows and pursed his mouth into a little *O* that drained all of the color from his lips.

The morgue was colder than any of the other rooms in GenH1, physically and aesthetically. The far wall was stuffed with long tubes that fitted lengthwise into circular compartments in twenty rows of twenty, forming a perfect square that from a distance could pass as modern art. One capsule was out of place, hovering above the floor.

With a wave of Dr. Little's hand, the top of the floating capsule slid open. Inside lay Travel, his arms at his sides, his eyes closed. His skin was ashen and thick like he had been carved from a block of wax. His brown wavy locks were tucked behind his ears on both sides, but several stray strands spread like fingers above his head.

"He's still L-Banded," I said. My bottom lip quivered. My heart ached.

"Yes, the preparation of the deceased does not include the removal of the wearer's L-Band, therefore, becoming a permanent method of identification above and below the ground."

So L-Bands continued to live on a wrist without a pulse, making the wearer a permanent prisoner.

Taking Travel's cold hand, I held it tenderly against my palm and wondered if David Casper lived a full life or, like Travel, died young from an injury or a disease.

Travel told me he had a lot of regrets, and now I couldn't help but wonder if joining the program became one of them. He was a father, the father of a baby girl named Victoria, and the first father of the thirty-first century. He would never hold her again, kiss her, recognize his features in hers, or watch her grow up, but his DNA was there, embodied in a new life. Twenty-three of his chromosomes had combined with mine to create, not clone, a one-of-a-kind human, something no one had done for over six hundred years.

Travel would live on, not only as a memory, but through the vitality and jubilance of a little girl. This gave me some hope, but at the same time, I couldn't help but think "what if" and question all of the decisions I made.

I drew in a deep breath, so deep I thought I couldn't catch it. "I-I'm ready to go."

As Dr. Little escorted me back to my apartment, there was no conversation between us, only the soft sounds of our shoes on the rubbery floor and a few cracks from my throat when I tried to stop my tears. Anger rose inside me, a deep pool of revenge that was about to overflow.

"Miss Dannacher—" Dr. Little started to say.

Without a word or a glance at him, I stepped inside my apartment and shut the door.

The replacement MED was clunky, looking more like an overgrown toaster than a robot. It asked if I wanted a painkiller. I said "yes." It asked if I wanted a sedative. I said "yes." In less than a second, two small tablets, one purple and one orange, slipped from a tube in the bot's abdomen and fell into my hand. I pretended to lick the pills into my mouth with my tongue but snuck them into the inside pocket of my robe instead. Great. Let them think I'm doped up, too tired, and too emotional to think about an escape. A lactation inhibitor was the only pill I actually swallowed.

There was a knock on my door, no *ding*, no face on my L-Band, just an old-fashioned rap of knuckles against metal. I slipped Magnum's device under my L-Band as a precaution, but when I unlocked the door, it only budged an inch before stopping.

"Is your L-Band 'free?'" asked a whisper.

"Yes."

"Feed this to your MED," came the whisper again, followed by a thin coin of black plastic held through the crack in the door by two fingers.

"What? You mean put it in its mouth?"

"Yes, do it now, quickly." I took the plastic piece and palmed it like a poker chip.

The MED was unsuspecting. "Do you require additional services?" it began. "I can dispense..." And pop, the chip dropped like a coin in a vending machine. The bot's eyes flashed with lights that turned first green, then blue, then red before a last bright flicker left the bot immobilized and unresponsive — dead.

"Is it done?" said the voice again.

"Yes, it's deactivated."

The voice belonged to Magnum, who entered my apartment, followed by Michael.

"This apartment is 'free' for now," said Magnum. "I've tricked the system again, but I can't do it for long periods of time or someone will notice and become suspicious."

He hugged me first with a hard pull against his chest and a clap of both hands against my back. Michael's hug was the opposite, soft and snugly, with his nose nuzzling against my hair and shoulder.

"Michael told me about Travel, Cassie. I'm sorry."

"So am I. He was a great guy."

Magnum cracked a smile. "But we shouldn't be too sad. Part of Travel is still alive. We just need to find her. At least he made his mark on this sterile planet before he left it." His attitude was slightly skewed, believing Baby Victoria was an equivalent substitute for Travel as if she actually embodied his soul.

"Did you get the maps and the files?" I asked Magnum, my heart racing.

"I did." His cheeks dimpled with a wide cutie-pie smile. He was a true radical, eager to pull something off on the establishment. "Here're the schematics of the region, and the latest copy of the Van Winkle files, even the classified sections," he said with pride. He presented a paper-thin monitor, holding it open before rolling it into a one-inch diameter tube and unrolling it again. "This is called E-Paper, which isn't connected to Liaison One, so it can't be detected by the system. The information it reads is contained in memory pins."

The E-Paper lit up with trails of different colors, winding and turning their way across the paper. A tap to an area either reduced or zoomed the image while two taps to a building switched between floors.

"With the data I collected, you'll know the position of every obscura, and once I block your locators and replace your L-Bands, you'll be able to travel anywhere in the world without being seen. You have everything you need to leave tonight if you're ready."

"Travel but without Travel," I said. "But I'm more than ready."

Magnum's dimples disappeared as his smile retreated. "I know, again, I am so sorry about him." He shook his head.

"What is it?" I asked.

"One of my crew was just directed to put a locator on every vehicle parked in the employee lot. They aren't taking any chances with you. They know how resourceful you are."

"Then we'll have to remove it from my car," Michael said. "I want to avoid the use of public transportation as much as possible."

"No problem. I can disable the locator."

"Can you do it in time for us to leave today?" Magnum gave me a nod. "Good. I think we need to get out of here as soon as possible," I announced, rolling up the E-Paper and shoving it up my sleeve. He handed me two memory pins, and I carefully wove them in and out of my cuff for safekeeping.

"Ella, Dr. Love, and the two of you have also been

placed under twenty-four-hour surveillance," he said.

"Me?" Michael asked. "Those sons of a—"

"I guess you're not a very good actor, Dr. Bennett." Magnum laughed and gave him a pat on the back.

"Apparently not as good as you, Magnum."

"So far, none of the hover terminals have been upgraded to maximum security. That probably won't happen until they realize you two are gone, but when it does, it'll happen quickly. People with babies will be detained and their L-Bands checked."

"So we'll take turns holding Victoria," I said to Michael. "One of us will walk far enough behind the other to make it look like we're not together."

"That won't matter," said Magnum. "They'll check anyone with a baby. Unfortunately, your baby will stick out like a sore thumb. It's going to make getting to Sector Nine incredibly difficult."

"We'll figure something out," I said confidently.

Michael sucked in his bottom lip. "If we're asked to raise our wrists for a band reading, we'll have to do it, or that will be a sure sign of our guilt. And besides, we'd never be able to outrun a SEC."

"Then we'll just avoid every SEC we see."

Michael sighed. "That may not be possible. A SEC could be stationed at every hoverbus depot, checking passengers with babies as the passengers board."

"Then we'll have to come up with a way to hide her, and—"

"Or, you can"—Magnum put his hands on his hips— "you can leave her with me."

"What?" I asked, spinning on my heels to face him directly.

"Just until you reach Region Three. My L-Band is legit and I have access to infant bands. I'll fit her with a modified L-Band and then bring her to you. Until then, my house is perfect. I tricked my obscuras over a year ago." He laughed. "No one would even know she was there."

"Magnum." I gasped. "You don't know how to take care of a newborn, and besides, you have to work."

"I wouldn't be the one taking care of her, my mom would. She retired last year. I'd have her move into my house while Victoria's there."

"Would your mom really do that for us?" asked Michael.

"Of course she would."

"Wait!" I interjected. "Why are we even talking about this? The answer is no. There's no way I'd leave my baby behind or even think about putting your mother at risk. Enough people already have their necks out for me. I'm not going to add one more."

"Cassie, think about it," said Michael. "She would be perfectly safe with Magnum's mom. No one would suspect a thing, and it would give us a chance to get away from here without the added threat of being caught. Even if we could hide her, what would happen if she started to cry?"

"Michael's right. If the baby's with you, your chance of getting caught more than triples."

I shook my head and crossed my arms.

"It would only be for a few days, Cassie, and then I promise I'll bring her back to you once you reach Sector Nine."

I trusted him, but could I trust his mother? Victoria was my responsibility. I couldn't pawn her off on someone else, and what if Magnum was caught on the way to Region

Three?

"Just a few days?" I asked while cracking my knuckles.

"Three tops," said Magnum.

"Okay." I sighed.

Michael patted my shoulder. "It's for the best."

I said, "I know," but inside I still felt torn.

"Now, there's a heartbeat reader embedded in the wall of your bedroom," continued Magnum, "but I have a solution for that, too." He pulled a small red pillow out of his pocket. It was the size of a man's wallet but twice as thick. "When you leave this apartment for the last time, set it on your bed and press its center. It'll mimic your heartbeat."

"That's it, huh." Michael was sarcastic, but he said it with an optimistic smile.

"Since Liaison One's original purpose was to connect all of us together for safety and convenience, it was never meant to be used as a means of manipulating or controlling behavior. Within the last twenty-four hours, protocol has had to install and upgrade additional equipment just to keep tabs on all of you. Cassie's right—the sooner you two leave, the better."

"What time do you normally leave GenH1?" I asked Michael.

"It depends—normally about six, but it's not unusual for me to stay until seven."

"Then that's when we should leave. What about these?" I asked, lifting my wrist. I pinched my L-Band. If it had been made of living flesh, it would have cried uncle. "The inhibitor only blocks communication—not our locations, right?"

Magnum scratched the top of his head. "Right. I'll come up with a solution for that, too."

"We need to be out of the GenH1 compound by seven, so we'll need to meet up again in about three hours. Will that give you enough time to get the rest of the things we need ready?" I asked.

"It should, and if it isn't, it'll have to be." He smiled. "We'll meet at the north end of this hall at four thirty, and if everything goes as planned, you two will be out of the zone before they even realize you're gone."

"Magnum," I said, taking his hand. "Thank you. Thank you for putting yourself at risk for us. I can't tell you how much we appreciate it."

"What they did to you was wrong from the very beginning, and trying to switch babies—that's unforgiveable. I'll do anything to help you out of this situation. Besides, I like the challenge." He saluted, turned, and strolled out the door with both hands in his pockets.

Chapter Twenty-Two

Dr. Love whimpered softly into the back of her hand. Her fixed smile collapsed into a ball of moist redness that contorted as her sobbing gained momentum. "Life is so precious," she cried. "What a horrible, tragic accident."

"We are so, so, sorry, Cassie," said Ella, pressing a tissue under her eyes.

"I know, I know," I lied for the obscuras in the room. "I just can't stop thinking that maybe there was something I could have done differently so Travel wouldn't have left the program. I never *ever* should have protested about the baby. I should have accepted the one they gave me and kept my mouth shut. Then maybe he wouldn't have left, and he'd still be here with us today."

We cried for the next hour, not only for Travel's death, his real cause of death, but also for my secret departure with Michael. Their words were forced and rehearsed, but convincing enough for the obscuras, while each blink, nod, and squeeze of the hand reflected the true sarcasm and disgust we all felt for the corrupt Van Winkle team.

When they left, Ella was still lightly crying, but Dr. Love's eyes were dry, her smile hard, and posture stiff. "You just need to stay strong, and above all, never lose hope," she said with intense eyes and condolences disguised as good-byes, since there was no guarantee that we'd ever see or talk to each other again.

Four fifteen came almost faster than I wanted it to. Waiting until the last minute to stuff three days' worth of clothes and a few toiletries in a large handbag was necessary but almost more stressful than creeping to the end of the hall and hoping my location wouldn't be detected.

When I came to the end of the corridor, a set of fingers enclosed around the top of my arm and with a quick tug, I was pulled around the corner to meet Michael.

Magnum popped his head out of the door across the hall. "In here, both of you." The room we entered was a bot closet, barely big enough for three, or I should say, the four of us. Though the JAN occupying the closet was inactive, it remained a wicked reminder that no matter where we went, electronic eyes could be following us.

"I did it. I found a way to make you both invisible, not literally, of course, but you know what I mean." Magnum's smile was wider than the loose bands he pulled from his pocket and almost twice as thick. "No one will ever suspect this."

"Are we going to travel through the vents or the walls?" I asked, imagining Michael's fingers stretching through the grate in my isolation cell.

"No, the vents won't lead you two to where you need

to go, and traveling through the walls won't work, either. They're wide enough, but one wrong turn, and whack," he said, smacking his hands together. "Meet Mr. A.G.-lift."

He exhaled. "So here's the plan. Michael, go to your office. Put this band on your wrist directly above your L-Band. Wait thirty seconds. The new band will unlock the old. Let the L-Band fall onto your office chair, but then don't touch it. It will reset if it feels a pulse." He dangled the bands from his index finger. "These dummy bands randomly change their identities to citizens in this region, so your real identities won't trigger any body count detectors. And when you board a hoverbus, credits will be deducted from your current identity's bank account instead." He chuckled.

"Awesome," I said, raising my hand for a high five and lowering it quickly when I realized they had no idea what I was doing.

"There's only one problem." Magnum frowned. "Your current identity and the wearer of the real L-Band can't be in two different places at once. If one of Liaison's security programs picks up on this, the nearest SECs will be sent to both locations to investigate, so...tap here if you suspect you're being tracked. It will make your band completely inactive and bots won't be able to recognize you. That's when you'll truly be invisible to Liaison One."

"But in that mode, we won't be able to board hoverbuses or open doors, right?" I asked.

"Right, so only use it if you have to."

"Okay, we will," said Michael as he stuffed a modified L-Band in his jacket pocket.

The stale, warm air of the closet began to make me feel sick.

"Cassie, I'll come with you back to your apartment while it's free and the three of us will meet up here again before the two of you get Victoria. I have another memory pin for you, too, showing Victoria's new location. I was ordered to L-Band her an hour ago," he said, handing me the pin.

"You saw her? How is she?" I asked, trying to contain my excitement.

"She was asleep and remained asleep during the L-Banding. I'm not sure, but she might have been sedated. She hardly moved."

"I hope she's okay." My throat tightened like I was about to cry.

"I'm sure she's fine—more than fine. She's constantly being monitored. They won't let anything happen to her. And lucky for us, the Liaison One system was never meant to be used as a security system. Therefore, the room Victoria's in wasn't designed with obscuras in its walls."

"Geez, I can't believe she's already L-Banded. They usually wait a week with newborns," said Michael.

"Yeah, but they weren't going to take any chances with her. No L-Banding ceremony either, just like with you, Cassie—just an L-Band in a fancy box. I met Dr. Pickford in the primary nursery, and he led me to a secondary nursery in the back. Victoria was the only baby in there, but there was a woman taking care of her, a private nurse."

The E-Paper exploded with light as I unrolled it and inserted the memory pin. A flash of yellow came next as our route from the hall to the nursery, and from the nursery to Michael's car developed onto the screen.

"The route I created for you to follow will wind you into areas of GenH1 that you didn't even know existed, and it will all seem very convoluted. At times you might think you've gone the wrong way, but don't worry, you haven't. You just have to trust me. I know the location of every obscura and sensor in this building, which means that I know how to avoid them. Remember that I've had to guide you away from their eyes, which will take you off the beaten path."

"From the looks of this"—I ran my finger along the yellow trail—"it will take at least an hour to get Victoria and then meet you at the mover."

"That's what I've predicted," said Magnum.

"I don't know, Magnum, do you really think we can pull this off? Without my L-Band, I won't be able to unlock any doors in this building, even low security entrances," said Michael. "A randomly selected identity may not have my level of security clearance."

"That's why you're going to use this." Magnum dug into an inner pocket of his jacket and jerked out a flat, circular object made from the same spongy material used for L-Bands. "This is your key. It will open any door in GenH1." His white teeth glistened in the low light radiating from his modified L-Band.

"You're a genius, Magnum."

"I know. I know." He laughed. "I've only left one thing for you two to figure out—what to do about the private nurse."

"That's easy. We'll hold her down and sedate her before she has a chance to call for help. Michael, you must have access to tranquilizers," I said.

Michael exhaled and crossed his arms. "I do. I have access to sedatives." He shifted his weight between his feet, looking nervous for the first time since we began our escape planning. His recent crack at violence must have been about all he could bear for now.

"Don't worry. I can do it by myself. I'll take her down," I said as Michael cringed.

Not that I was accustomed to violence, either, but I'd witnessed my fair share on digs. The heat, the boredom, the crack of dry skin against a dusty fossil after hours of excavation led to irritability and hot tempers.

And I wanted my baby back. Desperation would make me do anything I had to for her.

"Michael and I can get Victoria," Magnum suggested. "From there, I can take her straight to my house."

My heart sank. "I want to go with Michael to get her no matter what. I need as many minutes with her as I can get before I let her go."

"Okay, you and Michael will go."

"Then we're ready," I said, putting my hand up for another high five out of habit and dropping it again. "We can't thank you enough for all your help, Magnum."

Michael gripped both of his arms. "This wouldn't be possible without you."

"Hey. I'm doing this because I know it's the right thing to do. Now go," he said, embarrassed.

Michael gave me a tender squeeze, a look of reassurance, and headed to his office while Magnum and I made our way back to my apartment.

He drew the comforter and sheets away from my bed and pulled a modified L-Band from his waist pocket. He stretched it like a slingshot and let it snap back into shape before draping it just above the active L-Band on my wrist. The new band clamped shut and within seconds, my old

L-Band disengaged, shriveling apart and falling onto the bed with an inaudible thud. Then he set the little red pillow in the place where my heart would be if I was lying down, and pressed its center.

"Okay, that's done. Here's Victoria's new L-Band," he said, handing me the tiny, dummy one. "Now help me. This has to look like you just in case they send someone to perform a visual inspection." Magnum crammed two pillows under the sheet.

I found another pillow in the closet. "You won't believe this, but I've always wanted to do this so I could sneak out of a bedroom and go to a party that wasn't chaperoned."

"Why didn't you? Too afraid of getting caught?"

"No, not that," I groaned as I molded the stuffed figure beneath the covers with my hands, bending it where the knees would be to add to its legitimacy. "I never had the opportunity. We were hardly ever home, and when we were, there weren't any parties to go to, or at least any I knew about or was invited to, because I didn't know any kids my age in our neighborhood."

"I understand now."

"Understand what?"

"Your need and Michael's need to keep Victoria from having to grow up here at GenH1. To an outsider it doesn't sound so bad, but after Michael told me about what his childhood was like, I felt for the guy. I wouldn't wish that on anyone either. The dude didn't have anyone to play with unless you count the laws of physics and a periodic table of the elements as friends."

Yes, Michael and I definitely had more in common than any other two people in the world.

We took a step back to survey our handiwork. "This would fool anyone."

"Magnum, I'm really going to miss you."

"I'm going to miss you, too."

"So you don't blame me for running away from the program and leaving the world in a…in a bind?" I asked. A bind? That was certainly an understatement.

"No, I don't. Especially after reading the Van Winkle files and seeing what kind of life it really promised for you and your daughters."

"Honest?"

"Honest. We better go. This ruse might only buy us an hour. That's enough time for the two of you to get out of the zone and on a hoverflight to Region Three, but that's all. Once we're back in the hall, I'll reset the obscuras in your apartment. Ready?"

"Yeah, as ready as I can be." My heart pulsed hard enough to pound in my ears.

"Okay, follow me."

Outside my apartment, I quickened my pace to match his while carrying my overstuffed handbag. He was light on his feet, almost graceful, as he took the turn down the hall, hugging the wall with his back as we slipped into the bot closet undiscovered. A small light shone in the corner. Michael was already there. His breath hit the back of my neck as he moved in behind me.

"Michael, you made it." I turned and cupped his face in my hands.

"Of course I did. I wouldn't let anything stop me," he said.

Magnum bounced with excitement. "Okay, you two get

Victoria. I'll debug your mover and meet you in the garage."
He slid out the door as he gave a fist pump in the air, and I
matched it with one of my own.

I pulled the E-Paper from my sleeve and unrolled
it. Once fully extended, it stiffened into an eight-inch by
eleven-inch rectangle that was as thin as a sheet of paper
but as hard as a piece of steel.

Michael looked over my shoulder. "I've never read
schematics before. I've just heard about them." He exhaled
loudly and a strand of hair fell against his forehead.

"It's a complex map. That's all. I can easily figure this
out."

"You can?"

"Of course. I'm surprised you can't."

"I don't know how because I've never had to. Most of us
spend our whole lives using public transportation, and when
private movers are used, there's an assisted driving system
that directs the mover to its destination."

"Well then it's a good thing I know a little something about
maps."

The glove box of my mother's jeep and the space between the driver's seat and the console were stuffed with
folded paper maps, courtesy of the American Automobile
Association, even though her vehicle was equipped with a
GPS tracking system and on-screen navigational display.

Sometimes the maps we read were no more than a
scribble on a napkin or the inside of a candy bar wrapper,
but we never got lost. My mother used to tell me I had a
special gift when it came to following my nose.

"I can read this. We're right here, and we need to end up
there. Here's the path we're supposed to follow. Come on," I

said, my smile a tremble from nerves.

"Wait." Just as I was about to step forward, the JAN behind us vibrated and hummed. Michael grabbed my hand. "Quickly, make your band inactive so it won't recognize us." We tapped the screens of our L-Bands and stood still. The bot's eyes flickered, the door slid open, and it walked into the hall, zombie-like, without giving us the time of day.

"Okay, our turn. Let's go," he said, pulling me by the hand.

The map took us down several extended hallways and passages that Michael had never seen before. Most of the corridors were maintenance routes, so periodically we'd pass an inactive JAN that was attached to the recharger with a twisted rope. The inactive bots made me cringe, but Michael passed by them without a flinch.

Magnum was careful to choose the least-used, windowless passageways, but it took twenty minutes of walking before we reached the first A.G.-lift we were instructed to ride.

"Michael, according to these schematics, we're in the north wing. Does anything here look familiar to you?"

"Nope. If this is the north wing, it's a section I've never seen."

The A.G.-lift's doors opened in response to the flat, spongy key in his pocket. He surveyed the inside of the A.G.-lift before we entered. "Since we're no longer connected to Liaison One, how are we going to tell the A.G.-lift which floor to take us to?"

I examined the E-Paper. "Well, according to the schematics, this particular A.G.-lift can only go up one floor."

"Then I guess we're going up."

The lift doors closed as we entered, and although I had

several thirty-first-century A.G.-lift rides under my belt, I was still amazed when the chamber rose and its doors reopened before I could count to one in my head.

The room we entered was dimly lit and shadowed by rows and rows of rectangular boxes poised neatly on three-foot risers. The capsules appeared seamless, gleaming as if their metal exteriors were hand-polished by a bot.

Michael moved away from the lift, sidestepping while keeping his back against the wall. "Why in the world did Magnum bring us here?" The room was so quiet and the air so stale that his voice echoed despite his controlled whisper. "Why here?" he mumbled, followed by what I thought were the words, "damn it."

"Because this room isn't equipped with obscuras or voice detectors and the door on the other side of this room will take us to the far end of the secondary nursery," I said, looking up from the schematics. "Baby Victoria should be just on the other side of that wall." I pointed across the room with a hand that shook, rolled the monitor until it was no more than the size of a thick straw, and stuck it back in my bag.

"Then let's go," he said, urging me forward.

From this distance, the gray, unmarked door on the other side of the room that looked no larger than the size of my hand called to me. My vision, hindered by my intense desire to see Victoria, tunneled as I snuck cat-like on raised toes toward the other side of the room without looking down or left or right.

He was behind me, his steps ringing against the concrete floor, but before I reached the other side of the room, the shiny, rectangular boxes to my right finally caught my attention, seeming eerily familiar.

"Oh God." Through a square window on the lid of one of the boxes, I peered into the face of a boy, someone about my age, with pale skin, pink cheeks, and red lips, lying in a capsule that was obviously designed to provide cardiopulmonary support to someone on the edge of death.

Michael didn't have to tell me who they were. The containers held my brethren, fellow members of the S.T.A.S.I.S. program. Lifeless, but with their organs in stasis, waiting for an awakening. Each corpse silently called to me, pulling on my heart as they lie in this secret tomb, a holding dock for the half-dead.

"You didn't tell me there were more." I gasped. "You kept this from me. How could you?" I stormed through tight teeth.

"I promise to explain everything later." He grabbed my hand, but I shook it away. "Please, you'll understand once I—"

"Whatever," I snapped. But there was no time to be angry. Right now I had to focus on saving Victoria. Later, I'd cry for them.

Chapter Twenty-Three

"I need the sedative," I said with my back to the cryonic capsules.

Michael produced a small, liquid-filled cylinder from his pocket. "This sedative is a strong one, but remember, the nurse might have to be restrained and prevented from speaking while it takes effect."

"I know. No problem. I can do it. According to this," I said, unrolling the E-Paper, "Victoria's in room SN Three, which is obscura free, but the primary nursery, PN One, *is* under surveillance. In PN One, there are four obscuras with audio in each wall." I enlarged the image on the E-Paper.

"So once we enter SN Three, the only way they'll find out we're here is if we make a mistake and accidentally alert them."

"I hope you're right," I said, wiping sweat away from the back of my neck. "We can't make any mistakes."

Michael held up the spongy disk. With a tiny *clink* instead of its identifiable *ding*, the door unlocked like all the others we'd found so far.

With my first step, the cold metal door slid silently, but the rustle I expected to hear from the room, a rubbing of fabric followed by footsteps, never came, and after I peered inside, I understood why. With its back to me, an automatic rocking chair swayed up and down, emitting a sound like a rhythmical snore with its occupant sound asleep, mimicking the rocker's ticking with its own set of Zs. The white bassinet by the door was empty. Where was Victoria?

Shadowed by a solitary light source in the corner of the ceiling, the room was dim and fantastically warm, unlike the morgue we left. Room SN Three was large but cozy, just like the nurse who slept in the rocker with her back to me, holding a thick blanket across her lap.

I motioned for Michael to follow behind me, giving him the all-clear sign. We crept on our toes, hoping not to awaken the large figure before I could sedate him or her with a quick hit to the arm.

When I rose onto my toes and stretched my neck to peer over the round shoulder of the nurse, I found the most beautiful baby I had ever seen. It was my baby sleeping peacefully, wrapped in a pink blanket, and with an automatic pacifier perched on her lower lip.

As her pacifier clicked in time like a miniature heart, I came around the other side of the rocker to meet my target—the exposed forearm of the caretaker.

Transfixed by the sweet baby face before me, it took two blinks before I realized that Victoria's chubby nanny was Kale.

"Magnum should have told us." I hissed in fury.

"He probably didn't know. When he L-Banded Victoria, it was probably during the previous shift, which means a different nurse," he whispered back.

"I can't believe you agreed to be her caretaker," I said as I jabbed the vial in Kale's obese upper arm, the thin needle easily penetrating her skin.

The liquid dispensed quickly. Kale's eyes popped open and she flailed one robust arm, holding my baby with the other and reaching for her L-Band. When her jaw dropped, I clasped my hand over her mouth and pressed harder when her teeth came in contact with my palm. Several seconds later, her legs unhinged, her head fell backward, and one arm dropped from the armrest.

In one motion, I scooped Victoria out of her arms, drawing her instinctively into my chest, letting her cheek rest comfortably against my shoulder. She hardly stirred, the pacifier continuing its soothing magic, and my heart settled with the euphoria of a mother's bliss.

While I held her, Michael replaced the baby's L-Band as instructed, letting the old L-Band fall gently onto Kale's lap. Then he stepped backward toward the door and motioned for me to stand next to him. "Which way do we go, Cassie? Are we supposed to go back the way we came, or are we supposed to leave through the primary nursery?"

"Back the way we came, but only until we reach the A.G.-lift. Then I think we go right. I'll have to check the map again."

The route back through the hall of caskets was completed in less than twenty swift strides, centering my thoughts on Victoria instead of the twentieth-century bodies to my right and left.

The ride in the A.G.-lift brought us back to the corridor outlined in red on the E-Paper. I stopped and said, "Take her, Michael. I need to check the schematics."

"What if she wakes up and cries?"

"Then improvise. Do you think I'm any better at this? I've never been a mother before. I've never even babysat," I spat as my buried anger toward him began to resurface for not telling me about the others in the S.T.A.S.I.S. program still locked in half-death.

The pacifier started to slip during the transfer, and he had to awkwardly push it back into place with his index finger. He kissed the crown of her head and said sweetly, "Hi, I'm Michael. I knew your father."

"Two lefts, three rights, and one more ride in a service A.G.-lift. That will take us directly into the parking garage," I said, pushing the rolled-up screen into my bag so Michael could place the slumbering infant back into my arms.

A tiny noise came from Victoria's throat as she stretched, but the pacifier stayed intact, continuing to tick.

After tackling a zigzag of hallways, we entered the last A.G.-lift on Magnum's itinerary to freedom, which took us to Garage C, Level Two, the location of Michael's mover. Magnum was there as promised, leaning against the seamless hood of the hovercar, looking like the spokesperson for a cigarette ad, with his legs crossed at the ankles, arms folded, and a white rag hanging from his back pocket.

Magnum pulled out the rag and whipped it across the front of Michael's window. "You're all set. Your mover's invisible, too. I hinged the tracker to the ground." He pointed to the floor directly under the mover where something the size and color of a pie tin lay. "I also disconnected the vehicle's interior sensors, so the mover can't detect how many passengers are inside the cabin, and I disengaged its L-Drive, which means you're going to have to manually program each turn at least one hundred feet before you reach it. Do you think you can do that?"

"Yeah, we'll work as a team. Cassie, you'll have to call out each turn well in advance."

"Okay, that won't be a problem." Victoria sighed, almost losing the pacifier.

"Michael, put the key I gave you on the dash. It will activate any toll, gate, or tunnel without recognizing or registering your vehicle. Oh, and I also removed the hoverment restrictor." Magnum grinned and his dimples appeared. "Just in case you need to exceed the road codes."

Michael moved forward. "You're something else, Magnum. We can't thank you enough."

"I told you before that you don't need to thank me."

I turned so Magnum could see the tiny face of the baby peeking up above my shoulder. Her eyes opened, and when she yawned, the pacifier disengaged and dropped. Magnum quickly snatched it from the air before it hit the ground and handed it to me.

"So this is Victoria."

"This is her." I repositioned the baby in my arms and rocked her slowly, feeling complete for the first time since she was taken from me in the delivery room.

"She's beautiful, Cassie. She looks just like you."

"Thanks, Magnum. Thanks for everything." From the look on his face, I already knew his next question.

"So, are you ready for me to take her?" he asked carefully. "My mother said it would be an honor, and I promise you, she'll get the best care. I mean, look at me. My mom did a great job, right?"

"Yeah, she did a great job…" I paused, caught my lips with my teeth before they started to quiver, and said quickly before I changed my mind, "I'm ready. She'll be safer with your mother, and it will give us a better chance to make it to Region Three, where we can be together again."

Michael caught one of my shoulders with his hand and massaged it in an "atta boy" type manner. All I could do was shrug.

"I'll be in Trail's sector watching for you, and when it's safe, I'll bring her there."

"We need to go," said Michael sympathetically.

Could I really do this—watch her go a second time? But I had to, if Michael and I were going to make it safely into Sector Nine. "Okay, sweetheart." I drew in a deep breath to halt my tears. "Mommy loves you. I'll see you soon."

Victoria's forehead was smooth, soft, and baby fresh. I gave it a kiss and held her plump little hand between my two fingers. She whimpered for a moment, making cute, half-cry noises like a kitten in the middle of a yawn, and I gently placed her in Magnum's arms.

Michael grabbed me at the waist in a side hug, and as our shoulders met, he said, "It's better this way. It's just for a few days."

"I know. It's just hard." My last word wavered. "Bye, Magnum. Thank you, and tell your mother thank you for me, too." I kissed his cheek while he held Victoria against his chest, and then I gave my baby a last kiss on the top of her head, hoping it wouldn't be the last time I ever saw her.

"Let's go," said Michael. He opened the mover door and

I slide into the front seat. As it rolled away and lifted from the ground, Magnum lifted her little hand and moved it up and down in a wave. When we cleared the parking structure, we reactivated our modified L-Bands, and I broke into an uncontrollable sob.

Chapter Twenty-Four

"I still have Victoria's pacifier," I said softly. I gave it a squeeze, mimicking the clench of a baby's gums, and it clicked back soothingly. "I forgot to give it to Magnum."

"That's okay. He can always get her another one. You know how resourceful he is. He's probably shopping for baby supplies right now."

The first time Victoria and I were separated, she was ripped from my arms, and my elation was replaced with panic and loss. This time, I handed her over willingly, and I felt exactly the same way, yearning for the tiny little thing I hardly knew but loved so much simply because she was mine.

Michael gave me my peace while we traveled, letting me cry in silence as I was hit with the reality of what I had done and what we were doing. It came as a stream of questions, wave after wave, and with each pass he squeezed my knee, but I rocked it away, turning from him.

What if Magnum was caught before he made it to

his mother's house? What if his mother ended up being arrested? What if he wasn't waiting for us at Trail's house? The "what ifs" built up until it was hard to catch my breath between each flow of tears.

"Everything is going to be okay," Michael finally said when I wiped my face and took a deep breath.

"I hope so," I said, looking out the window for the first time.

"So, this is your first time in a hovercar," he said in an obvious attempt to take my mind off Victoria. "What do you think?"

My anger toward him still lurked, waiting to strike, but at that moment, my battered spirit prevented it from taking root. "It's kind of scary. I know we're only five feet from the ground, but it's just so different from what I'm used to," I said, looking across the twilit sky. Egg-shaped cars soared past silver buildings, many structures at least two hundred stories high. I couldn't help but smile at its technological beauty.

As the official navigator, I kept the E-Paper unrolled on the top of my knees, trying to estimate at least one hundred feet of road before each turn, so I could direct Michael right or left, and he could program it into the dashboard display. He used the time in between to educate me on movers, hoverbuses, and flyers, pointing at each as we passed and identifying each make and model.

The roads were full of hoverbuses, with or without passengers, following their assigned routes, and many of them were patrolled and flown by bots.

The universal key provided by Magnum sat on the dash like a good-luck token, and at each toll a floating arm lifted, letting us through without registering the vehicle's passage and deducting units from some poor, unknown clone's transportation account. My good-luck tokens were in my pocket—the two pieces of pottery. When I thumbed the one Michael found for me, recognizing it by its shape, it was enough to keep my anger toward him at bay.

"Michael, do you think they know we're gone yet?"

"I don't know. I hope not. I want to make it to our first hoverflight before they do, since it's easier to find and track a public mover than a personal one."

Magnum's itinerary had us switching hoverflights several times before boarding a transatlantic flight that would take us directly to Region Three, Sector Nine, or what I liked to call it: Australia.

Magnum's route also consisted of the less-traveled toll roads and highways that were considered no-risk zones, thus they were unmonitored, void of fixed obscuras on every post, but it made our journey so convoluted that at times we felt like we were going in circles.

"How long will Kale's sedative last?"

"For several hours, so that means she won't be the first one to alert the authorities, unless her shift ends before then and another nurse comes in to relieve her. We just need to hope that your long nap won't become suspicious until then."

A long nap, that's what I needed, anything to take my mind off Victoria, and keep my rage at Michael from surfacing.

"We only have a few more turns," I said with zero enthusiasm, "and then we're supposed to leave your mover parked on the street outside the Shopping Precinct and walk to Hover Terminal Thirty-Six."

Two turns and ten minutes later, Michael lowered the mover and eased its wheels against the curb, picking a section of the street already dotted with a row of parked vehicles of the same make and color, which wasn't too hard to do considering that only three models from one factory and two possible paint colors existed in this region.

"I need to get out of this uniform. It's too obvious." He kicked off his shoes, slithered out of his pants, and started to pull off his shirt.

Damn, he was hot, though I tried not to watch. My best peek came when his tunic caught under his chin, and it took him a few seconds to pull it free and tug it over his head. His abs were well defined, rippled with hard muscle, along with his pecs, shoulders, and arms, bringing me back to the kiss when my fingers rode the path of each one from under his shirt.

Men's boxer briefs hadn't changed much from my century. I'd seen enough advertisements on Liaison to know, but now I saw a pair in real life, black stretchy fabric hugging down to his upper thighs. It was enough to raise my body temperature.

I shifted uncomfortably in my seat to face the window as he dug in his bag and produced a pair of tan pants, black shirt, and a pair of smooth, black shoes.

From the window, I caught my breath and watched the people in the Shopping Precinct bustle from one store to another, some pushing hovering carts with the ease of using just one finger. A mother and daughter walked hand in hand across the square. The little girl stopped to pet a dog on a leash as it and its owner passed, and the mother gave her daughter's arm a gentle tug to move her along. I frowned and wished Victoria was in my arms.

These peaceful clones moved in and out of their busy lives, oblivious to the fact that in ten to fifteen years, the world they knew could be gone, replaced with chaos, fear, and a survival of the fittest mentality.

Could I sit by and watch it happen, knowing I could turn the key? It was different now that I was a mother. Could I really be that selfish and let Victoria and all of the other children on this planet inherit a society gripped by fear and death?

If they'd just asked me first and allowed me to make my own rules. With Michael, the genetics genius, at my side, I knew we could have made the program work. Maybe we could come up with our own program, and once established, we could try to work out a deal with Region One that included the awakening of the other men from my time.

"So," I began. "This secret place you're taking me to, is there a genetics facility there—one that could house something similar to the Van Winkle Project?"

Michael turned to me. "There is, but don't worry. Nobody there's going to force you to continue with the project. They don't know the project exists, and no one will ever find out that you and Victoria are fertile."

"Unless, um, unless I wanted them to."

"What do you mean?" He drew away from me.

"Well, I might be willing to continue the project in this secret place if and only if it's completely under my terms, and with you in charge."

"Really?" With wide eyes, he gripped the steering console. "Are you sure?"

"Yeah. Not for Gifford or Dr. Little, but for my friends, and for you and Victoria, too. I've already put enough people in danger. I don't want to let the whole world fall apart. And," I continued, smiling and lifting my shoulders, "you can teach me about genetics, and I can help you. I can't be a paleontologist, but maybe I can be a geneticist assistant or something. I already know a lot about science. It's something I love. We'll reinvent the Van Winkle Project—turn it into something ethical and humane."

"Yes, of course, we could do it," he said with so much enthusiasm, his words ricocheted off the windshield. "I know we could, and I know the people there would be willing to help, too, and let us take the lead."

My shoulders relaxed as the weight of my words, something that gave me new strength, settled in my heart. I could only hope he was right, and I didn't just make the biggest mistake in my life.

"We just have to get there first," he said.

With a voice command, Michael made the car door open, and he helped me step out of the mover, proving chivalry still existed in 3025. My offer seemed to give him a new round of enthusiasm.

"We'll put our bags in these"—he opened the trunk— "so we look like commuters instead of people who plan to be gone for a while." With the pull of an orange tab, a slab of plastic the size of a brick unfolded, taking the shape of a thick, small trash bag."

"Wow, what are these things?" I asked as he handed me the other plastic brick.

"They're metered grocery bags, designed to count and deduct units from the buyer's account as items are placed inside them. Everybody owns one, and during this time of night, we'll fit right in."

At the depot, we quickly spotted our flight number and stood on the platform. The hoverbus, an extra, extra-large version of a hovercar, lowered next to the curb and we boarded, relieved it had three empty rows near the back. We kept our heads down as we walked, hiding our faces from any obscuras, and avoiding direct eye contact with the other passengers even though we knew our false identities should help us remain safe.

"Scared?" he asked when I grabbed his hand.

"A little."

"Don't be. You'll get used to it. We aren't as high up as it looks."

"How fast does this thing go?"

"Once we're over the ocean, between eight hundred to nine hundred miles per hour, but don't worry. It won't feel like we're going that fast."

I cringed and whispered, "What about the bot?" The seat next to the driver was occupied by the most human-looking bot I'd seen thus far. With a full uniform and lips that moved in perfect cadence with its words, I didn't realize it wasn't a person until after we boarded, and it said, "Good evening, ladies and gentlemen, welcome to Hoverflight Fifteen."

"PORTS announce flights and help passengers with their baggage. They occasionally walk the aisle, sometimes more than once." Michael leaned lightly against my shoulder and whispered, "Let's inactivate our bands just in case it makes more than one pass and the identities we entered with have changed. I'm not sure a PORT could pick up on that, but it's better to be on the safe side."

"How do you know they haven't downloaded our faces onto every Liaison in the world and offered a reward for information leading to our arrest?" I murmured, scanning the people sitting ahead of us. Even though it was late in the evening, no one looked as tired as I'm sure I did, especially the women with their stiff hairstyles and tailored shirts made from fabric that refused to wrinkle.

"Well, for one, it's never been done before. Our crime rate is so low, and the crimes that are committed are mostly pranks, nothing too scandalous. The public wouldn't know how to react other than panic, and I'm sure the president doesn't want that," he whispered back, his lips practically brushing my ear.

"So you don't have any regrets coming with me?" I turned and noted the soft blue of his eyes, the perfect angle of his nose, and his shoulders, broad and strong.

He stroked the side of my arm. "I don't regret coming with you. I only regret," he continued, firmly planting his cupped palm on my shoulder and dropping his voice to a whisper, "not telling you everything I knew about the S.T.A.S.I.S. program."

This wasn't the place or the time for my anger to resurface, but I couldn't contain my rage as it swept through my being and settled in my heart. I crossed my arms over my chest hard.

"Please forgive me. I didn't tell you because it wasn't something you needed to know."

"I'll forgive you—eventually," I said, a little louder than I meant to and turning onto my side, so he'd know I didn't feel like talking about it anymore. This conversation had to take place when we were alone.

The cry of a baby behind us made me jump, and after its cry turned into a full-blown wail, its mother made her way to the bus's changing station, a plastic, rectangular table that was folded flush to the wall and of the same color. The only distinguishing mark was a small symbol in its center in the shape of a diaper.

Michael and I sat, barely exchanging words, my thoughts too full for small talk until the baby being changed began crying again. Infectious like a yawn, another baby somewhere near the front of the hoverbus started to cry, too.

"Like coyotes," I said, imagining Victoria in my arms.

"What do you mean?"

"One starts to howl, and then all the others join in. I love the sound of coyotes howling in a pack, especially when there's a full moon."

I unrolled the E-Paper and elbowed him as he was also drifting off into slumber. "According to this, when we land we'll be in Region Two, Sector Five, Division Thirteen. That's London, England," I gasped when I recognized the country's distinct shape on the map. "Is that even possible?"

"Yup, we'll be in Region Two." He didn't even sound surprised. "We're traveling a lot faster than it feels. Once these buses are out of the zone, they increase their speeds. We've been flying over the ocean for at least thirty minutes."

"According to Magnum's notes, once we land we need to take two additional hoverflights. The first flight doesn't drop us off in the zone where Travel's brother lives, so we'll have to walk to his house. He's continuing to take us off the beaten path."

"He sure is," agreed Michael as he yawned.

An hour later, the hoverbus stopped and lowered but

continued to float, sending an inaudible vibration throughout the bus.

"Reactivate your band," I reminded him as I touched the screen on mine and the hoverbus landed.

"Damn it," I heard him say as he walked down the aisle behind me.

"What is it?" I whispered, turning my head.

"My band. It won't reactivate. Quick," he said. "Trade places with me. I can't be the last one out."

Knowing he'd be invisible to not only bots but body counters, he dodged past me as I momentarily cut back into a row of empty seats so the automatic door wouldn't start closing before he reached it. Minutes later, Michael was safe, and I became the last passenger on Hoverflight Fifteen to step onto the pavement.

It was dark outside, but the sun was just begging to rise, casting a natural glow that sharply contrasted with the artificial lighting of the terminal. We waited for the other passengers to disperse before we turned to locate our next flight.

"These are early commuters. What time is it?" he asked. He lifted his inert L-Band, repetitively tapping the screen, but nothing he tried gave it any life.

"5:32 a.m." Too early for me, though the thought of going to Australia, a country I always wanted to visit, gave me renewed enthusiasm. "How long do you think it will take to get to Sector Nine?"

"I'm not sure with all of this backtracking, but according to Magnum, backtracking is the best way to keep the authorities off our trail."

All of this region-sector-division talk was so confusing.

But I figured it out, and basically after London, we were going to Australia, back to London, and then on to New Zealand. After New Zealand? Well, that was still a mystery—at least to me.

I turned until I was facing the terminal sign. "This is not the way I remember London. Everything looks just like it did in Los Angeles: the buildings, the streets, the people. It's so sad. I mean, where's Big Ben?"

"Who's Big Ben?"

"It's not a person; it's a clock, a large clock tower that reigns over London, shadowing the River Thames."

"I'm sorry, Cassie. I've never heard of it."

"The essence of what makes London, London is gone."

During our wait, a bot walked into the terminal. I put my head down and moved closer to Michael.

"Don't worry, it's not a PAT," he said.

"A PAT?"

"Patrol bot. Now those," he said, giving a discreet point, "those are PATs."

"And check out what they're doing," I whispered.

The pair of PATs stopped a couple pushing a stroller. The stroller settled to the ground and one PAT read the couple's L-Bands with a hand scanner while the other picked up the dainty, banded wrist of the baby and did the same.

Satisfied with their readings, the PATs passed along a row of waiting passengers and stopped once again when they reached a woman with a baby in her arms.

"There's another PAT and another one," he said with a tap of his elbow against mine.

"What about that guy?" A human matching the PATs in terms of uniform strolled into the terminal, his head shifting from side-to-side like he was examining paintings on the wall in a museum. He stopped periodically to talk to some of the bystanders, his nods and expressions indicating that he was asking questions.

Michael looked at his wrist, forgetting again that his deactivated band wasn't automatically displaying the countdown for the arrival time for our next flight. "That's a government patrol officer."

The officer pointed to a woman with a bundle of baby in her arms. In the next minute, he read the mother's L-Band and then the child's. His upper lip stiffened, and he moved casually until he spotted a stroller.

"See? It's a good thing Victoria's not with us," Michael whispered. "Especially since my band is broken."

"Yeah, you and Magnum were right," I said, though it still gave me little comfort in the fact that she wasn't with us.

"And they've obviously discovered we're gone, but it also means they don't have Victoria because if they did, they wouldn't be checking babies."

"Exactly. We're safe for now." I sighed.

The officer approached a young couple, a girl with flowing brown hair and a guy whose hair was short, like Michael's, with longer strands at the crown. The two held out their wrists, and their bands were scanned.

"They match our descriptions," I whispered after a bump to Michael's ribs.

"It might just be a coincidence." His eyes flashed to the monitor above our heads. "The bus will be here any minute. They're always on time."

"Let's split up until it comes. If they are looking for us, they will be looking for a man and woman. I'll stand next to those two women, really close, so it looks like I'm with them. You move over there," I ordered, motioning behind me.

"Good idea."

He strolled away to stand among a pack of male commuters, and I made my move to fit in with the other women at the edge of the curb and twisted the length of my hair into a bun, fastening it with a locked strand of hair. From our separate places, we pretended to be minding our own business as the patrol officer and PATs made their rounds, first questioning parents and young couples, then moving on to men and woman in our age range.

"I need to see your band," said the officer to a lady just ahead of me. She held out her banded wrist unconcerned, and the officer swiped it across his Liaison. "Thank you," he said, and asked the gentleman next to her to do the same thing.

No, no, no! Did I trust my L-Band? What if mine suddenly stopped working, too, or my band told the officer my name was Fred? Were Magnum's modifications gender specific?

I took two steps backward, allowing a man to my side to slip ahead of me, just in case. Our hoverflight came into view and landed. Yes! I circumvented the officer and boarded, breaking a sweat and holding my breath. I could only hope Michael was able to sneak aboard, wedging himself between commuters.

Rushing to a seat, I turned to see him coming down the aisle with his hands in his pockets. When he sat behind me, I heard him exhale and take another deep breath. We'd made it before being interrogated.

Once we were hovering above water, I inconspicuously

unrolled the E-Paper and examined the route we would take on foot once we landed and had to backtrack to a different terminal. Periodically I turned my head to gaze out the window.

The sea below was deep blue, marked with white lines of surf, the bus's regulated hoverment low enough for its exhaust system to blow downward into the ocean, sending the body of water into a state of unrest just like me, my feelings turbulent, unsuspecting, and unpredictable.

He moved into the seat next to me and leaned his head on my shoulder and whispered, "We're safe. For now."

Chapter Twenty-Five

"This flight's a lot longer than the flight to Region Two," I said to myself.

Michael's closed eyes fluttered, and his chest noticeably expanded as he took a deep breath. "Sorry, I fell asleep. I wasn't much company."

"That's okay. I already had my nap. It was your turn to get some rest. Look," I said pointing out the window. "The moon's following us."

"Cassie, the moon doesn't—"

"I was kidding. My mom used to tell me that when I was little. When you look out the window from a moving car, it looks like the moon's following you. Didn't you ever notice that before?"

"No, you don't notice something like that when you've spent most of your life on the fourteenth floor of a two-hundred-story building." He sighed and stretched into a yawn. "You still think about your mom a lot, don't you?"

"Every day."

Michael set his hand on top of mine.

"Hey, I think we're flying over Sector Nine," he said as he looked out the window. "Clear to Region Three and then back to Region Two. We're certainly doing a lot of backtracking, but it's working. If they were on our trail, they would have grounded our flight."

"Or they could be waiting for us when we get off."

"Hopefully not. We'll find out in a few minutes."

The terminal was empty, with the exception of a handful of late commuters. There was a light breeze cascading against the landscape, and Michael had to brush his hair with his hand several times against the current of wind to keep it in place.

Australia looked exactly like London—tall metallic buildings and crisscrosses of roads with oval- and egg-shaped cars and buses either parked, hovering, or in flight, following the lines of the road below. I didn't see Sydney's famous Opera House at the water's edge looking like an alien ship with its concrete sails, but I didn't bother to ask him about it either. Just like Big Ben, I'm sure it was gone, making this city a clone of the one we just left.

"It's 6:20 p.m.," I said, as I glanced at my L-Band before examining the evening sky.

"It's hard to keep track of the passing hours when we've been in three different time zones." He readjusted the tote strap on his shoulder, put his hands on his hips, and took a whiff of the night air. "It's a strange feeling."

"What?"

"Not being connected to the system. It's disabling in some ways, but in another way, I feel so liberated, free. It's a type of independence I've never felt before."

"I know exactly what you mean. My L-Band never made me feel like I belonged to the thirty-first century. I always felt like an intruder on an invisible leash. Besides, my L-Band made everything too convenient. I wasn't used to that," I said, staring at the moon and deactivating my band for the time being. "I like this feeling. It's called freedom. It reminds me of home."

We hastened to the next terminal on our itinerary, four blocks east, and three blocks to the north, in order to catch a hoverbus back to London before returning once again to Australia. I shivered. "We're in a different season, too. Our summer is their winter," I said, looking down at my short-sleeved shirt and Michael's T-shirt. "I wish we'd had more time to prepare for this."

"We're mentally prepared, and that's all we need." He smiled, and the golden specks in his blue eyes became visible as we passed under an obscura-free light post.

We shared the sidewalk with three additional couples and a handful of stray commuters who also chose to hurry against the sharp wind. The others were dressed more appropriately than us, but no one seemed to notice. He visually checked every pole and sign, fixed or hovering, for obscura lenses, like he did every time we were on foot, but again, he didn't see any. Magnum's schematics were accurate and up to date. So far his diligence kept us safe and undiscovered.

"That's the terminal, Michael."

The terminal was busier than I expected. Small groups of travelers stood huddled together and lone shoppers stood or sat with metered grocery bags or compact, bag-loaded carts floating next to them.

There were two PATs on patrol. One had his hind wheel down, chasing a small dog that had managed to get away from its owner, while the other one stood at attention, watching a row of passengers descend from a bus that just arrived. It approached people at random and scanned their bands.

Michael pointed to the illuminated numbers on the front of the hoverbus at the north end of the terminal. "Check the map. Is that our flight?"

"Yup, and a line is already forming. Let's break up like we did before and get in line," I said, reactivating my L-band.

Nodding and walking forward, he waited until there was a sufficient distance between us before making his way toward the grounded hoverbus.

Trying to look calm and ordinary, I casually looked behind me to see where he was in the crowd. Crap. I ended up in the middle of the line, but he was last. An unsafe position while his band was inactive.

From his frown, I could tell he was angry at himself for not reaching the line before the two women in front of him. He scowled and rotated his jaw as if he was chewing a wad of gum. A gray-haired man with stiff legs and an equilibrium cane walked toward the back of the line but was called to move to the front and board first due to his disability. Darn.

The driver was a middle-aged man, and the porter was also human. Darn again. Unlike bots, a human worker was more likely to notice if the bus doors started to close before Michael reached the first step.

The seat I chose was an empty bench near the back and next to the window. Geez, Michael practically rode the back of the lady in front of him. She felt his unnatural proximity, and turned to look back at him, but he only smiled and then pretended, I think, to trip as the woman entered, so he could bump her forward with his chest, temporarily making them one person according to the bus's sensors.

The door slid, but he turned in time to squeeze through without being pinched.

"Wow, I've never seen that before," said the porter, a tiny, bald man with an extra-large mustache.

"Yeah, that's never happened to me," said Michael. "You need to get that door checked. I could have been killed!"

Good job playing the role of disgruntled passenger and blaming the hoverbus's sensors. It worked, bringing an apology from the porter and easing the man's suspicion.

"Well, I don't know about being killed, sir," said the porter, "but you might have gotten a nasty bruise on your shoulder."

Michael tapped the screen of his L-Band and reacted as if it responded perfectly to his commands. "Well, it's not my L-Band." He proceeded down the aisle without further interaction.

He took up a row to himself directly in front of me. There wasn't a wink, smile, or nod between us. He kept his arms crossed and his head down. Something had happened to make him memorable, and I didn't want it to make me memorable, too.

"I see you're from Region One," said a girl directly across the aisle from Michael. She gave a nod in the direction of Michael's band and flicked her brunette hair from her shoulders. Her red L-Band and comparable accent to Travel's told me she was not only from Region Three, but she was also a born—if that's what you can call it—and bred

Australian.

"Yeah, Region One, Sector Three," he fibbed. If my memory was correct, Sector Three was Canada.

"Visiting family?"

"Yeah."

The girl paused, waiting for him to ask her the same question in return, but he didn't. He stared at the floor instead.

"I was visiting my cousins. I used to live in R3, S9, but now I live in R2, S5, D11. Have you been there before?" the girl asked in a barely distinguishable Australian accent.

"No." His answer almost made me laugh, considering that we were in Region Two, Sector Five, Division Thirteen—London—less than three hours before.

"Oh, well, if you want someone to show you around, I don't have any plans or anything when we arrive."

Oh my God. Are you kidding? Why don't you go put some shrimp on the barbie and eat a vegemite sandwich while you're at it, Aussie girl, or should I say, "Sheila."

"No, actually, I'm going to be really busy with my family. I won't have time for any sightseeing. Thanks, though," he said with a blush.

Good answer, Michael, but I shouldn't be so mean. He was a total hottie after all, and she was just doing what I never could—starting a conversation with a cute boy. Besides, it wasn't like he was my boyfriend. My jealousy said I'd begun to forgive him and at least wanted to get closer.

"Oh, okay." Miss Australia was defeated. She left a few minutes later, strutting down the aisle toward the bathroom.

When the porter was preoccupied, I leaned toward the back of Michael's neck and whispered. "G'day, mate."

"What?"

"Nothing, um, this flight should be short compared to the others. We'll be off in less than half an hour according to Magnum's notes."

He whispered out of the corner of his mouth, "I've been calculating the hours in my head. We've been traveling for about seven to eight hours total. That means it's between 1:00 and 2:00 a.m. in L.A."

"That sounds about right," I said, moving closer to the window to survey the night sky and the flickering surf below as the porter moved down the aisle.

He nodded and smiled at everyone he passed, but when he got to me and the empty seat next to me, he asked, "Traveling alone?"

"Yeah. One of my friends is getting married this weekend."

"You mean next weekend? Today's Sunday. The weekend's almost over."

"That's right. I meant next weekend. I'll be there for the whole week."

"Congratulations to your friend," he said, and smiling, the porter walked away, but I didn't like the way his mustache twitched when he turned to leave.

"Now we are both memorable," I whispered to Michael.

Through lips that barely moved, he responded. "It'll all work out."

The terminal was more crowded than it was the first time we were there, making it easier for us to blend in with the commuters. He kept his distance from me until Little Miss Aussie ended her flirting with a final "good-bye" and a wave before disappearing into the crowd.

It was strange. We were in Australia, but the people

didn't sound like true Australians, their accents being too weak. In London, it was the same thing. Was it the result of being able to travel from one region to another in just a few hours? Whatever the cause, I was glad there was still enough diversity in their cadences for my twenty-first-century ears to hear them.

"Now where do we go?" asked Michael, still blushing. The Aussie was probably the only girl, besides me or a tier two GenH1 employee, who ever flirted with him.

"Terminal Three. Over there," I pointed.

But over there was a place we didn't want to be. Two PATs stood at attention while three patrol officers directed a small crowd of people into two parallel lines. Now it was the PATs' turn to scan L-Bands with their built-in readers. All passengers who approached to board our next flight were asked to make a third line behind the other two, and everyone with a stroller or carrying a baby was immediately escorted into a fourth line where they were questioned and scanned.

"Michael, what are we going to do? Our flight leaves in five minutes. If we don't go over there, we'll miss it, but if they scan your band, you'll be caught."

"And if I'm caught, I can't take you to…um." He surveyed the terminal, his lips pursed. "We need a distraction. Follow me."

"Are you crazy?" I whispered as we joined the third line.

"No, not yet. You'll see, I think." He nodded toward the lady in front of us who was holding a white and gray spotted cat in her arms. He fumbled in my bag and produced Victoria's magic pacifier, holding it in his open palm. The synthetic nipple throbbed and clicked, sending the cat into a hypnotic state of desire, and me into a rekindled state of want for my baby girl.

"Simon owns an overweight Persian cat named Tom. One day when we were working in the lab, he told me about Tom's favorite toy, a baby's pacifier. Watch this." He snickered and flicked the pacifier like a bottle cap, sending it into a crowd of passengers twenty yards away.

The cat leaped from its owner's arms. "Oh no, my cat. Someone help me!" the woman shouted. Three additional screams followed as the naughty kitty darted between the legs of two women who were standing within inches of the clicking pacifier. Both PATs lowered their back wheels to make the chase.

"Go, now," he said, darting toward the first line of scanned passengers who were already boarding the bus. Michael pushed me three passengers ahead of him, creating a bit of distance between us, and we made it down the aisle and into two empty benches across from each other in the rear.

The flight back to Australia seemed longer than the first, especially since we pretended, once again, to be strangers. After our quick escape, my adrenaline was high, keeping my heart beat strong and my nerves on edge, but after a nap, we were finally back in the land down under.

"I need to check out the map again," I told him after we unloaded at the terminal and he jogged up to my side. "There's a park. We can make a pit stop there." I pointed to a large patch of grass with a hoveryard in one corner.

Two unsupervised children in the hoveryard bounced weightlessly on plastic animals with exaggerated, cartoon-like faces. One waved to me, and I waved back, before we sat down on a bench, and I suddenly missed Victoria all over again.

I unrolled the E-Paper and examined it, regarding Magnum's personal notes and instructions. "It's not far. We're at the edge of Division Three, Subdivision One, and Travel's brother lives just down the street in Division Three, Subdivision Two." Melbourne, Australia, was the twenty-first-century translation. "I sure hope he's home."

He looked up at the sky and held out his hand as if he was trying to catch a drop of rain. "He should be. If I'm remembering correctly, Sector Nine is eighteen hours ahead of L.A. I'm guessing it's around seven thirty in the evening here."

"You're spot on," I said, looking at my banded wrist.

After studying the map, Michael and I walked through and behind several subdivisions, or neighborhoods, following footpaths that kept us from the obscuras aimed at various angles and at the houses clustered in each block of land. Travel's brother's house, 2-27, was the last home on the end of the street, and being last, it was set slightly farther apart from the others on a larger parcel of land.

My anxiety level doubled. "Magnum should be there waiting for us, and he'll have Victoria," I declared, my voice breaking as I was overcome by the thought of my sweet girl.

"He said he'd be watching for us. That doesn't mean he'll be there the minute we walk through the door, so don't be disappointed."

From a field behind the back fence, we could see the back door clearly. A pair of boots layered in fresh mud lay next to a dirty shovel on the back porch. Two birds, mechanical ones, I might add, sat on a metal perch, twitching their wings above an overturned self-watering dog bowl.

"It looks like he's home. Are you sure he'll help us? Travel and his brother kind of grew apart."

"Yeah, I'm pretty sure he will. I read his profile. He works at the local power plant. He's a low-wage earner, but his worker's benefits earned him the use of this house and a hovercar. And here's the interesting thing. Last year he filed two complaints against his employer for privacy breaches. He thought the company was trying to brainwash him. Now he's labeled a non-conformist with paranoid tendencies—just the guy we need right now. Come on. Follow me."

The back gate opened easily. "There's an obscura," I said as I skirted behind a pair of trees.

"Magnum said that the houses in this section of the region were part of the first development, which means that each home has an independent security system, one that can be turned on or off by the owner. That's another reason why we decided to ask Travel's brother for a safe place to stay."

"If Magnum's not already here with Victoria, we'll need to tell Trail to turn off the outdoor obscuras."

Magnum and Victoria better be there. The anxiety of not knowing was driving me crazy.

"And I know how to do that." Michael bent down and raked his hands across the dirt at his feet. "I'll throw rocks at the door. That should activate the birds."

"You mean those robotic things?"

"Yeah, those robotic things are a doorbell. They're called Whimsy Birds. They were popular about five years ago. The fad didn't last. They were too noisy and irritating…"

"Unless you're a guy who thinks the government's trying to control you."

"Exactly." Michael pitched a handful of pebbles at the

door.

"When he comes out, I'll call him over. I'll try not to let him speak until I get a blocker under his L-Band." Michael handed me one of Magnum's L-Band inhibitors.

"A guy with his track record might be on high surveillance even if they don't suspect he's going to help us. We're kind of taking our chances with him, but he's the best one we've got right now."

"Okay, I'm ready," I said, slipping out from behind a tree.

Another spray of pebbles set the birds into a squawk that made my ears ring with a clamor of metal wings reminiscent of a possessed pinwheel. Within minutes, the back door opened and a man stepped onto the back porch. He immediately noticed me and my signal to stay mute, a "shhh" with an index finger parallel to my mouth.

When he was close enough, I grabbed his wrist—no L-Band blocker—meaning Magnum wasn't there yet. My heart dropped as I slipped the disk under his L-Band. "Now you can talk."

"Wow. I must be dreaming because it's been a long time since a pretty girl tried to get my attention." He laughed.

"I wish it was a dream."

It was cold. A thick cover of clouds filled the sky during the last half hour, bringing a sprinkle of rain that could be felt as the wind picked up. "Well, if it was a dream, it's over now." Trail frowned as Michael made his appearance. "The pretty ones are always taken."

"We need to talk to you. Can you please turn off your outdoor security system, just until we get inside?" He was puzzled, but he stepped backward, almost tripping as he entered the back door. "And don't remove the chip under your band," I added.

After Trail leaned through the doorframe and shut off the alarm, he waved for us to join him on the porch. "Don't tell me you work for Region Control," he said as we entered a small living room with slick, white walls and beige, boxy furniture.

"No, far from it," said Michael. "I'm Michael Bennett and this is Cassie Dannacher." Michael offered his hand for a shake. Trail hesitated and then took it.

Trail's hair was light blond, almost white, with eyebrows and eyelashes to match, causing his pale-blue eyes to pop above his cherub-like cheeks and broad nose. I held my gaze and added a smile.

"We're friends of your brother," Michael added quickly.

"As long as you're not from Region Control," said Trail. "When I came home from work, I found my dog dead in his bed. German Sheppard named Elk. The poor boy was half blind and could hardly walk, but he was still the best guard dog ever, even better than those damn birds out there. I took care of him the old-fashioned way. Buried him right out back less than an hour ago. I thought my neighbors saw and reported me to the region."

Way to go, Trail. I liked this guy already even if he hadn't been Travel's brother. He was very short, shorter than me, and wide enough to take up half the couch he was offering us to sit on. It must have been difficult for him to grow up with such an attractive, athletic brother, especially with Travel having enough charisma for the both of them.

"Oh, I'm so sorry to hear about your dog," I said.

"Thanks. He was old, it was his time. I told myself I wasn't going to cry, but damn it's tough. I'm sure going to miss him," he said, shaking his head.

"Yeah, sorry about your dog," added Michael.

The gnawing intensity of our journey, the pressure, the fear, the close calls with the PATs and porters, a dead dog, and the knowledge that Magnum was not here waiting for us were enough to unbalance all of my stored emotions. Suppressing my tears was futile. Once my lower lip started to quiver, forget it.

"What's wrong? Does it have something to do with my brother?" Trail asked me when the first tear dropped.

Michael spoke first. "Yes, it does."

"Is he okay?"

"Actually, he's…"

Michael didn't have to finish his sentence. My tears and Michael's eyes held the answer.

"No, I don't believe it. Someone would've contacted me. I'm his only next of kin. I'd be the first one notified."

"Not when the government's involved with his death," said Michael.

We told our tale from the beginning, the very beginning, although Michael didn't disclose our final, secret destination.

During our bizarre story, Trail nodded and his eyes blazed with anger toward the president and the Van Winkle Project's false promises. Never once did he slip into a state of denial or disbelief. He cried when he reached the end of account.

Michael said, "You couldn't have helped him, but you can help us now, please, and in doing so help Travel's daughter. We don't have anyone else to turn to. We trust you."

"Yeah, yeah, of course. I'll do anything for my brother's baby, the mother of his child, and the man who tried to help him." Trail wiped his red eyes and snorted against his palm.

Where was Magnum and Victoria? I stared out the back window for the umpteenth time, hoping to see him slipping through the yard with my baby bundled in his arms.

"I don't think your house is under surveillance, at least not yet, or the authorities would have been here by now. But by tomorrow, that could all change. Magnum told me that a basic surveillance upgrade could be ordered by the team and installed by a bot in just a few hours. How many obscuras do you have on your property?"

"One at each door, front and back, but there aren't any obscuras inside the house. In fact, they just sent me a message today, saying they're going to send a crew to complete the necessary system advances."

"When are they supposed to be here?" asked Michael.

"Wednesday."

"Good, that gives us two days before—"

"Then Magnum needs to get here before then," I interrupted. "He should have been here by now. Maybe he's been caught or knows the authorities are on their way here and doesn't want to risk having to hand Victoria over to them."

"I don't think so," answered Michael as he joined me in looking out the window. "They don't know our current location. If they did, we'd be sitting in a detainment facility. Magnum's just being extra careful. He's probably watching the house and waiting for the right time to act."

Trail lifted his hand and looked at his altered band. "So do you think they're trying to listen to me right now?"

"I'm not sure, but we can't take any risks. Keep the disk in for the rest of the evening so we can talk freely, but tomorrow you're going to have to remove it and go about your normal routine in order to avoid any suspicion."

"You also can't tell anyone about Travel," I added. "Not even the made-up story about the hover accident."

"Okay, what else do you want me to do to help?"

Michael licked his lips and straightened his back against the chair. "There's a man I need you to contact for me. His name is Saul Whittaker. He's a Region Three, GenH3 employee. We worked together for several weeks last year. He's a pilot and my transportation guide."

Transportation guide to where? This was obviously the point where Magnum's plan ended and Michael's began. We needed Saul to fly us to our final, secret location.

"Sector Ten is not going to be our final stop." Michael smiled. "Sector Ten has minimal security compared to the other sectors. They'd be less likely to look for us there but not unlikely. We'd still be fugitives, trying to fit in without working L-Bands and looking over our shoulder every minute. But once we reach this alternate location, they won't be able to find us, let alone bring us back to one of the regions." Michael's smile grew.

"Alternate location?" asked Trail. His teary eyes widened.

"I think it's time to tell you, Cassie." He squinted and the depth of his eyes glistened.

"Where are we going?" I urged.

"Tasma."

Trail reacted first. "Tasma? That's not a real place."

Tasma—the subject of Kale's playground song and sarcastic remarks from Dr. Love.

Michael leaned across the table, his eyes sparkling. "It is real. I know it is because I've been there."

Trail clenched his hands. "I knew it. Those bastards. There's another damn government cover up for ya."

"Wait." I said. "So where's Tasma? I don't understand."

"It's an island off the coast of Sector Nine." Which meant it was an island off the coast of Australia.

Trail interjected, "And it's not supposed to exist."

"And it doesn't exist. At least not on any map, not even the ones Magnum gave us. Only a handful of people know the truth. The less people who know about it the better. That's why I had to keep it a secret until now."

"But how can the government keep something like an island a secret?" I couldn't imagine the existence of an entire island being kept in confidence back in 2022.

"It's easy. The open sea south of Sector Nine is restricted due to high winds, whirlpools, high surf, tornadoes—you name it. But all of that's just a lie to keep people away."

"How come they don't want anyone to know about it?"

"Well, it was once one of the dead countries. After the plague, the new government believed that the island's inhabitants either left and returned to the mainland or stayed and died out, but it turned out that the country was never really dead. Apparently, there were enough rebellious, young survivors to stay and form their own government, a government severed from the rest of the world and Liaison One."

"But they were infertile, too. How could their society survive?" I asked after another peek out the window.

"At first they couldn't. Within ten years they were on the verge of extinction, but the remaining citizens refused to leave. They decided that they would rather die on their homeland than come under the control of the new-world regions."

I couldn't blame them for that.

Damn it! What was keeping Magnum so long? Where was my baby? Taking a deep breath didn't calm my nerves.

"And I'm sure the forefathers didn't want that, in case the mainlanders found out," said Trail. "That could have started a revolt." He smiled mischievously.

"Exactly. The forefathers were afraid that if the public knew about this small population surviving and building their own democracy, then more citizens would try to overthrow the new government or pull away from it to form their own bands, inspired by the success of the people already doing it. The earth had just lost over half of its population from a terrible disease. Life was too precious. The forefathers didn't want to punish or destroy the inhabitants of Tasma for their defiance, so their solution was to keep them happy and turn them into a distant memory, a made-up place."

"But they needed clones," I added.

"They did. So the forefathers made a deal with the islanders. They brought them baby clones once a month to replace the elderly who died, and in return, the islanders agreed never to leave their island or try to contact or recruit others from the three world regions. Over time, the island was erased from every map and obliterated from the memories of the survivors of the plague."

"So if this place is so top secret, why were *you* allowed to go there?" I asked.

"Well, when the regions recently became desperate for fresh DNA, the three presidents met and decided it was time to take a census of Tasma. Another geneticist hypothesized that some of the people who resided there might be able to reproduce. The presidents wanted to see if this was true, and that's where I came in. As a physician already handling your case, they felt that I was the only person qualified to take random fertility sampling."

"And?" I asked with minimal hope.

"They are as infertile as any clone."

"How many clones live there?"

"Less than fifty thousand."

"And you said Tasma's south of Sector Nine?"

"Yeah."

"Oh, my gosh. Tasma. It has to be Tasmania."

"What's Tasmania?"

"It's one of the islands of Australia, but during my time, it also had its own government. It was its own state just like it is now."

Trail pursed his pale lips. "So why do I need to contact what's his name, and what do I say?" he asked.

"Saul's one of the ten who know the truth. He's the only pilot whose flyer is not equipped with blockers to keep it away from Tasma. He stayed with me while I collected samples and examined some of the men and women, acting kind of like my assistant." Michael continued, "I need you to call him and tell him that you're from GenH1. Tell him it's a code 42/147 and that you're calling on my behalf. This code not only identifies the destination of the flight, but it also tells Saul that he's not to contact anyone, not even me, for verification or further instructions. His flight plan won't be registered, and his plane won't be tracked or monitored by Liaison One."

"So that's where we're going to live, Tasmania?" I asked.

"Yes. The population will welcome us. They trust me, and I made many friends. I'll admit that the buildings are older than what we're used to, some are hundreds of years old, but they've all been maintained. They have electricity, plumbed water, and many of our conveniences with the exception of Liaison One. There are no L-Bands, and most importantly, the residents live in a democracy, managed by an ancient constitution that's very similar to the one before the plague."

That meant Tasma had the resources needed for Michael and me to restart a Van Winkle Project on our own.

"So we can develop and start a program on our terms?" I asked.

"Yes, and we'll begin an organ cloning program, too. They've been doing transplants the old fashioned way, using a donated organ. But an organ from a clone doesn't have much life left in it, making their mortality rate higher than that of the regions." Michael gave my hand a reassuring squeeze. "But you and Victoria won't have to worry about that."

"But what about you?"

"Like any clone, I have a 30 to 40 percent chance of needing a transplant in the future, but I'm not concerned about it. I'll take my chances." He gripped my hand tighter, a sign that there was no point in arguing with him. "You'll like it there. Before my first trip, it was described to me as what the world was like one thousand years ago. You'll feel right at home."

"Will we be able to contact Shen-Lung and Tupolev from Tasma? We need to let the other presidents know Gifford plans to deny them of fertile females."

"To coordinate the delivery of baby clones, the Prime Minister of Tasma has a direct line of communication with the presidents."

Trail wiped under his nose with the back of his hand. "Michael, when do you want me to call Saul Whittaker?"

"Tomorrow morning at nine. Tell him he'll need to meet us at ten. He'll know where. One hour should give Cassie and me enough time to make it the pick-up location."

"But what if Magnum's not here by then? I'm not leaving without Victoria," I said.

"We won't leave without her. I have faith in him. He'll be here before then. I know it," said Michael.

Travel showed us to a guest room, and after Michael and I took turns taking showers, we lay side by side on the bed, my ears eager to hear the opening of a door or the sound of footsteps—anything to indicate that Magnum was finally here.

Michael hadn't dried thoroughly before getting dressed. His black T-shirt clung to his chest, and his thighs below the hem of his boxer briefs were damp. I picked at a loose piece of thread poking from the seam of my cotton pants, and from the corner of my eye, watched his abdomen rise and fall with each breath.

He rolled onto his side to face me, and when his knee touched my thigh, I inhaled through my nose to disguise my reaction, a pleasant heat shooting through my chest. As his fingertips brushed against my cheeks, I arched my back and welcomed his kiss.

With his hard shoulder against one hand, and my other at the back of his head, our kissing intensified. His lips trailed the length of my neck, and he drew one leg across mine as I bent one knee and lowered my leg to meet his.

When his mouth moved to my collarbone and the bit of

shoulder not covered by my shirt, I pushed against his arm, and he lifted away from me, his forehead glistening with perspiration. Rising up on my elbows, I sat up and raked my hands through his hair. Even with my wacked-out hormones, it was hard for me to stop.

"We can't," I said, dropping back to the bed.

"I know. I'm sorry. I just can't help myself when I'm this close to you." He lay on his back, with bent knees and his hands laced behind his head.

I stared at the ceiling, and as my breathing slowed, I thought about rescuing Victoria, and the rows and rows of S.T.A.S.I.S. capsules resurfaced in my mind.

"You didn't tell me there were more like me," I said, trying to keep my voice from rising.

Michael didn't say anything, but I heard him exhale through his nose.

"How many are there?"

"Sixty-two," he finally admitted after a long pause.

"So why am I the only one who…?"

Michael sat up and frowned. "Because you're the only female who survived the awakening."

I gasped, rising to sit next to him.

"I tried, I really did," he continued. "I tried to revive them all, but I failed. You were the only one who survived the fluid replacement and cell repair. I saved you for last, hoping that by then I'd find a solution to the problem. I just wanted you to live so badly." He turned to meet my eyes.

"Then the other women are dead for good?"

"Yes." A deep sigh dropped his shoulders.

"How many?" I groaned.

"Before I was old enough to join the program, there

were two teams trying to bring them back to life. There were thirty-seven pre-menopausal females in total, but by the time I came along, only seven of them were left, including you."

"Wait. This doesn't make sense. If the program started before you were a doctor then…then how long was I here before I was awakened?" My heart jerked in my chest.

"Cassie, don't ask me that now. You have the Van Winkle files. You can read them later, and then you'll know everything."

"Just give me the number, Michael. How long was I there?" I demanded.

"Thirty-one years," he said so softly I could barely hear.

"Thirty-one years?" I shouted.

"Please, don't be angry with me. Remember, I've only been involved with the project for five years, and I didn't want to awaken you, or any of them, until I knew all of you would survive." He reached for me, but I pulled away. "And finally we did it. We regenerated your cells and filtered your blood. Your heartbeat was strong and steady, and—"

"Then it's no accident that I'm here. They knew I was in that warehouse, that we were miraculously still hooked up to an energy source, didn't they?"

"Yes, and I'm sorry." He sighed. "I didn't tell you at first because I was following the plan, and then after, it didn't seem to matter anymore. I knew it would upset you. I wanted to protect you from the things you didn't need to know. You've already been through enough. I planned to tell you everything once we made it to—"

"Don't! I don't want to hear it," I said, flopping back against the bed.

Thirty-one years. It wasn't a coincidence that Travel was a twenty-year-old clone in the year 3035. They reinvented him especially for me. Bastards!

"So what's going to happen to the ones who are left?" My tone was desperate but bordering on demanding.

"Simon's saving them in case he finds a use for them in the near future. He refers to them as 'fresh DNA.'" Michael lowered to his elbow next to me. "And there's something else." He licked his lips, and his chest expanded with a steady breath. "Your grandfather is one of them," he said quickly.

"What? Are you sure?" I asked, twisting to face him.

"I'm sure. Each chamber was opened and resealed, so the team could retrieve the paperwork inside. We needed ages and the causes of death. Marshal Miles Dannacher is one of them."

It was as if time stopped. I couldn't blink, only stare. I couldn't speak, only think. My grandfather was here. Besides Victoria, he was the only person on the planet with whom I was genetically connected. But he was frozen, in a state between life and death, stored like a time capsule.

Full of worry for Victoria and too mentally spent to argue and ask my questions, I turned away from Michael and closed my eyes.

Chapter Twenty-Six

Trail did not own a house bot. In fact, he thought all bots were spies and was detained once last year and fined five thousand credits when his neighbor's GROW came too close to the edge of his yard and he smashed its face with a shovel. Trail was my kind of guy.

"Good morning," I said. He was already dressed for work, wearing thick canvas trousers and a shirt that read "L-Energy Plant" in red letters that matched the puffy spots under his eyes. "How are you doing? Are you holding up okay?"

"Yeah, I think I'm ready to face the day. If anyone asks why I look like crap, I'll tell 'em I'm sick, ran out of anti-virals, and was too tired to go to the dispensary and get some, so I didn't sleep very well. They know I don't own a house bot."

"We're so grateful that you agreed to help us. I don't know what we'd do without you. Thank you."

Trail made the coffee himself, pushing buttons and

watching the brown liquid flow, hot and savory, into mugs before setting them on a tray he positioned in the middle of the kitchen table. A plate of scrambled eggs and toast he pulled from the food heater joined the mugs in the middle of the modestly set table.

The coffee was thin but creamy, coating my throat on the way down as I drifted back into the bedroom to give Trail some alone time. Michael emerged from the shower wearing only one thing—a towel wrapped around his waist. When he gave his head a quick shake, a spray of water droplets hit my upper arm and he smiled apologetically. He sat down next to me and leaned his cheek against my shoulder, making a wet spot with his hair.

His damp skin was cool against mine, and as I eyed a bead of water trickle down the contour of his abs, I couldn't help but set my hand on top of his thigh. From under the towel, his muscles moved against my palm as he scooted even closer.

"It's almost nine, Michael," I said. "Magnum's not here. We'll have to stay here another day and wait for him."

"I know," he said in the same disappointed tone. I turned my head and walked to the window while he dressed.

The clouds hung low in the sky, draping across the building in the distance as a peek of sun broke the horizon. My eyes, blurred by a ray of sun, refocused, and from the corner of my eye, there was a flash, something dark and quick, and a body stood mute behind the largest tree beyond Trail's backyard.

"Check this out," I said excitedly.

Still pulling up his jeans, Michael hobbled to my side as the figure made a second dash to the back gate. It was

Magnum, and Victoria was in his arms.

"He made it," I cried, running to the back door to momentarily turn off the Whimsy Birds and meet him. "Magnum's here," I shouted as I passed Trail, who was taking a long sip from his coffee mug.

"I told you I'd make it," Magnum said as he presented Victoria to me and let a canvas bag slip from his shoulder and land on the floor.

"My baby girl," I said through a smattering of kisses to first her forehead and then the tops of her hands as my heart swelled with love.

After giving him a big clap on the back and handshake that turned into a hug, Michael's chin rode over my shoulder as he came up behind me and looked down into Victoria's sweet face. From atop my other shoulder, Trail did the same after introducing himself to Magnum.

"Here, Trail. Hold her," I said, giving Victoria to her uncle for inspection. He took her in his arms and stroked the back of her fisted hand with his index finger. "This is really Travel's baby? His actual baby, blood-related and all?"

Michael grinned. "Yes, she's the first one of her kind, not a clone, and she can have babies of her own someday."

"I'm her real mother, and your brother is her real father," I added.

Another touch to Victoria's hand triggered more tears as Trail cried into the sleeve of one arm while he cradled the baby in the other.

"So you didn't have any trouble sneaking here?" I asked Magnum as Trail transferred her back into my arms.

"Not an ounce, but security has picked up everywhere. You guys need to catch your last flight to Sector Ten as soon as possible." Magnum didn't know the truth. Like Michael said, the less he knew, the better. "Everything you'll need for Victoria during your trip is right here." He gently kicked the bag he'd brought with him.

Magnum and Michael clapped each other on the back, and when it was my turn, Michael held Victoria and cooed at her.

"I'll never forget you, rebel."

"And I'll never forget you."

"You've covered your tracks, right? You won't get caught?"

"Me get caught? Hell no. I'm too cool for that, remember?"

That was something I'd always remember.

Before Magnum left out the front door with empty arms, he gave Trail a strong handshake, me a long hug, and Victoria a gentle kiss on the forehead.

"Come with us, Trail, to Tasma," I said after the door closed, my eyes damp with tears.

"Yes, come with us," Michael interjected.

"No, I can't." He shook his head. "It's tempting. It really is, but I've got something here I need to do in the regions. Something I can't leave." What that was, I couldn't imagine, but Trail's eyes told us not to ask. "Thank you, though. It means a lot to me that you'd want me to come."

"Of course we would. You're Victoria's uncle, after all."

Just as I was about to hand her to Trail for another hug, the birds at the back door went crazy, producing a frenzy of squawks and clanking metal. "Oh no. Who's here? Why use the back door?" I asked, dashing across the room to get away from the window.

"To the bedroom, quickly," said Trail. "Maybe security

officers questioned the neighbors and one of them reported seeing someone other than me come through the back door."

Michael grabbed the bag Magnum prepared for Victoria. "If it's trouble, we'll find a way out of here. Just remember, Trail, once we're gone, call Saul, give him the code, and tell him one hour."

"Got it." Trail threw us a thumb's up behind his back as we ran to the bedroom and kept the door open just a crack.

The bird's quieted down, and we heard the back door slide open and closed.

"Good morning, Mr. Carson," said a male voice. "As you know, you're home is Liaison non-compliant."

"Yeah, so?" said Trail. "It's being upgraded on Wednesday."

"So, manual readings must be taken regularly," said the other male voice, "to ensure the safety of the subdivision, of course."

"Yeah, so?" Trail repeated in a tone that was more believable than I would have had at that point.

"L-Band readings from your house indicate there are three people inside, but thermal readings from the street show four separate life forms. A strange phenomena, something our security team hasn't seen before."

Damn it! We should have had Magnum fix Michael's band while he was here.

"Why are you taking thermal readings of my house?"

"It's something we do on a regular basis in the older subdivisions." Yeah, right. Whoever that officer was, he was a terrible liar. They suspected we were here, and maybe even Victoria.

"We need to go. Now," I whispered, collecting all of our

bags. "Through the window."

The window slid open easily without triggering an alarm. Michael climbed out first. Then I handed him the baby and made my own pathetic climb over the window ledge and leaped to the ground, lacking Michael's athleticism.

"We'll run to those trees," he said, taking my hand.

The Whimsy Birds made their third debut since our arrival, bursting into a chorus of eccentric shrieks as we sprinted toward the trees. Neither one of us dared to look over our shoulders but we heard a man shout, "Hey, I just saw two people running out of the backyard, a man and a woman." At least they didn't see Michael holding a newborn against his chest.

Our run slowed to a brisk walk once we were several blocks away. "Do you think they'll be able to find us?" I asked as Michael handed Victoria back to me and I deactivated her band and mine.

"As long as we stick to Magnum's map to avoid obscuras and stay behind the trees when we can, we should be okay. We can only hope Trail's able to call Saul for us. If not, then I don't know what we'll do."

Victoria blinked against the harsh morning sun. I readjusted her blanket until a small flap of cloth folded over her head to cover her eyes, and then I looked at Michael. He, too, was squinting against the sun, his sensitive blue eyes trying to shield themselves from the glare as they worked to identify the buildings in the distance and scan the horizon for PATs.

But his eyes also held fear. If something happened to him, I could never forgive myself.

"Michael," I said as he pulled me with him to cut across a tree-lined lot. "No one knows you're involved in my escape.

Magnum can cover your tracks, and you can come up with enough lies to explain where you've been. Stay here. Just show me where to go. I'll find Saul. I'll give him the code, and he'll take Victoria and me to Tasma, no questions asked, just like you said."

"What are you talking about?" he asked, almost tripping on a curb.

"This is your world. Not mine. You've dedicated your whole life to your career, to the program, and now if we don't make it…"

"My life has been dedicated to the program, but that's not the life I chose for myself, remember? As far as I'm concerned, this isn't my world, either."

"But if we make it to Tasma, we'll never be able to come back here, right? You'll be stuck there and—"

"And I don't care about that, as long as I'm with you." We stopped our jog, and he held me by the shoulder, his words tugging on my soul.

"I can't let you give up everything for me. If something happens to you, it'll be my fault. Please, stay here."

"I'm not leaving you." He let out a big breath.

"But what if you need an organ transplant?"

"Don't worry. After we get the Van Winkle Project started, that's the next thing I'm going to do—start an organ cloning program, so transplants can be performed. Many lives will be saved. It's something we can do together."

"Thank you," I said with my voice and with my eyes.

We broke into a sprint, darting in and out of trees. Victoria wiggled in my arms, made a sweet sound, and looked up at me when we re-entered the sunlight and jogged toward a busy intersection.

Chapter Twenty-Seven

"Quick." Michael pulled me behind a parked transport mover as a PAT on a hoverscooter came into view. It rode by, slowing down when he passed, but with our deactivated bands, we were just another part of the car.

"That was close," he said. "I'm sure there'll be more, but we're almost there. If Trail made that call, Saul should be waiting for us outside the hoverbus terminal.

A row of hoverbuses in the distance shone silver in the morning sun, and just outside the entrance sat a miniature hoverbus with a single-bladed propeller attached to the top of its egg-shaped body. With its golden sheen and thin black stripe, it eerily reminded me of the helicopter I died in. A man casually leaning against the cabin door waved when he saw us hurrying toward him.

"Hey, nice to see you again, Saul," said Michael. "This is Dorothy, my assistant." Michael had remembered my middle name. "And this is clone X-465382," he said, pointing to Victoria. After exchanging handshakes, Saul opened the cabin door and took his own seat as pilot and we buckled into the seats behind him.

We hardly spoke during the flight, but Victoria cried, and I did everything I could to sooth her.

"How are you doing?" whispered Michael to me.

"Okay, considering. We're so high this time."

"This bus doesn't have hoverment restrictions. Are you scared?"

"A little. You know what happened the last time I flew this high." The inside of Saul's sky mover was angular despite its round exterior, and the lack of dashboard dials, switches, and what I considered a decent-sized steering wheel, made me especially nervous.

Michael laughed and squeezed my knee. "It's okay. A lot has changed since then."

It was difficult to interact with Victoria without accidentally saying her name, and just when I was about to slip and call her "my sweet Victoria," an island came into view. She magically stopped crying as if she sensed my relief.

"That's odd." Saul peered over the steering knob, trying to get a wider view of the sky in front of him. With a voice command, he activated the external obscuras and inspected the empty sky.

"What is it?" Michael unbuckled his harness and slid into the seat next to Saul.

"You didn't hear that?"

"No." Michael put his hand to his ear. "I forget my L-Bud in my hotel room."

"We were just ordered to return back to base."

Michael grabbed his arm. "But you can't, Saul. Please,

just drop us off. We're almost there anyway."

"There's nothing I can do. The blockers have been enabled. We have to go back."

"Blockers? But I thought this flyer didn't have any blockers."

"No, it does, always had. They've just been disabled until now, and there's only one man who has the authority to turn them back on."

"Who?"

"Shen-Lung."

The flyer continued to hover within miles of Tasma. It rocked slightly, and its muted hum rose several octaves each time Saul tried to defy the fixed controls.

Victoria's pink lips curled into a frown, and she cried again, louder than before.

"In Chinese mythology," I said above Victoria's cries, "Shen-Lung is a mythical dragon who controls the wind, clouds, and rain. He's a weather-making dragon."

Shen-Lung had the power to manipulate the fate of farmer's crops, giving it control over life and death in China, and now the man named after him, a clone, was holding our fate in his hands.

Saul removed his L-Bud and jammed it in his pocket. "They keep calling me. If I don't turn around, they'll send out another flyer with a boarding team, and I won't be able to stop them from entering this flyer." Michael sighed. "Shen-Lung knows you're on board with a woman named Cassie and a baby. I've been ordered to subdue you if you resist." Saul put up his hands. "You know I won't do that, but I have to turn back. Please don't try to stop me. There's nothing I can do."

Holding my wailing baby against my chest did little to stop her crying, and her hot, red cheek against my skin made me want to cry, too.

"Saul, there's something you should know. Cassie's baby is not a clone—she's biologically made. President Gifford tried to take her away from her mother, her birth mother." Michael emphasized the word "birth." "See why we can't go back? Tasma is the only safe place for them."

"If I could, I would, but the flyer won't go in any other direction. I've tried." The flyer pitched, dropped several feet, and rose again like it was fighting to free itself from an invisible string. "And here comes the boarding team."

An unmarked flyer identical to the one in which we were riding hovered to our left and our flyer bobbled.

"He's right. We have to go back. It's over," I moaned, remembering the helicopter crash more vividly than ever. Hollow screams pierced my ears—first my mother's, then Daniella's and Ian's, followed by my own final, frantic shriek. "Michael," I cried, snapping back to reality.

"I'm sorry, Cassie. I'm so sorry. I thought this would work. Go ahead and take us back, Saul. You won't be reprimanded. You can't be reprimanded for a code 42/147, and don't worry. I'll tell them that I prevented you from leaving right away."

The hoverbus steadied and rotated in its current position and retraced its course to Melbourne, Australia, in Region Three. Michael held me during the entire flight while the baby slept on my lap. This was the last I time we'd probably ever see each other. We'd be separated for good, with him jailed and me a secret prisoner within the walls of GenH1. Travel was gone from me, and soon Michael and Victoria would be taken from me, too.

"I'm sorry. I tried, I really did. I thought my plan would work." Michael buried his face in his hands.

"I know you did. You did everything you could to help me, from the beginning all the way to the end." I patted the top of his thigh, and when I did, the memory pins in my sleeve pressed against my wrist. "Wait! It's not over yet. We have a bargaining chip." I beamed with joy. "The unclassified Van Winkle files." The pins sparkled in the light from the window as I lifted my arm.

"We do, we have the complete files, and that's why there's something else you need to know, something I wasn't going to tell you until we actually reached Tasma."

Oh no. What was it—another lie, another cover-up, something to reawaken the anger I already had for him? Anger softly brewed deep in my soul.

"What is it? Tell me now." I demanded as I held Victoria against my chest and dug into the bag Magnum left for us and found a bottle. Once she clutched the nipple with her mouth, she relaxed and stopped crying.

"In the files, you're referred to as VW-1."

"Yes, I know that," I interrupted, "and Victoria is VW-4."

He blinked watery eyes and sucked his lower lip into his mouth. Parting his lips was enough. He didn't have to say anything else.

"There are two more. I have two more daughters," I said in a slow whisper. My whole body trembled.

"Twins," said Michael gently. "Born before you were awakened."

My throat tightened, making it hurt when I tried to swallow. A surge of panic swelled in my chest, and a sick, empty sensation expanded in the pit of my stomach. The hum and bob of the flyer, the delicate *suck, suck* sound of baby lips upon a rubber nipple—I momentarily felt and heard none of it.

Michael took a deep breath and continued while I remained stunned, my heart racing, the pulse in my neck palpable. "After you were revived, we kept you comatose while your injuries healed, but it wasn't for two months like I said. It was for almost two years."

Was I really hearing this? Victoria ate and squirmed, but her warm body wasn't enough to counteract the chill developing in my arms. Her bottle almost slipped from my hand.

"At the time, we thought a full awakening would be impossible. You were artificially inseminated, became pregnant, a C-section performed, and you gave birth to twins—VW-2 and VW-3—identical. Healthy and fertile."

I had a cesarean? I didn't even have a scar.

"Then Dr. Pickford made the decision that you would never be awakened, that you'd continue to bear children for us while in a comatose state, but your health started to fail. You'd been in a vegetative state for way too long. Our only solution was to proceed with your awakening. But before your awakening, and against my better judgment, you were artificially inseminated a second time."

"Where are they?" I gasped, trying to catch my breath and clenching my free hand into a fist.

"That I don't know. But I do know this—they didn't stay at GenH1. After they were born, they were taken away, and I've never seen them again. I checked the VW files, even the classified sections, and nothing. I don't know what happened to them."

Their father, was it Travel? No, they'd want half siblings, not full. "The father? Do you know who it is?"

"It's me. I'm their father," he said between breaths.

My jaw locked. I couldn't speak. My shoulders tensed, and my bottom lip trembled. This whole time, Michael was the father of two little girls I didn't even know existed, a special connection to one another ignited when we contributed X chromosomes and created life. Now he was more than just my boyfriend.

A crease formed between his eyes, eyes frantically searching my soul for a sign of forgiveness and love. He inhaled deeply, his whole body shaking.

"But I didn't find out until after they were born, and when I did, I almost threw Simon up against the wall. My sample was supposed to be used for research purposes, not to produce another genetics genius, something Simon had planned all along."

My face grew hot, and my legs grew heavy like an impulse-regulator patch was affixed to my spine. I could almost hear the patch clicking, ticking like a clock, and then I realized the sound was the beating of my heart.

"Now do you understand why I'm so willing to leave the program at GenH1? Before Victoria, I didn't think about our babies. They didn't matter to me. I gave away my rights to them because they were born without my knowledge. It's something I've regretted ever since. But then you were awakened and... I want our babies back." He shook his head and blinked out a tear. "I was a fool to ever believe in the project."

"I-I..." But the words didn't come.

"I've been looking for them. While you were pregnant,

I spent every spare moment searching files and questioning the staff. They're three years old now. With the files, we can bargain to get them back. That's one of the reasons I went along with the program, not telling you anything. I didn't know what you'd let slip, and I couldn't risk getting fired because I had to use all their resources. To find your daughters. To find *our* daughters."

Michael shared my pain, but I'd never known it—the pain of being separated from one's child—but his pain went deeper than mine. With his pain came the regret of knowingly signing away his rights as a parent.

Could I continue to blame him for not telling me the truth about my stasis, the other participants in the program, and holding his tongue about our daughters until now?

Telling me about the twins beforehand might have resulted in an act of desperation, like me holding a steak knife against Dr. Little's throat.

Michael did what he thought was best, a product of his upbringing and the society that raised him. I believed him, and now, as I looked into his eyes, apologetic eyes full of sorrow, I forgave him. He was the father of two of my children, after all.

"Are you mad at me for not telling you sooner?" he asked anxiously.

"I'm mad, but I forgive you," I said.

Four uniformed men were waiting at the hoverbus depot to escort us to the capitol of the region. The clouds shifted above, blocking the sun, casting gray shadows across their grim faces. The four men did not converse other than commanding us to enter a private mover and then exit when the vehicle settled to the ground.

Michael and I didn't speak, but like me, I could tell he was full of anxiety and disappointment. Our original plans were ruined, but maybe we could still salvage some of our freedom with the information contained in the pin. If anything, I could make a case for Gifford's impeachment.

We weren't immediately rebanded as Michael expected, but the faces of the four men were stern, fixed without smiles, warning us that we shouldn't try to run away.

Shen-Lung's presidential building was impressive. A multi-inclined roof with sweeping curves made it ancient and historical, a piece of art. The corridor we entered matched the building's exterior with its high beams and load-bearing columns.

A relief of mythical dragons decorated the door at the end of a long hall. In its center, encircled by a hoard of serpents, was a carving of the benevolent dragon, Shen-Lung, blowing a billow of clouds above its great head, and for a moment I imagined fire escaping its gaping mouth of fangs and pointed teeth.

Attached to its doorframe by wrought iron hinges, the majestic door swung open as we approached it, reminding me of the entrance to my beloved botanical garden, making me smile at the pleasant memory.

In the middle of a fiery red rug stood a man, large of waist, but not height, with his arms spread in a welcoming manner. "I am Shen-Lung." Shen-Lung's features were distinctly Chinese, and surprisingly, I wasn't as intimidated by him as I expected.

"President Shen-Lung," I said, stepping forward before he could say more. "Before you decide our fate, there's something we need to share with you." I held out the memory pin, my hand shaking, as Michael drew me close to his side. "It's-it's the Van Winkles files. Unedited."

The president's eyebrows came together, and he cocked his head to one side, taking the pin from my hand.

"President Gifford wasn't planning to share any of my babies with your region or President Tupolev's. The proof is in the pin," I continued.

"Then my suspicions were correct." Shen-Lung lifted his chin and released an audible breath through his nose.

"And there is something else," I said, taking another step forward.

"Michael and I don't want this world to end at the grip of a population shortage. The Van Winkle Project can continue, but it needs to do so on my terms in Tasma." The less government control, the better. In Tasma, Michael and I would serve a greater purpose than we would here, and my children, our children, would grow up in a world more reminiscent of the one I held dear. Michael gave my hand a warning squeeze like he thought I should have kept my mouth shut and waited to hear Shen-Lung's plans for us first.

But as much as I despised William Gifford, Dr. Little, and Dr. Pickford, I respected the innocent clones who held the "life is precious" motto blindly in their hearts.

"That is very noble of you, Miss Dannacher." He made a second bow. "But before we can think of the future, on behalf of President Tupolev and myself, I must first apologize to both you and Victoria." He shook his head. "President Gifford is an evil man, consumed by power and greed, but I am a man full of hope and generosity. It is an honor and a pleasure to welcome you to my home. I will do everything to make things the way it should have been from the beginning."

"Thank you," was all I could say, as my heart continued to rap noticeably in my chest.

Shen-Lung whispered into his L-Band and within seconds two women entered. "You both must be tired and hungry. Li Na and Zhang Min will take you to your quarters while important decisions are being made." He bowed a third time before he left the room, and from the corner of my eye, I saw him hold up the memory pin and smile.

We padded down the paper-walled halls, following the women whose light steps were inhibited by the tightness of their uniforms: full-length dresses patterned with cherry blossoms. Michael was escorted to the room next to mine, but the minute after the women left, he joined me in my room, and the two of us, with Victoria nestled in between, lay on the bed and stared at the ceiling.

Michael rolled onto his side. "The files might not make any difference. For all we know, Shen-Lung is as power hungry as Gifford, and now that Shen-Lung has you and Victoria—"

"Don't even say that. I don't even want to think about that right now." My muscles were tight, on edge, but my mind was as mushy as a sponge. "But I do know this—I want out of the regions, and I want this thing off my wrist," I said, making a face at my L-Band.

I couldn't take any bad news or bad thoughts, so Michael and I lie in silence, his hand in mine as Victoria sucked from another one of the bottles Magnum's mother packed, and I imagined two little girls holding hands, identical to one another like clones.

After a *ding*, Li Na entered with a hovercart. She set

a ceramic teapot, two matching cups, and a plate of hors d'oeuvres on the table and left, giving a bow, but the savory odors coming from the Chinese dumplings and spring rolls did little to give Michael and me an appetite.

Fifteen minutes later, Li Na returned to escort us back to Shen-Lung's office. While we walked back through the halls, my body shook with the thought of Victoria being taken away again, but at the same time, a bit of hope lingered in my soul, a knot of faith in man.

"Much has changed in the last two hours," said the president when we approached the fiery red rug. He clasped his hands behind his back. "For one, William Gifford is no longer the president of Region One. He was asked to step down shortly after I finished reading the files and shared them with President Tupolev."

Yes! My whole body tingled, and when my trembling hand met Michael's, I could feel him shaking, too.

"You were right about Gifford. He wanted complete control over the repopulation process. He planned to rebuild his region first while letting the populations of Regions Two and Three grow at one-third the rate. He disregarded one of our basic beliefs. 'Life is precious,'" he said with conviction before leaning over to peer at Victoria, who was cradled in my arms. "You are both free, free to fulfill the destiny, the destiny that you desire."

Could this be possible? Were we dreaming? "Thank you. Thank you so much, President Shen-Lung." Michael's grip tightened as he repeated my thanks.

But can we trust him? I wanted to whisper to Michael even though his misty eyes and soft smile told me he thought we could. This seemed way too easy.

"Yes, I know my new destiny," I said, releasing Michael's hand and stepping forward. "And I can fulfill it with Michael's help."

The president bowed, his eyes laced in tears, his smile earnest and genuine.

On our terms, the Van Winkle Project would continue in Tasma, and in the process, we would find our daughters, VW-2 and VW-3, and develop an organ-cloning program.

This time *we* held the cards in our hands, and together with hope and faith, Michael and I knew how to play them.

• • •

"I love you, Cassie," whispered Michael as the Tasmanian horizon came into view, the hum of the flyer vibrated through my soul, and Victoria happily drank from a bottle.

"I..." My lips parted, but the words he wanted to hear didn't come. Did I love him? I wasn't sure, but I did know one thing—at that moment, I was truly happy for the first time since my awakening. The flyer lowered, bobbing a few feet from the ground. Michael placed his warm hand on my cheek and said, "Welcome home, Cassie."

Acknowledgments

Thank you to all of my readers for your enthusiasm, dedication, and support. My hope is to write entertaining and captivating novels that all of you will love as much as I do.

My amazing critique partners, Jennifer Anne Davis and Tania Hutley. Your feedback is invaluable. I'm a better writer because of you two!

To my extended family and in-laws for your continued support and inspiration. I love you all.

To the staff and students of Santana High School, especially my work family—the English Department—Andrea, Angela, Barbara, Carolyn, Eileen, Emily, Jamea, Janelle, Marla, Marty, and Sophia. Thank you for seeing me through this amazing journey.

To my street team, The Street Angels, for helping me spread the word about my books. I appreciate and value your special commitment to the team.

To my sister and beta reader, Korina Kramer, for your

encouragement and constructive criticism.

And finally, to Entangled Publishing. It is an honor and a privilege to be a part of this incredible team. Robin, Kerri-Leigh, and Liz—you are editing geniuses.

About the Author

Growing up in San Diego, California, Karri Thompson spent much of her years at the beach, reading novels, tanning, and listening to music. At SDSU, she earned a BA in English, MA in education, and her teaching credential. As a wife, mother, and high-school English teacher, she began writing novels, giving all of the compelling plots and unique characters in her head a home. Victorian literature rocks her socks, and when she's not writing, jogging, going to concerts, or watching her son play football, she's reading Dickens.

BONUS
MATERIAL

Deleted Scene

Ascendancy

"Um, so what's that?" I asked, pointing to the box at the end of my bed.

"It's a game. Ella told me that you were bored, so I thought I'd keep you company for a while—that is, if you don't mind," said Michael.

"No, I don't mind. What kind of game?"

"Let me show you." He brought the box to my bed and lifted the lid. A thin, rectangular slab of metal floated from its container and unfolded. "Oh my gosh, that's amazing."

With a tap, he knocked the board into position, where it remained suspended, inches above my lap.

He leaned forward to steady the game board, and the muscles in his forearms flexed. My lips parted, but I held my breath until he was seated with his heels resting on the bed frame.

His eyes darted from mine to the game board, and he cleared his throat. "So, um, do you want to be the mover or the L-Band?" he asked, pointing to the game pieces.

So they called cars "movers." "The mover," I announced. Cars were cool. L-Bands were ugly, and I didn't know enough about them. I took the tiny, metallic mover, inspecting its bullet-shaped body and running the tip of my finger against its four fixed wheels. Hmm, maybe their cars didn't fly.

"So this game board represents this hospital?" I asked, shifting my eyes from Michael's to study each square outlining the board where it read "GenH1."

"Yes, but not just the hospital. It includes this subdivision, division, sector, our region, and Regions Two and Three." He touched the center of the game while he spoke, and what appeared to be a solitary board, sliced horizontally into four additional boards stacked offset from one another with a hand's width of space between them. "But since this is your first game, I think we'll just stick to this city." He touched the uppermost board, and they collapsed back into one. His tone was playful, borderline flirtatious, definitely not as doctor-like.

Score.

"Wow, I've never played a game like this before." I grinned and my whole body tingled.

"Now, we both begin with ten thousand credits." Michael pulled what looked like two mini Liaisons from the box and handed one to me. "The object of the game is to become the wealthiest player by buying and renting property, which is actually kind of ironic considering that the government owns all property."

"Buy and rent property? Then it's just like Monopoly," I

said, scanning the board until I found the words "Community Chest" and "Chance," but instead of the four Railroad spaces and two Utilities, I found the squares "Hoverbus Depot," "Liaison One," and "Obscura Preservation" in a subdivision adjacent to the hospital.

"It's based on an ancient game. I was hoping you'd recognize it." His eyes gleamed. "It's called Ascendancy." He tapped the board's center, and a 4-D image of the game's title rose in a slow spin, each bold, red letter flashing for several seconds, before disappearing with a silent sizzle.

The innocent-sounding word gave me chills, especially when I saw that the "Jail" space was replaced with the not-so-innocent title of "Prison," a place where a felon could end up serving a life sentence. I wasn't sure what to make of that.

Michael showed me how to navigate through the screens of the mini Liaison, the Banker's page, the property page dotted with Liaison-generated houses and hotels, and explained how each sector was separated into divisions, then subdivisions, and how each region was broken into sectors. And every time he reached across the game, stretching his muscular arm and letting his shoulders settle back into place, my heart danced, and I caught his eyes grazing over my body.

"Oh, I get it. Now I understand," I said as he recited the rules from memory. Our eyes met, and he beamed, his knee bobbing up and down a few times during the silence — maybe from nerves. Like being on a first date.

On his first turn, he landed on Community Chest. He tapped the game's Liaison and read the virtual card: "You've won second place in a flyer race — collect two thousand credits."

"Flyer?" I asked.

"Movers with high-hoverment capabilities."

"And what exactly do you mean by hoverment?"

"All modes of transportations—movers, flyers, hoverbuses—fly, or hover, at designated height restrictions. It eliminates traffic congestion. Flyers travel in the least-restricted environment at a minimum of one thousand feet."

"Great," I said sarcastically. After the helicopter accident that killed me, flyers were something I wanted to avoid.

And their cars did fly after all. "And movers?"

"Personal movers are restricted to five feet."

Michael's liaison flashed like a casino game as two thousand credits were deposited into his Ascendancy account. "Thank you, Community Chest," he said, pleased with himself.

Now it was my roll. The one-dimensional dice flashed with the numbers five and two. The seventh square was Chance. "Go directly to Prison—do not pass Go, do not collect five hundred credits." Bummer. I dropped my tiny mover into a computer generated prison cell that sparked when my game piece hit the vertical bars.

Michael moved ahead eleven spaces, placing his marker on a brown square decorated with tiny slabs of wood. "The botanical garden. I think I'll buy it."

"The botanical garden?" I sighed. "That's the first place I want to go when I can leave this room."

"How did you know about the botanical building?" he asked, his grin growing.

"Ella. I asked her about trees and flowers," I answered softly through a smile of my own.

"When you're ready, I'll take you there. I promise," he

said, leaning close enough for his breath to hit my lips. "As for this botanical garden, I changed my mind. You can buy it when you land there." His cheeks rose and the light in his eyes danced when he laughed.

I was only eight spaces away from that special place, but instead I rolled a three and my marker ended up on a government-run high school called "Educator 7."

"Do you want to buy it?" Michael asked.

"Sure. Why not?" The balance of credits on my game liaison dropped by six hundred credits, and a virtual house appeared on the board, a single-story green home with a chimney looking so real I tried to touch it, but my fingers felt nothing but air. I remembered the small bungalow that belonged to my mother. When I drew my hand away, the house fluttered and re-solidified.

"So if the government owns all property, what happened to the house my mother owned? And my father's? He had a house, too."

"I'm sorry, Cassie, but all property was absorbed and redistributed by the government after the plague, and"— he sighed and set his hand on my knee—"your bloodline ended."

"Ended? Are you sure?" My hands trembled in my lap.

"Yes, we traced your genealogy thoroughly." He pulled his hand back, making the game board teeter and reset itself. "I can't. I've already said too much. I hadn't planned to—"

The game board dropped into his hands. He folded it, placed it back in the box, and powered down the miniature liaisons.

Though they begged a good stretch, I kept my legs crossed, silently urging him to stay where he was instead of returning to the chair.

Tightening my stomach muscles, ignoring the pain, I tilted forward until the space between our faces was less than two feet.

"Kiss me, Michael," I whispered so quietly I wasn't sure he heard me. Or that I really meant to say it.

He caught me by the waist and brushed his lips against my cheek as he pulled me in for a short but firm hug. He was exciting to hold, exciting to touch. His indigo eyes split my soul, and his kisses produced sparks.

He kissed my lips, a soft, short kiss.

Yes. Finally.

"Don't worry, this room is 'free,'" he said before kissing me again. I accepted his tongue on the third kiss, not really knowing what I was doing, but I didn't want him to stop. Holding my face in his hands, his kisses became firm, passionate, and unguarded.

"You're so important to me, Cassie. You're the only thing I need in this world to make me truly happy," he said, bringing his lips against my neck. "I—"

My fierce embrace took him off guard, nearly causing him to stumble and fall backward, but it was welcomed, and he held me with the same fervor and enthusiasm I was feeling. I didn't want to let go. The warmth of the back of his neck against my arms and his soft breath upon my shoulder made me feel loved instead of empty in this strange world.

I pulled him against me, pressing my mouth against his, and he kissed me hard, massaging his fingers into my back. My last conversation with Magnum flitted through my mind.

"Michael's never had a girlfriend. He's never even been with a girl"

"You're kidding?"

"Nope, he told me so himself. Hasn't kissed a girl, either. How could he, growing up in this hospital."

"Then he's as inexperienced as I am."